Dangerous
Pleasures

Books by Fiona Zedde

BLISS

A TASTE OF SIN

EVERY DARK DESIRE

HUNGRY FOR IT

DANGEROUS PLEASURES

SATISFY ME
(with Renee Alexis and Sydney Molare)

SATISFY ME AGAIN
(with Renee Luke and Sydney Molare)

SATISFY ME TONIGHT
(with Kimberly Terry Kaye and Sydney Molare)

Published by Kensington Publishing Corp.

Dangerous Pleasures

FIONA ZEDDE

KENSINGTON PUBLISHING CORP.
www.kensingtonbooks.com

KENSINGTON BOOKS are published by

Kensington Publishing Corp.
119 West 40th Street
New York, NY 10018

All Kensington titles, imprints, and distributed lines are available at special quantity discounts for bulk purchases for sales promotion, premiums, fund-raising, educational, or institutional use.

Special book excerpts or customized printings can also be created to fit specific needs. For details, write or phone the office of the Kensington Special Sales Manager: Kensington Publishing Corp., 119 West 40th Street, New York, NY 10018, Attn. Special Sales Department. Phone: 1-800-221-2647.

Kensington and the K logo Reg. U.S. Pat. & TM Off.

ISBN-13: 978-0-7582-1740-0
ISBN-10: 0-7582-1740-4

First Printing: February 2011
10 9 8 7 6 5 4 3 2 1

Printed in the United States of America

Dangerous Pleasures

Chapter 1

"**Y**ou should fall to your knees and thank God that you're single again."

Mayson turned away from the view of the San Diego hills, shaking long, wavy hair out of her eyes. She leaned back against the terrace wall and squinted at her best friend sitting at the nearby table.

In the sharp sunlight, she could tell that Renee hadn't slept well the night before. Faint shadows lurked under her eyes and the corners of her narrow mouth were tight with tension. But a restless evening couldn't erase her effortless beauty. The short, natural hair. Twin dimples in her cheeks. The slender body in its usual weekend sundress that left her shoulders bare.

Renee paused with the glass of grapefruit juice near her mouth and looked at Mayson, a reluctant smile on her lips. "Just like that, huh?"

A light breeze stirred up, fluttering the hair around Mayson's face. Ink-black strands against her oak-brown skin. Renee thought briefly about going inside for her camera to capture the contrasts of her friend. Beautiful/strong. Jamaican/Chinese. A centered hurricane.

"Of course," Mayson said. "Linc didn't deserve you. I told you that the first day you brought that needy fucker home." She bent down, her body supple and graceful from over ten years of practicing and teaching yoga, and grabbed another strawberry out of the almost empty bowl. "Usually divorce is a sad thing but you just dropped a big piece of shit off your shoe when you unloaded that moron."

"I loved him, though," Renee said, defensive.

She swallowed more of the tart juice, lowering her lashes against the sunlight blanketing the rooftop terrace. Her hand fumbled on the table for her sunglasses.

"You *wish* you loved him." Mayson sank her teeth into the deep-red strawberry, sighing in brief pleasure at the sweetness that exploded in her mouth. "One day you'll realize that it's okay *not* to love everyone who loves you."

The two women faced each other on the rooftop terrace of Renee's seventh-floor condo. Below them lay the city of San Diego, tumbling hills dotted with other houses, other condos, other rooftops, the green interruption of trees, the gaze rolling down the hill until it fell into the sharp blue water of the Pacific.

Remnants of their Saturday brunch—a joint effort prepared in the kitchen nearly two hours before—lay scattered on the table. A bowl that was once full of fat red strawberries now contained only their lonely stems. Two empty plates with golden crumbs from the long-gone waffles, flecks of powdered sugar, and haphazard stripes of maple syrup. A small saucer still held half a sausage patty. It sat far away from Mayson, who, though not a nazi sort of vegetarian, didn't want the meat anywhere near her. She was never in the mood to smell pork.

"It's a good thing I already love you or I'd be following your advice already." Renee gave Mayson a sour look.

Her best friend grinned. "Don't shoot the messenger, honey." Her rough-soft Jamaican accent curled lovingly around the words.

"You are being such an A-hole."

"Ooh," Mayson teased, grinning. "Are you actually cursing at me?"

"Shut up."

Mayson stuck out her tongue at Renee and grinned.

Her friend never cursed. Never. The summer they turned eleven, the two of them had gone off to camp together. One of the counselors at Camp Minnehawk had had the filthiest mouth Mayson had heard before or since. She'd stood in awe of the girl's inventiveness with the English, and some of the Spanish, language.

Renee's reaction to the girl had been just the opposite. If she'd even been thinking of uttering a curse word before hearing Contessa Stephens swear like a drunken sailor on the last day of leave, that summer had effectively cured her of every single impulse.

The warm stone of the terrace pressed against Mayson through her thin T-shirt and jeans as she leaned into it, still smiling. "What's up with Linc, anyway? I thought he was dating somebody else?"

"He is." Renee paused. "I just woke up thinking about him this morning." And those thoughts had led her to call him. Bad idea. On the phone, he'd acted as if *she* was the one who had asked for the divorce.

"I'll forgive your subconscious for that lapse in judgment," Mayson said.

"I can't just forget him like that. He was a big part of my life for four years. We shared a life and a mortgage."

"The house was in his name, Renee. You didn't share anything more than the burden of that pseudo-marriage."

"I'm just not there yet, Mayson. I can't see it as a complete mistake. Even after everything that happened." Her glass clinked against an empty plate as she put it back on the table. Linc was the future she had chosen for herself. At the time, her choice had felt like the right one. She looked at Mayson, then away.

"Fine. I'll let you keep your illusions. But we both know you're better off now. I'd rather you be vaguely uneasy without him than miserable with him. You may have short-term memory loss about how things were between the two of you, but I don't."

Renee winced. "Leave it alone, Mayson."

The soft voice resonated faintly with pain. And that more than the words themselves stopped Mayson. The last thing she wanted to do was hurt Renee.

"Fine. Sorry. I got carried away, as usual."

She dropped into the chair across from the bowed head, an apology on her face. "You want to go to the movies later? Djimon Hounsou is in a movie that just came out."

Renee's eyes met hers, the pain clearing from the sunlit brown. "Okay. But you're buying the tickets *and* the popcorn."

The pressure lifted from Mayson's chest. She sighed through her smile. "No problem. That shouldn't break the bank."

Chapter 2

Mayson's booted footsteps sounded cautiously in the damp alley between First and Second streets. The three whiskeys she'd had flowed pleasantly through her system, provoking a tuneless hum, a half dance through the darker than expected night; unexpected because she hadn't planned to be out much later than sunset.

She'd dropped Renee off at her condo hours before. The movie was good and at the end of the evening her friend had been laughing again, flashing the familiar white smile. One day she'd learn to keep her mouth shut about Linc. Obviously today wasn't the day.

Mayson sighed and kept walking. Something lurked in the shadows nearby, teasing her with its definite presence. She should have been frightened. She should have walked quickly toward a better-lit street. Instead she sauntered peacefully with that presence, away from the women's bar that had been nothing but boredom, boozy girls, and too many drinks.

"Mayson."

The soft voice—with a hint of Southern peach—sounded like a hallucination. Peaches like that didn't often fall in San Diego.

"You left the bar too soon, darling. The fun was just getting started."

She slowed down to allow the peach to catch up with her

from the hidden corner of the alley. Although it was a voice she vaguely recognized, she wasn't sure from where. After a few moments waiting in the dark with nothing and no one materializing, Mayson dismissed the voice as a definite hallucination and continued on her way. Her feet itched to move.

She emerged from the dark street onto University Avenue. It was alive this time of night. Boys in tight pants, their gestures urgent and electric. Chic gay girls with their short haircuts and newsboy caps perched on one side. Stylish heels tapping like music against the sidewalk.

"Mayson."

The voice came again, closer.

She turned around.

A woman stood under the streetlights. She had short hair just beginning to curl against her scalp, shining dark eyes, and a body like a high summer peach in the Southern California heat. Round. Firm. Delicious. The red dress she wore flattered her dark skin, fluttering around her knees as she walked. The woman came closer on high heels that brought her within kissing distance of Mayson's six-foot height.

Ah. Now she knew why she recognized that voice. This was one of her students, someone who regularly took yoga classes at Dhyana Yoga. And she'd been in the club Mayson just left. She remembered her from the bar, leaning over to get the bartender's attention as every woman nearby leaned over to check out her ass. Mayson included.

"This is a far way to walk in those heels," Mayson said.

"Not too far since I have what I want in sight."

Oh.

Friday evening traffic trickled past, fluttering the hem of the woman's red dress.

"I'm Fatimah," she said.

Mayson's mouth twitched. "And I think you already know my name."

They smiled at each other.

The dress Fatimah wore was one of those wraparound

kinds. It lay snugly over her breasts and the thick nipples that seemed determined to press back against the fabric. The tie at her hip fluttered in the breeze and begged to be loosened.

A wicked grin curled Mayson's mouth. She reached out her hand. Between her fingers, the fabric felt like silk. Maybe it *was* silk. The tie slid between her fingers, whisper-soft beneath the lazy caress of her thumb.

Under her light touch, Fatimah fidgeted, shifting from one leg to the other, rubbing her thighs together under the dress. Mayson didn't put her out of her misery. Fatimah had been so confident before. She released the bit of silk but did not step back.

"I was surprised to see you at the club tonight," Fatimah finally said.

"Why?" Mayson thought she knew the reason but wanted the other woman to say it.

"All this time I *thought* you were into women but I wasn't sure." Fatimah tossed her head back like she was used to having long hair. "You're always so impersonal in class."

Mayson hid a smile. She *had* noticed Fatimah in her classes, her subtle and not-so-subtle cues that she was available. But Mayson was very, very careful. There were always women in the studio giving those signals. But no matter what the women said with their bodies, she took care never to let her hand linger too long, avoiding the thrust of breast or curve of ass casually thrown in her way as she guided the students through their poses. Dhyana Yoga was her business, not a pickup spot.

But she and Fatimah weren't at the studio tonight.

"Just how personal did you want me to get in class?" she asked the woman.

Fatimah lowered her gaze. "There are a lot of people at the studio who'd like to have you."

"Really? I hope they come for the lessons, not just to look at me."

"Trust me, they want to do more than look." Fatimah smiled

in renewed confidence, full lips parting over white teeth. "*I want to do more than just look.*"

Mayson's smile joined hers. "Well, I'm pretty sure we can do something about that," she murmured. "Would you like to go back to my place for some coffee?"

The walk to her house was short. They didn't waste the anticipatory silence by talking, only walked close together, the backs of their hands occasionally touching, Mayson inhaling the night and becoming more sober with each step. She hadn't been looking for sex tonight, but she was glad it had found her.

It felt like a long time since she'd had a woman in her bed. But it had been only two months. Two months wasn't a long time for her to go without sex, especially when she wasn't in a relationship. The last time Nuria, her sometime lover, came into town, they'd had eight days of incredible I-can't-bear-to-leave-your-skin-much-less-the-house-for-an-hour sex that left Mayson raw and her muscles aching for days afterward. She and Nuria had had a mutually satisfying casual relationship for almost ten years now. The bloom had never gone off that rose. But Mayson knew it was only because they lived on separate coasts and saw each other only once a year.

In her house, she stood on the threshold of indecision. The kitchen for coffee or the bedroom for what they really came here for? She could feel the other woman's quiet but slightly accelerated breath near her, almost at her back. The anticipation rose inside her, flaring her nostrils, tearing her patience to shreds.

The decision made itself. "Come here."

The dress was beautifully easy to take off. With one tug the string loosened and Mayson unwrapped the body that had been promised to her. Fatimah's pleasure rumbled deep in her throat at Mayson's appreciative and hungry look.

The last time she'd had a woman in her house intent on sex, Nuria had backed her against the door as soon as they walked in and demanded that Mayson fuck her. It had been her pleasure to take the reins then, lifting Nuria against the door, tearing her panties away from the already wet and welcoming pussy, and sliding her fingers home.

But that was another time.

She and Fatimah came together, mouths, bellies, hands on skin. Through her clothes she could feel the other woman's heat. Her hard nipples. The damp skin already ready for the tasting.

"Fuck me," Fatimah hissed against her ear.

Perhaps that time and this one weren't that different after all.

She licked the soft, salty throat, gripping a fleshy hip while her fingers delved into the dense hairs to find the slick pussy. Two fingers. They both gasped and Fatimah fanned her legs wider against the back of the sofa, arms braced wide as Mayson fucked her slowly, relishing the pleasure of her pussy and the soft, sighing moans, and the hips rushing up to meet her fingers.

Her nipples were fat and eager for Mayson's mouth. *Ah!* She groaned into the abundant flesh, licking and sucking at the stiff nipples, fingers working, curving up, sliding deep, exploring and taking.

With one hand, she abruptly lifted Fatimah up until she sat on the back of the heavy couch, legs spread wider. Her gasp of surprise turned into a groan of pleasure when Mayson slid her fingers deeper. Her head fell back, hips diving up for Mayson's seeking fingers, her head thrown back to release a continuous chorus of moans.

"Yes! Oh yes!" She thrust up against Mayson's fingers, the juice from her cunt slick and plentiful.

Her nakedness and Mayson's clothed body. The rising heat in the room. The leap of her breasts with each movement of Mayson's fingers.

"Mayson!"

Fatimah gripped her arm, fingers sinking into the skin. That pain joined the nearly unbearable fullness between Mayson's thighs, her pussy molten from the noises the woman made. Fatimah threw her head back, screaming. Her pussy clutched and spasmed around Mayson's fingers. Thick juice rushed down her fingers.

Fatimah's breathing sounded loud in the room. "Oh my God, that was—that was perfect." She laughed into Mayson's neck.

The soft breath fanned against her sensitive skin, sending goose bumps dancing down her chest. She pulled Fatimah from the back of the sofa away from the living room and up the stairs.

"We're not done yet."

Breathless laughter bubbled again from her guest. "I hope not. I haven't gotten to touch you yet."

"You'll definitely get your chance."

Mayson pushed open the bedroom door and guided Fatimah with steady, devouring kisses—her hands on her breasts, the lush ass—into the room already glowing with light from the bedside lamp. On the bed, Fatimah twisted in her arms to turn off the light.

"Leave it on," Mayson growled.

She liked seeing what she was getting. Lights-off sex was never her scene even when she had briefly slept with men in college. The movement of light over sweating flesh was an endless source of pleasure for her. Rippling, sweat-soaked skin. Bared teeth. She liked to see the animal her lovers became in that intimate act, stripped bare of everything civilized and wanting nothing more than to satisfy that down-low ache.

"I like that you like to look," Fatimah whispered.

She flicked open the buttons on Mayson's shirt one by one, revealing skin an inch at a time. Mayson's nipples pebbled, eager for more contact, but she forced herself to be patient. Fatimah didn't seem to be in a hurry.

The woman dipped her head to enclose a newly bared nipple in her hot, wet mouth. Mayson groaned low in her throat, reveling in the tongue licking slowly at her nipples, circling the hard tips, then the mouth sucking again until she thought she would wash away on the river of lust between her legs.

"Yes...," she hissed, gripping Fatimah's head tight against her.

She squeezed her legs together to hold the sensation close.

"No, baby. Let me in there." Fingers slipped between her parted thighs, stroking her dripping pussy.

"You're so wet." A low gasp of surprise and delight. Fingers swam inside her, playing over her clit. "You feel so damn good."

Fatimah's mouth wandered low, licking its way down her tightened belly. That mouth on her clit stopped her breath. Then started it again.

"Christ!" She arched up in the bed, into the heated mouth, into a hungrily lapping tongue that knew its way around a wet pussy. "Fuck, yes." She urged her on with low growls.

The tongue flicked her clit faster, alternating licks and sucks until Mayson's body was a tight arch, ready for its release. Fatimah's greedy mouth dove into her pussy. The wet slurps, the groans of her enjoyment.

"God, yes. Yes!" Her body exploded. She crushed her pussy against Fatimah's face.

The woman crawled up her body, face wet. "I hope you can go again," she murmured. "The way you taste made me so hot." She licked Mayson's mouth, flooding Mayson's nostrils with the salty scent of her own sex.

"Kiss me," Fatimah murmured. "Turn around so I can kiss you, too."

She waved her sexy pink cunt in front of Mayson's face.

Light played over Fatimah's body as she sat up in the bed and stretched. Under Mayson's hands those curves had been inspiring, a pleasure to caress and taste and stroke against the sheets. Her mouth watered for another taste. A smile played on Fatimah's face as if she knew Mayson was watching. She raked her hands through her short hair, fingers making the sound of a sigh through black curls, and got out of the bed.

Her body was soft, symmetric seduction as she sauntered naked across the room. At the low oak bookshelf that also served as a padded window seat, she knelt. Spine arched, ass out. Heat flared between Mayson's thighs. Fatimah trailed her fingers along the spines of Mayson's leather-bound set of law books.

"This is pretty heavy reading," she said, picking one at random, flipping it open to a page.

"I was a lawyer once upon a time. Some books I couldn't throw away."

Her guest made a noncommittal noise, then rose gracefully, a book held open just below her breasts.

Fatimah's lips parted and she began to read a paragraph on tort law.

"Does that turn you on?" She looked up at Mayson with a raised eyebrow, the book still framing heavy breasts and dark nipples that Mayson longed to pinch and lick, then pinch again.

Some women are into the strangest things. Mayson allowed her smile to show. "What you read, no. How you read it, definitely."

To prove it, she touched herself very lightly with fingers that came away wet.

"Hm." The woman smiled and closed the book. To her credit, she put it back exactly where she found it, lining it up with the other spines before getting once again to her feet and giving Mayson a slow, considering look.

Whatever game she was playing, Mayson liked. She'd never had a groupie before, and this one was certainly sexy enough to make the bother worth it. As interested as Fatimah was in fucking her, she also seemed intent on peeking into Mayson's life. She moved from bookshelves to paintings to

photographs to sculptures, taking in everything she saw as
eagerly as she'd taken Mayson's fingers inside her pussy.

Fatimah pulled open the closet doors and stepped inside.
The light clicked on. "My God, you are *really* organized."

From her position on the bed, Mayson could see the curve
of her arm, the hint of her bare backside. Without seeing it
happen, she knew Fatimah ran her fingers along the clothes
suspended from their hangers, organized by garment type,
color, and fabric weight. When the woman started opening
drawers inside the closet, Mayson decided she'd had enough.

When Mayson walked up silently behind her and touched
her hips, Fatimah startled, abruptly slamming the sock drawer
shut. "You moved so fast," she said breathlessly.

"You just weren't paying attention." Her heart thumped
wildly under Mayson's hand.

Mayson soothed her with a light caress, stroking her hip
with one hand, the satin curve of her breast with the other. A
nipple hardened between her fingers. Heavy thighs parted.
Fatimah leaned back into her as the wetness between her legs
thickened.

Satisfied, Mayson bent to lick the curve of her ear, her
throat. Fatimah groaned and dropped her head back in surrender. Her clit plumped and Mayson's fingers slid easily inside her warmth.

"Can I fuck you again? Or do you want to keep snoop-
ing?"

The woman chuckled hoarsely. Her hips moved hungrily
toward Mayson's fingers. Sweat broke out in lovely prickles
against her skin and Mayson licked her shoulder, down her
back, the gloriously thick curve of her ass. Salty sweet. Her
fingers didn't pause their motion as she went to her knees,
pushed Fatimah back against the low bank of drawers, nudged
her thighs wider.

"Yes," Fatimah moaned. "Fuck me." Her fingers clamped
onto Mayson's shoulder and squeezed. "Fuck me, please."

And Mayson was never one to deny a woman her request.

* * *

"Thanks. I knew you wouldn't disappoint."

Standing in the doorway, once again in her street clothes, Fatimah looked well-satisfied, well-relaxed. An echo of the feelings that sat in Mayson's body. The woman slid her fingers up the lapels of Mayson's robe and pulled her down for a kiss.

Damp lips. Wetter tongue. The lazy exploration of mouths that was both a hello and a good-bye.

"Glad I could be of service," Mayson murmured, licking at the corner of her mouth.

"I hope you enjoyed it as much as I did."

Enjoy was an understatement. Fatimah, she found out in the course of their abbreviated pillow talk and third round of spine-melting sex, was a massage therapist who knew her way around a woman's body. Her fingers, short and agile, delved into places that made Mayson gasp in surprise, then in hedonistic satisfaction.

Mayson chuckled. "Absolutely."

Fatimah's round cheeks creased with laughter. "See you around, teacher."

She tucked her purse under her arm and turned to walk down the short flight of stairs leading to the circular drive and the street. The hem of the pretty red dress kissed her knees with each step. Mayson watched her for a while, enjoying the simple pleasure of woman and early morning before going back upstairs to her thankfully empty bed.

Chapter 3

"Tell me again why I allowed you to talk me into coming with you to this party?" Mayson narrowed her eyes at Renee. She shifted her shoulders under the long-sleeved shirt and vest, wishing for the umpteenth time she'd worn something cooler. Already she could feel the sweat gathering at the small of her back.

"Because I've done stuff like this for you more times than I can count."

Mayson grunted. She shoved her hands into the pockets of her slacks, looking around the room full of corporate types who worked with or for Renee's firm, Banes Unlimited. Her best friend was easily the sexiest woman there, in her peach-colored dress draped Grecian style around her slender form.

"Come on, honey." Renee looped her arm through Mayson's. "Lighten up. I know you could be at the club getting ass from some hot girl, but explore the possibilities here." She flashed her dimples at Mayson. "Besides, you're here to support me, not have fun."

Mayson chuckled wryly. "As long as I know the real deal."

They strolled together through the crowd, Renee pressed to Mayson's side as they took in the eye candy, such as it was. In a ballroom full of suits, self-identified corporate studs, and the very occasional attractive woman under fifty-five, Renee was getting the better end of the deal.

Walking so closely together, Mayson knew they ran the usual risk. People often thought they were a couple. Some asked; most just assumed and treated them as such. But Mayson would tell anyone who asked that they were best friends and had been ever since Renee beat the crap out of a schoolyard bully who'd tried to rally the rest of their four-year-old classmates into making fun of Mayson and her accent, both newly arrived from Jamaica.

Renee's parents were from Jamaica and, although she never had the accent, she passionately loved all things Jamaican. Even the new girl in class whom she hadn't spoken to until the bully hit the dirt, holding his nose and calling for teacher.

"There's my boss," Renee hissed as they moved through the arched entryway leading to another crowded ballroom. "Let's not walk that way."

At Renee's direction, they made a sharp right toward a smaller room decorated like a seventeenth-century French palace complete with over-the-top Louis XIV–style furniture and a large portrait of the Sun King on the wall. A jazz quartet played a lazy number in the middle of the room.

"Alonzo is such a waste of space," Mayson muttered. "I don't know why you don't just knife him one night and have done with it."

"Because I would go to *jail.*" Renee emphasized the last word with a light pinch to Mayson's side.

Laughing, Mayson jumped back from her.

"Alonzo has been a dick since the day you started working for him, Renee. It'll be a relief for us both when you quit and leave all that stress behind."

"Yeah..."

Mayson spied the chocolate fountain at the back of the room and homed in on it, pulling Renee in her wake.

"Keep talking," she said. "I'm listening."

An infusion of chocolate would be the perfect thing to make the evening more bearable, Mayson thought. As they

moved toward the chocolate, the band started playing a live-
lier song. Some brave souls got up to dance. A short Elvis
look-alike balancing three glasses of champagne in his hands
stumbled toward them. She pulled Renee closer to her side
and maneuvered around him.

"Anyway, quitting is easier said than done," Renee said.
"When I leave, I want to do something on my own, not keep
slaving to earn someone else a paycheck."

Mayson nodded but kept her mouth shut. For the past two
years, at least, Renee had been miserable working for Alonzo
Banes. She knew what she wanted to do. She knew how to do
it. She was just scared.

When she grunted, Renee looked at her sharply. "What?"

"Nothing."

At the chocolate fountain, she stopped to take a deep and
respectful breath. The dark, rich scent of melted chocolate
made her taste buds all want to hop in for a swim. By mutual
agreement, they put the discussion on hold. Renee held a
skewer lined with strawberries under the chocolate stream.

Mayson plucked one of the berries off the bamboo skewer
and bit into it. "Thanks." She grinned down at Renee.

"Renee, you're looking delectable as usual."

Mayson heard her friend groan with irritation, but the smile
she turned to face her boss was absolutely brilliant. Wearing
his signature gray—sport coat, jeans, a darker gray handker-
chief stuck in the breast pocket—Alonzo Banes stood much
too close. Mayson never understood why such a relatively
young guy would wear such an aging color. The perpetual
gray of his outfits only emphasized the few streaks of silver in
his thick hair.

"Interesting word choice, Alonzo. I didn't think you knew
any with that many syllables." Renee flashed her boss her
pearly whites while her brown eyes remained cold.

Mayson would never want to be on the receiving end of
that look.

"For you, I'd happily extend myself." He stared at Renee like he wanted to devour her.

Jesus.

"Mayson, you remember my boss, Alonzo."

Mayson nodded at the man. "Evening," she said.

He didn't offer his hand and Mayson didn't put hers out either.

"A pleasure, ladies."

Mayson felt his eyes on her trying to see past the starched front of her button-down shirt and black vest. He licked his lips, looking from her to Renee, a fantasy obviously playing through his head.

Yeah, definitely a knife for this asshole.

"It's been fun." Renee looped her arm through Mayson's again and steered her away from her boss. And away from the chocolate. Mayson sighed.

Once out of earshot, Renee made a sound of disgust. Mayson allowed herself to be pulled into a smaller room with comfortable chairs, a few people scattered around, and a breeze blowing in through the open French doors. They sank into a green velvet love seat, sighing in unison.

"You know that chocolate fountain was the highlight of my evening," Mayson muttered. She leaned back in the chair, trying to decide how annoyed she wanted to be.

"I know." With a flourish, Renee produced a plate of chocolate-covered strawberries and cream puffs. "For your trouble," she said with a teasing laugh.

"If I ever doubted your love..." Mayson pounced on the plate.

Renee laughed. "You are so easy."

"Yes, and don't you forget it." Mayson split a cream puff with her tongue, enjoying the thick, semisweet cream sliding over her taste buds. *Heaven.*

Renee laughed again as they settled into the sofa to people-watch in silence. The pretty boys were in plentiful supply tonight. The pretty girls were not.

Ah well. Mayson shrugged.

"As much as I love my gay brothers, I have to wonder if there are any straight men aside from Alonzo"—Renee made a face—"at this party?"

"If that's what you're looking for, I can't help you with that." Mayson grinned around a strawberry. Its juice was even sweeter with the chocolate.

"I don't know why. I've helped you find girls before."

"Nothing I could keep."

"As if you're really looking for anything permanent. I love you, Mayson. But you're just too damn picky."

"I think you just hurt my feelings."

"Doubtful." Renee snagged a glass of champagne from a passing tray. The light filtering through the liquid and bubbles and glass shimmered against her cheek as she lifted the wine to her lips. Renee's laughing eyes drifted up to catch Mayson's.

"Once upon a time I would've—" Something bumped into Mayson's shoulder from behind, stopping her words.

Wetness flooded down her neck and shoulder. Mayson jumped up from her seat.

"Shit! I'm *so* sorry." A woman materialized from behind the love seat, frantically wiping at the spreading stain on Mayson's shirt and the front of her vest.

How long had she owned this vest without anything spilling on it? Mayson turned to the woman with irritation. Big brown eyes framed by a thicket of black lashes stared up at her. A full mouth, brightened with lipstick, smiled in apology.

"Sorry," the woman said again. She shoved her empty wineglass onto a nearby shelf and bent to wipe again at the stain on Mayson's chest and shoulder.

Beside her, Renee smirked. She stepped back and allowed the woman to clean. Mayson frowned at her friend. *This shit is not funny.*

The woman stopped wiping and straightened. "I'm so

clumsy. Please let me pay for this." She paused at the look on Mayson's face. "Please. I insist."

"It's only white wine," Mayson finally, grudgingly, said. "I'm sure it won't stain."

"Still, it needs to be cleaned." The woman reached into her purse and pulled out a card. "Let's exchange cards and I'll get this taken care of as soon as possible."

Her long, manicured fingers curled around a piece of cream-colored stationery. When Mayson didn't immediately reach for the card, she tucked it into the damp vest pocket.

Mayson didn't bother reaching for a card of her own. "Really, it's okay. Don't worry about it." She tugged at the damp collar of her shirt and loosened the first two buttons.

The woman stepped close enough for Mayson to smell her perfume, a mixture of citrus and roses. "Please. It would make me feel so much better if you accepted my offer to clean your beautiful suit."

The woman's voice vibrated with seduction.

She wasn't bad looking, Mayson decided, watching the burgundy mouth and the way the black dress clung to her breasts and hips. The woman was slender, but beautifully proportioned with a thick ass and hefty breasts. She smiled, as if Mayson, the slow kid, had finally moved to the head of the class.

"I'm Kendra," she said. She offered her hand, palm down, intimacy in her gaze.

Beside her, Renee muttered something about getting a room. Jolted from the other woman's slumberous gaze, Mayson turned to her friend.

"Ah, this is my friend, Renee."

The gaze Kendra turned on Renee wasn't a friendly one. Mayson watched with amusement as the woman gave her what amounted to a visual strip search, the eyes tearing apart Renee's outfit, jewelry, haircut, how close she stood to Mayson.

"A pleasure," Renee said, although her voice said the opposite.

The women shook hands coolly before Kendra turned back to Mayson. "Call me," she said, and walked slowly away, hips swinging under the black dress.

"That was interesting," Mayson said. It wasn't often that she got picked up at a straight event.

"*That* looked like trouble," Renee muttered. "Did you see the way she stared me down like she was ready to wrestle me to get to you?"

"That would be fun to see." Mayson twisted an invisible mustache and grinned.

"Pig."

"Heartless. I thought you were ready to do anything to get me laid tonight."

"Me, not you." Renee sipped her champagne.

Mayson shook her head. "And selfish too."

A chuckle spilled from Renee's lips.

With a frown, Mayson looked down at her shirt. "Let me run to the bathroom and clean up this mess while you go mingle with your people."

Renee sighed. "Fine. I suppose I do need to do some networking."

"Don't have too much fun." Mayson laughed.

When she came back from the bathroom, instead of going to find Renee she continued out to the balcony. The Friday evening air was crisp, even in San Diego, where the rest of the world thought it stayed a balmy eighty degrees all year long. They had just left behind a particularly brisk winter and were getting back into the sweet monotony of surfing days and hammock-swinging nights.

She leaned her forearms against the steel railing and drew in a deep breath.

"I thought that was you out here, Mayson."

Grant Chambers appeared at her side with a beer in hand. She glanced at the solidly built man in surprise.

"Hey, Grant. What are you up to?"

"Enjoying the party, what else?"

"Did you come all the way down here just for this shindig?"

"I've come down to San Diego for less." He eyed her meaningfully and smiled, white teeth flashing in his brown face.

Her mouth twitched with amusement. Grant had lived next door to Renee's parents in Dana Point for as long as she could remember.

Although he'd been the charming boy next door, he and Renee had never connected in the way Mayson knew he wanted. And when he went away to school at Berkeley, everyone thought that his earlier ambition to court and eventually marry Renee was over. But after finishing his graduate degree in criminal justice, he moved back to Dana Point as a police officer and had been there ever since.

He'd never made any secret of his intentions regarding Renee. And she just ignored him and carried on with her life.

It was too bad. Grant was a good guy; nice but not boring. Mayson liked that about him. With his endless optimism and ability to turn every setback into an opportunity, he was like a big, happy kid.

"Have you seen Renee yet?" Mayson asked.

"I've seen her but we haven't talked." He sipped his beer. "She looks good."

"Doesn't she always?"

"Very true." Grant laughed but there was something less than amusement behind the sound.

Maybe the wait for Renee's attention was getting to him. *She* wouldn't have held out that long for a woman who wouldn't give her the time of day. Was he even dating other women?

She turned to look at him and found his eyes already on her.

"Word around the neighborhood is your parents moved back to Jamaica. Is that true?"

"Yes. They went back down a couple of months ago." The familiar sadness sank into Mayson's belly at the thought of her absent mother and father. "It's something they talked about doing for years. A part of me is glad."

"But I'm sure you miss them."

"I do, but—"

"Mayson, I've been looking for you."

She swallowed the rest of her words and pushed away the sadness. This wasn't the time or the place. Grant squeezed her shoulder.

"And you found me," she said to Renee's pronouncement.

She turned in time to see Renee wrinkle her nose at Grant. The source of her friend's dislike of the muscular police offi- cer was a mystery. Renee could do much worse than Grant. She had in the past.

"You following me, Grant?" Renee asked, her voice only slightly teasing.

"Ah, if only I had time for such pleasurable pursuits." His gaze on her was mild, taking inventory of her. An approving light winked in his eyes. "But I'm actually here with a friend."

"Really?" Renee gave the room behind her a cursory glance. "Where is she?"

"Networking. I'm just the arm candy." He flashed that dazzling smile of his. "Whenever she's ready for me, she knows where I am."

"I'd love to meet this woman and see what your type is."

"All you have to do is look in the mirror to see my type, Renee. But my date is nothing like you."

Just then, a tall woman appeared on the balcony, obvi- ously looking for someone.

Damn. If Mayson had known how to wolf whistle, she would have let one loose then. Big, thick hair like a halo framed her beautiful face. Black-coffee skin. Breasts plumped up in a pale yellow dress that rode the fine line between tasteful and tasty.

"Grant, I need you," the woman said in a rough voice like she'd smoked too many cigarettes. Or just woken up.

He took one last drink of his beer and straightened to his full height. "I'm right here." He aimed one of his infectious smiles at Mayson. "It was good to run into you, Mayson. Renee. See you around sometime soon."

The two looked after him, Renee with a considering look on her face. "I didn't think that was his type at all," she said.

You got that right, Mayson thought. The woman looked hot and fast. As if she'd try anything to get off. Not at all like a side of homegrown sexy like Renee. "I guess you don't know him as well as you thought," Mayson said.

"Believe me, I know everything there is to know about Grant Chambers and that's why that tricked-out little sports car can have him."

Mayson stared after the girl who had already disappeared into the crowd with Grant on her arm. *Or that tricked-out ride can have me, if she ever gets tired of driving stick.*

They left the party a few hours later after Renee, tired of mincing around on her high heels, suggested they go for a drive to La Jolla. In Mayson's drop-top Toyota Solara, they sped away from the Hillcrest party, heading up the 5 under the bright moon.

"Why don't you give the guy a chance?" Mayson raised her voice to be heard above the wind.

"Don't start. You sound like Mama."

"Your mama has been known to be right about a thing or two."

"The last thing I want is the boy next door. I know him. He's boring. If you like Grant so much, why don't you take him home to your parents?"

"Fucking men is something I'll leave to you. If he had a

cute sister, we could talk, but as things stand…" Mayson shrugged.

Grant had two brothers, both older than him, already married and gone off to New York to raise families of their own.

"All this isn't even about Grant. It's about most men that I meet. They all want to cling like parasites after the first time you sleep with them. That's not what I want." Renee dropped her head back against the seat to look at the stars.

"What do you want, then?"

"I want sex," Renee said. "With no complications."

Mayson raised an eyebrow at her friend. "Really?"

"Yes. Why are you so surprised? I hope you don't think you're the only one entitled to a little pleasure on the side."

Mayson nearly stuttered. "No. But I just thought you wanted—you know, a guy you could see occasionally, go out on dates with, eventually take home to your parents."

"That sounds nice, but I really just want the sex." Renee laughed at whatever she saw in Mayson's face. "You can be such a prude." Then she sobered.

"All the years we've been friends, that's what you had. Sex. The only long-term relationship you ever had was with Nuria and even that one was based on sex." Renee tilted her head, frowning in the sudden halo of light from a street-lamp. "You've been so happy. No one has broken you. That's what I want."

"You make my life sound so meaningless and empty," Mayson said, allowing the sadness to leak into her voice.

"No! It's just the opposite. You're the most fulfilled person I know." Her hand landed on her friend's arm.

Really? Mayson shook her head. "Don't use me as an example, Renee. Just because I haven't been able to commit to anyone doesn't mean I never wanted to."

"Was there someone?" Renee lifted her head.

Heat crept under Mayson's cheeks, unexpected. Unwelcome. "Yes. But it was a long time ago and things didn't work out."

Passing headlights illuminated the curiosity in Renee's face. Mayson shook her head in response to the unasked question. Renee pressed her lips together, then lay back against the headrest. Quiet.

The car sped toward La Jolla, wind dancing over their skin, other vehicles racing past. Their headlights blazed a path through the darkness ahead of them, illuminating the serpentine road. Around them, the hills of San Diego rose up silent and dark.

The leather squeaked as Renee rolled her head to look at Mayson. "Have you ever wanted to be free from yourself?"

Mayson nodded, releasing the threads of memory unraveled by Renee's earlier questions.

"Linc never knew me. Or I hope he didn't, because the person he saw was cold and unlovable and she complicated things. I don't want to be that person." Renee's voice was soft, lost.

Her dangling pearl and platinum earrings batted against her cheek as she raised her head to look at Mayson. "I want to be uncomplicated. I want to be in an uncomplicated situation."

"Isn't that what we all want?" Mayson looked briefly at Renee before giving her attention back to the road. "But as for your man problem, it's too bad you just can't get what you need—no names, no numbers—then leave. That way the guy can't complain that you're not there for him or whatever it is that men complain about."

Renee smiled faintly. "That's a damn fine idea but how do I even go about that?"

"Do what everybody else does," Mayson said, shifting into third and passing a black Bentley. She narrowed her eyes against the car's high beams before reaching up to tilt the rearview mirror. "Put an ad in the paper. Or online, since that's much quicker."

"You have a solution to everything, don't you?"

"Not really, but when life drops shit bombs, it doesn't make sense to lie there and wallow in the mess. Get up and clean yourself off."

The car sang with Renee's soft laughter. "Well, since you put it that way, wise one." She laughed again.

"Every problem can be solved, honey." Mayson grinned. "Never forget that."

Chapter 4

Renee let herself into her house with a sigh of exhaustion. When she and Mayson got to La Jolla, her friend exhumed a bottle of red wine from her trunk. Between them, they finished the bottle, talking loudly, laughing, their shoulders pressed together as they sat side by side on the hard cement steps facing the splash and release of the sea.

Now, slightly drunk and more tired than she'd been in a long time, Renee could barely navigate the dark interior of her condo without bumping into something.

"Ouch!" She bounced off the door handle, rubbing her hip through the dress.

With an aggrieved sigh, she kicked off her shoes, stumbling in the straps of the high heels as she made her way across the bedroom. Exhaustion tugged her toward the bed, but habit found her in the bathroom, stripping off her dress and stepping under the shower's scalding heat.

Afterward, she sat on the edge of the bed, naked, smoothing lotion into her skin. Tiredness still nipped at the edges of her awareness but it was something she could easily ignore. Now that the shower had cleared away the last of the fog, the haunting remnants of her morning conversation with her ex-husband came back to her.

Over the phone, his voice had been that same deep seduction she always had a weakness for. During their marriage, his voice was a comfort she relied on. She asked him to tell stories, to read to her, to talk about his day just so she could lose herself in the dips and heights of his profound voice. But what he'd said in the morning hadn't been comforting.

"I wish things could have worked out with us, Renee," he had said. "But you weren't willing to change for the relationship. You're as much a stranger to me now as when we first met. I need someone who can open up to me and who will trust me."

Renee hadn't fought the divorce. She couldn't say that she would have filed if he hadn't done it, but the marriage had been spiraling down the drain almost from the start. Linc had wanted too much emotional intimacy from her too soon. And later he became intent on devouring her personality and converting it into something more suited to his life. He wanted her to be someone more attached to him, someone more stylish whom he could show off at work functions. The relationship had been destined to fail. Still, she missed him. At times, familiar intimacy was better than none at all.

"I can't do anybody any good right now," she'd confessed to Mayson, sitting on the cool steps overlooking the ocean on one side and the seal refuge on the other. Even though she knew Linc had been an emotional leech, that didn't stop her from feeling worthless as a partner and unable to provide the most basic of emotional reassurances.

"If what you need is a good fuck, go out and get it," her best friend said as the surf pounded against the hard packed sand, misting their faces with sea spray. "Forget any so-called emotional inadequacy. You've done okay with me for the past twenty years." But even Mayson's words couldn't make her feel better.

Renee ached for a solution to the chaos swirling inside her.

"Do what you do best, honey." She heard Mayson's voice as if she lay in the bed next to her. "Take care of yourself. There's no one else to consider in this. Take what you need and move on with your life."

And what I want is sex. That would help her to forget about her insecurities, about Linc and his damn voice pouring poisonous doubt into her ear.

Renee pulled her laptop from the drawer in her nightstand and booted up the machine. It flickered on from hibernation mode and immediately found her wireless connection. Within a few keystrokes she found a familiar Web site, one that she and Mayson had often browsed out of boredom, laughing at the desperation of some of the ads from people "looking for companionship." Tonight she wasn't looking for companionship. She wanted even less than that.

The words came to her and she drafted her ad. As she wrote what she wanted and what she didn't want, the lyrics of Rupert Holmes's Piña Colada song ran through her mind. Her fingers slowed on the keyboard. And sadness caught the edges of her mouth and turned them down.

Unlike in the song, there was no chance that she and Linc would end up together after discovering new and appealing things about each other that four years of marriage had never revealed. Even when they'd first gotten together, she and Linc never seemed to fit. They never liked the same things. Their friends never got along.

And it wasn't until they separated that Renee realized that she'd become estranged from her own friends during the course of their marriage. His friends had become hers and after the divorce she was left alone.

Renee shook herself out of the stupor, quickly finished the ad, and uploaded it to the Web site. *Nothing is going to come of this,* she thought, turning the computer off and getting ready for bed. This would be yet another of her failed attempts to reach out to another human being.

But just before she fell asleep, she remembered her question from earlier.

Was there someone?

Then Mayson's disquieting answer. "Yes."

"Who?" she'd wanted to ask. "Who had it been?"

Chapter 5

Life in a corporate office was slow death, Renee decided. She picked up the proofs from her desk and left her cubicle, heading to her boss's office, which was one of only six offices along the outer walls of their eighteenth-floor suite. The company had recently moved from a cozy two-story Victorian in Hillcrest, where most of the designers had private offices. In this cold building in the heart of downtown, she had been relegated to a "cubicle farm," losing her privacy and what she now realized was the luxury of being able to think in peace and quiet. Alonzo, of course, kept his office.

At his door, she knocked once before walking in.

"Here's what I have for Skarsgard," she said, dropping the proofs on the corner of his immaculate desk. Did he ever do anything besides surf the Net for porn and call his assistant to arrange expensive lunches the company had to swallow?

Alonzo looked away from his computer screen and leaned back in his chair. "Thanks." He smoothed his gray silk tie. "I'll take a look at these and get back to you by the end of the week."

"Thank you." She turned to go.

"You look a little out of sorts and frustrated, Renee." Alonzo stroked his tie again. "Like you need a good...date."

She continued out of the office. "That's sexual harassment, Alonzo. And I'm not afraid to press charges."

His secretary looked up as Renee passed but the older woman said nothing. She'd been working with Alonzo long enough to know his pattern and how Renee responded to it. Renee didn't know how much longer she could deal with her situation at Banes Unlimited. It had gotten old long ago. Even now she remembered the feel of Alonzo's eyes on her, following the way the black pinstriped slacks clung to her backside and thighs.

Mayson was right. She needed to find her way out of this corporate mess and into something she could actually enjoy. Photography. The problem was she wasn't sure she could financially survive doing it.

At her cubicle, she grabbed her still-hot cup of coffee and logged back on to her computer. The white mug with the company's logo warmed her palms. After sending off the on-line ad last night, she'd been anxious to check her account. Simultaneously scared that no one would respond to her message and also that someone actually *would* respond, Renee hesitated before finally logging into her account.

Nine messages.

She stared at the number of responses, surprised. Most of them had come in late at night, within an hour or two after she'd posted her ad.

"I'm not sure about this one, Renee."

She abruptly closed the browser window at the sound of Alonzo's voice. He appeared at the entrance to her cubicle holding the thick rectangular card stock like it had a bad smell. "This might not be what Skarsgard and the group are looking for."

She swiveled in her chair to face him. "Why don't you let *them* decide that?"

Her boss looked at her as if she'd lost her mind. His hand stiffened at his side.

"What I mean is, why don't we plan to present that to Skarsgard in the meeting? In the meantime, I'll work on at least two alternative mock-ups so if he doesn't like that, there are other directions that we can go."

Before he could say anything, she spoke again. "That's probably the most cost-effective way to go about it." She quickly explained the cost benefit to him. Bringing it down to money always made Alonzo see the light.

He nodded. "Okay. I think that can work. I knew you'd see things my way." With a grin, he gave her body the obligatory leer and walked away.

She rolled her eyes and turned back to the computer. The nine messages sat tantalizingly in her profile inbox. Nine responses. She should wait until she got home. That would be the sensible thing to do. Renee clicked on the first one.

HungCaliStud: You want sex, I want the same. Name the time and place and I'll be there with my rubber on.

The attached photo showed a shirtless man in black leather pants. A pretty face with the muscled chest and belly of a gym regular. Or a soldier. *Nice.* If that was his real picture. Renee hit the "save" button. What was a man like that doing online looking for hookups? If he walked into any straight bar in San Diego, he'd have a swarm of girls hovering in no time. Maybe something was wrong with him.

Not that it matters. It's not like you're going to date or marry him. Her inner voice (which sounded distressingly like Mayson) dismissed her concerns.

"Jesus, get a grip, girl," Renee muttered to herself and clicked on the next message.

The others were more of the same, pretty boys, pretty bodies. One scary GI Joe type with the crotch cut out of his fatigues and a cock ring tight around his balls and fully erect penis. Renee quickly looked away from the photo as soon as she saw it, just seconds before she clicked the "delete" button.

It was like shopping. Renee smiled to herself, the mouse clicking through the finite but interesting list of men, each offering himself up for her pleasure.

At the sight of number eight's Village People mustache, her thighs twitched in remembered discomfort. Her first boyfriend grew a beard a few months into their relationship and had never learned how to give head without rubbing her skin raw.

Delete. She clicked on number nine. A picture opened up on the screen in front of her but she barely paid attention to it. She read his message.

> *You're a stranger, so am I. Let's keep it that way*
> *and only exchange what we both need.*

She liked his words—no bull, no attempt at trying to lure her in. Just like her, he had something to offer. He put it out there and it was up to her to take it. She looked at the picture. It only confirmed what she had seen in his words. A strong face, all angles and darkness, not pretty but straightforward. He wore a simple gray T-shirt and jeans, peering at her, unsmiling, from a photograph that looked like it had been taken by someone who didn't know him. The wall behind him was the same gray as his shirt.

Renee clicked on the link to his e-mail and, after making a couple of quick decisions, sent him a message.

> *Perfect. Come to me at the Hotel Continental in*
> *Old Town at 9 o'clock tonight. Ask for Lola*
> *Divine at the front desk.*

As soon as she pressed "send" she called Mayson.

"I did it," she said when her best friend answered the phone.

"Okay," Mayson paused. "So now I'm waiting for the rest. Don't make me ask that stupid question."

Renee laughed. "Fine. I took your advice."

"Oh shit." In the background, she could hear rustling of cloth, like Mayson was still in bed. "What dumb advice of mine did you follow this time? I thought I already told you years ago not to listen to me."

"You did, but I do it anyway. Sometimes you actually make sense."

"Notice that you said 'sometimes.' "

"Noted." Renee took a breath. "I put an ad online and got some responses."

The phone fell silent.

"Well, don't you have anything to say?" Renee demanded.

"Are you going to meet up with any of these guys?"

"I just set it up with one of them."

"Oh my God." Cloth rustled again. "I'm not sure this is the best idea I ever had. This guy could be a killer or a rapist."

Renee picked up a pencil from her desk, chewing at the rubber tip. "I don't think he is."

"But you don't know for certain."

"You're right, I don't know, but I'm going to meet him anyway." She sighed, irritated by Mayson's lack of support. "I'm tired of doing the safe thing, Mayson. I really am."

"Fuck." Her friend sighed too. Renee could almost see her sit up in the bed, scrub a hand over her face. "If anything happened to you, your parents would kill me."

"You were the one who even gave me the idea. Why are you all of a sudden against it?"

"Because I never thought you would take me seriously. I just thought you would jack off to the idea and go to bed to wake up to another day."

"God! That sounds so boring." *So like me,* Renee thought.

"Not boring, sensible. Jesus, Renee!"

"Mayson, of anyone, I thought you'd support me in this." Renee didn't bother to keep the annoyance from her voice. "*You* would do something like this and not think twice. I doubt you'd even tell me about it."

Mayson sighed. "Fuck. Okay, fine. I'll stop being an over-protective asshole now." The sound of glasses clinking, liquid being poured, trickled through the phone. "What time are you meeting this guy? Should I come with you?"

"And do what? Watch? No thanks!" Renee nearly laughed at the thought of Mayson lurking in the darkened hotel room with her rolled-up yoga mat ready to do damage while Renee's stranger pounded into her from behind. "That definitely wouldn't work."

"Honey, you could get killed." Mayson's voice deepened. "I wouldn't be able to forgive myself if that happened."

"I absolve you. This is my decision to make and I'm making it."

"Okay. Okay. Just—just tell me where you'll be and when so I'll have the information. Then call me when you're done." Renee heard the distaste in Mayson's voice. "Shit. I can't believe I'm letting you do this."

"You're not *letting* me do anything. The last time I checked I was still a grown woman."

A rustle of papers from the adjoining cubicle reminded Renee just how little privacy she had. She lowered her voice and leaned close to the phone. "Look, if you're not going to say anything useful, I'm going to hang up."

"Renee, I don't—"

"Nope. I have to get back to work anyway. Talk to you later." She hung up the phone.

But it wasn't that easy to shut Mayson's voice out of her head. The closer it grew to nine o'clock, the more nervous about the date she became. She sat at her desk and worked on the alternate drafts of the Skarsgard proposal. But the thought of her meeting with the stranger sat, uncomfortably, at the back of her mind.

At 5:48 she looked at her watch but made no move to get up and leave the office. She didn't call the hotel to reserve the room. She didn't do anything. At 7:22, with her work done, she put away the proofs, locked her desk drawers, and left the building, her car turned toward home. 9:13 found her stretched out in the tub, bubbles up to her throat.

The lavender scent from her bubble bath swirled in the bathroom with the steam and the mournful saxophone from her iPod. Renee closed her eyes and tried to forget there was someone out there waiting for her. But she couldn't forget.

Chapter 6

"**M**ama? Daddy? You here?"
Renee pocketed the keys to her parents' house and
dropped her duffel bag. She closed the door behind her and
called out again.

At the bottom of the stairs, she hesitated. There had been
numerous unfortunate incidents during her childhood when
she'd walked in on her parents' very active sex life. Like too
many times in the past few months since her divorce, she felt
a dull throb of envy. Why couldn't she have found something
like what they had? All her life she had memories of them
being affectionate, respectful, and passionate with each other.
Twenty-nine years of beautiful, though sometimes cringe-
worthy, memories. But she was their daughter; how come she
hadn't been able to make *her* marriage last more than four
years?

Renee started up the stairs, but the sound of a car door
made her turn back the way she came. She opened the front
door.

"Hello, darling!" her mother called out from the passenger side of an unfamiliar SUV.

Renee's father climbed out of the backseat and waved.
"We didn't expect you until later this evening," he said, the
words rolling music in his strong Jamaican accent.

The trunk of the SUV eased slowly shut to reveal a familiar face. Her father took a bag from Grant with a smile at the younger man, moving quickly despite his snowy hair and thin frame. Grant carried the two remaining cloth shopping bags from the trunk and laid them at Renee's feet.

She frowned back at his smile. "Hey, Grant."

"Renee." He said her name once, nodded, and smiled again, a blinding flash of white teeth that softened the harsh planes of his face.

Somehow it confused her to see him here in her parents' driveway after the last time she had run into him. The man who'd taken up so much space at Mayson's side—then walked off with that stunning woman—was nothing like this tame creature playing bag boy for her parents. She turned to look at them. "I—uh...I decided to take the afternoon off from work and drive up a little early."

"An hour earlier and you would've missed us." Her mother, cool-looking in beige linen slacks and a pale blue tank top, slipped around the SUV to pull Renee into a hug. Her heavily powdered cheek brushed Renee's.

When Renee was a child, her mother had never worn makeup. She was beautiful and natural, giving color-free kisses when she squeezed Renee against her soft mommy's body. But as she'd grown older and the years began to tell, her mother began to wear makeup and lose weight, more and more so until her cushy size fourteen was barely a four and her kisses always left stains behind.

"Where were you?"

Her mother looked Renee over, plucking a stray hair from the collar of her sweater. "All over the place. Since Grant had the day off we asked him to go with us to the gem mines in Pala."

Her father kissed her cheek with a loud smack.

"Daddy!" Renee giggled, unable to stop herself. He grinned back at her.

Her parents' hard work and skilled investments had earned them a plush retirement six years before.

Her mother tugged her into her arms again. "You should come in and have some lemonade with us, Grant."

"Thanks, but no, Mrs. Matthews. I have some work to catch up on at home."

He flashed the older couple an apologetic version of his smile and started for his SUV. Both he and Renee knew he had nothing better to do, but as interested as he was in Renee, he also knew that she didn't want him around. As a cop, Renee assumed, he'd learned to read people well.

"I'll catch you later on," he called out, climbing into the driver's seat.

Maybe it was an illusion, but Renee swore that he winked at her as he drove off.

"I wish you'd stop giving poor Grant the evil eye, Renee." Her mother picked a bag full of scarves from the doorstep and pushed open the front door.

"I did not!"

"Oh, darling, please." Her father patted her lightly on the shoulder as he passed, picked up the other bag, and made his way into the house. "If I was him I'd run away too. Your body language was screaming at him to stay away."

Renee shrugged dismissively, irritated at the resurrection of this old topic of conversation. "Mama, Daddy, I'm not interested in that man. How many times do I have to tell you?" She followed her parents into the house.

"We're not asking you to be interested, but we'd like for you to be *nice* to him." Renee's mother frowned at her.

"What's so bad about Grant?" her father demanded. "He's a good man with a successful career. He's single and, as far as I know, doesn't beat his women."

"Not to mention you've known him for years," her mother added.

"Exactly!" She sank into the living room couch and pulled her legs up under her. "I don't want a man I've known for years."

"And we all know how fishing in unfamiliar waters worked

out for you." Her father's remark whipped Renee's head around.

"That's not nice, Daddy."

"But it's true." Her mother's voice, threaded with only a slight Jamaican accent, floated behind her as she walked into the kitchen. "You barely knew Linc a month before you married him. Now according to you, you two are as much strangers now as you were when you met." She pulled a bowl of frozen strawberries from the freezer. "Four years, darling."

Even though all this was true, Renee didn't want to hear it from her mother. Yes, Linc had been a stranger. A seductive stranger with his jazz radio station voice, lean body, and hands that promised her so much.

Her love of the unfamiliar had been what drew her to him, and although she and Linc were still alien to each other after four years of marriage and nearly six months of mutually agreed upon divorce, it was the things she knew intimately about him that repelled her. His clinginess, the way he wanted to turn her life into a mirror of his, how his feet were like hunks of jagged ice in the bed against hers.

"Mama, Daddy, we don't have to talk about this any more."

"You mean you don't want to talk about this any more." The blender growled from the kitchen, cutting off whatever else her mother had to say.

"Isn't that what I said?" She eyed her parents firmly until her father laughed, chuckling merrily from his armchair.

"Fine, fine. Enough about Grant." He grinned, throwing up his hands. "No matter how much we talk you'll just end up doing what you want anyway." With a push of a lever, his chair slowly reclined.

"So true." Her mother came out of the kitchen balancing three strawberry daiquiris on a tray.

It was the same mahogany tray that had been there throughout Renee's childhood. Through years of her father taking her mother breakfast in bed. Her mother bringing her chicken soup through almost thirty seasons of cold and flu.

"Thanks, Mama." The cold glass bit into her palm.

"You're welcome, love." She passed her husband his daiquiri and he took it with a smile.

"The perfect end to a perfect day," he said, lifting his glass in salute to his wife.

Renee's mother settled down beside her on the sofa and took a long sip from the straw curved over the edge of her frozen drink. She echoed her husband's sigh of contentment.

"So tell us, darling, how are things going in San Diego?" Her mother's heavily mascaraed eyes watched her over the rim of her glass. "Obviously Mayson hasn't found Ms. Right yet. She's not even looking." Her mother laughed without making a sound. "How about you?"

Chapter 7

After the visit with her parents, Renee felt good. And bad. Without her telling them (it was probably Mayson who told), they had known about her renewed devastation over her failed marriage. During the visit, they plied her with drinks and food and jokes until she almost forgot her misery. But they couldn't let go of the topic of Grant Chambers. Every opportunity her parents saw to insert their neighbor, they took it, repeatedly inviting him over until Renee wanted to scream. Their insistence on Grant only made it more obvious that they thought Renee needed a man and couldn't get one on her own.

Although she had always been open with her parents, Renee didn't think she could just come out and say what she really wanted to: "I don't want another husband, Mama and Daddy. I just want sex."

So she returned home from Dana Point with sex on her mind and the determination to do something about it.

On Sunday, four days after the aborted first date, Renee contacted the stranger again. He responded with the same words and so did she. This time, she didn't tell Mayson about her date. She simply left work and went to the Hotel Continental, where she changed clothes in the lobby bathroom before heading upstairs to meet her stranger. Her heart banged painfully in her chest with each step. But she didn't stop.

At the door, she hesitated. What could happen to her here tonight? Mayson's words came to her again. A rapist. A killer. Renee took a deep breath. Or someone to give her exactly what she needed. Fulfillment. She slid the keycard in the door, opened it, and stepped inside.

The door clicked shut behind her.

"I'm glad you showed this time." Amusement threaded through the deep, masculine voice. "I'm not sure my ego is strong enough to take another disappointment."

Renee swallowed, uncertain about what to say. He sat in a chair near the bed, light from the bedside lamp illuminating the life-size version of what she'd seen on her computer screen. Long legs were crossed at the ankles. His sprawl in the chair emphasized the thick weight between his legs. He sat up.

"Does the light bother you?" he asked. "We can turn it off." He reached over and clicked off the lamp.

Darkness dropped onto the room, but his image had already burned itself on her retina. A muscled, dark-skinned man in a white T-shirt and dark blue jeans. His meaty fingers, oddly gentle on the tiny knob of the lamp when he turned it.

Renee walked deeper into the room.

"You don't want to talk?" he asked. "That's fine. Usually I'm not much of a talker anyway, especially standing in front of someone as pretty as you."

At that last bit, Renee smiled. Some of her anxiety disappeared. Even in the midst of an anonymous encounter, this man couldn't stop himself from tossing out the compliments, the bait, to lure her—the female—closer. His words *were* seductive even though she doubted he could see more than a vague outline of her shape now.

"A gorgeous body like yours is unmistakable," he said.

He took a deep, audible breath.

Her thigh muscles clenched and released at the power of it. He was being quiet because he thought she wanted it. He forced himself to be whatever she asked of him, because he wanted her sex. Renee's nipples tightened.

His silence now allowed the sex in the room to speak. The whisper of her gartered and stockinged thighs as she crossed the room.

The darkness moved as he stood. But Renee stopped him, pushed him back down in the depths of the chair. His chest was hard under her palms. Still saying nothing, she slipped off her headscarf, the thin trench coat, and dropped them at his feet. Heat caressed her bare shoulders, the tops of her breasts thrust up in the lacy black bra that he couldn't see. That he didn't need to see. She moved closer to give him a chance to feel her. The breath from his open mouth misted over her skin. His body heat scorched her.

It has been so long.

She reached for him and moaned silently when he pressed stiff and sure against her hand, his masculinity plain through his jeans. Her stranger came closer. Closer. Anticipation twisted like a wild tornado in her belly. She straddled him. His hands settled on her hips.

Her center, stretched wide between the black parentheses of her garters, ached to swallow his hardness. She unbuttoned his jeans. He breathed deeply under her hands, not moving, waiting.

His hands touched her breasts—finally—squeezing her nipples through the cloth, surrounding the gentle rise of flesh. Plastic crinkled and he stopped, chuckled, retrieving the condom from inside her bra. She heard him unwrap it, felt him move to put it on, but she stopped him with a press of her hands. Renee wanted this.

There were so many things she missed about sex, the intimacy of kissing, of sharing breath with her lover, but there were other things that she craved more and more these days, that made the blood run hotter under her skin. The simple act of rolling on a condom was one of them.

She sighed, taking his thick stalk between her hands, closing her hands around the throbbing heat that would soon be inside her. Delirium rolled inside her hips. She moved against his thighs, the sensation coming over her in waves as he played with her breasts through the cloth. He moved closer. She rolled the latex on him. His hands freed her breasts from the lace. His mouth claimed a nipple.

Renee couldn't stop the low gasp, the grateful squeeze of her hands around his maleness.

I need this. She felt the words in her spine. Said them silently as she mounted him and he gasped around her nipple. A groan worked its way past her throat at the tight stretch. *So good.* She pushed his shirt up and off, wrestling quickly with the cloth, crying out at the temporary loss of his mouth on her skin. But when it came back—*oh!* He licked her nipples, one after the other, squeezing her breasts, thrusting smoothly up into her. His grunts vibrated under her chest. All of him. Renee wanted to feel all of him. This stranger who seemed to want this struggle of the flesh as much as she did.

Renee dug her fingers into the back of his neck as she rode him. Fire pulsed through her thighs, up into her belly. His mouth locked around her nipple, sucking, teeth scraping, hips thrusting up into her as the rough denim rubbed the inside of her thighs.

The moans rose in her throat, but she swallowed them. She wanted to hear him, the sounds they made together, the grunt, slap, hiss of their sex and the chair slamming against the wall, and the tiny panting noises she couldn't prevent from escaping.

A hard knot of pleasure grew in her belly. Expanded with each breath and grunt and slam of his maleness inside her. She squeezed him, reaching for her satisfaction as surely as he was reaching for his. Her stranger's hands gripped her bottom, jerking her harder and faster on him. Her breast popped free of his mouth, the nipple wet from his kiss. Sweat dripped between them, down her belly, her face. He was full and hard inside her and she gasped with the molten delight of it.

He grunted, a freight train, thrusting harder, pistoning into her enough that she could—internal muscles straining, thigh muscles aching—push herself there. He arrowed up, shaking, coming hard and fast. And she knew she had to get hers now or risk not getting anything at all. She sank her nails deeper into the back of his neck, clenched her internal muscles around his already softening dick, riding him hard until—

"Oh my God!"

Her heart rocketed in her chest. Her body caught ablaze. And fell slowly back to earth. Thigh muscles twitching, gasping, she collapsed against him.

He breathed deeply above her, his body limp too, but his heart at a gallop under her cheek. The gallop slowed to a trot, then a slow canter. He grasped at her thighs again, pulling her against his damp body.

Suddenly, the sweat and bristly hairs on his chest were too much to bear. Renee gently disengaged herself from him, pulled her bra back up, and adjusted her panties. She leaned down and kissed his bristled cheek.

"Stay, honey." He snared her in a strong grip. "I have a lot more where that came from." His voice was a low, postorgasmic buzz over her skin.

Renee froze. Was this the point when things fell apart? She licked her lips and slowly straightened, anticipating the worst. But his hand dropped away harmlessly. He fell into silence again.

Renee swallowed past the lump of fear in her throat. Bending down, she felt around on the floor for her coat and scarf, pulled them on. She walked toward the door. This was the most daring thing she'd ever done. And with the minute tremors of orgasm still flitting through her body, Renee smiled.

In the dark hotel room, she could hear her stranger's deep

breaths, smell the sex they'd just shared. *This was worth it.* Exhilaration and satisfaction trembled in her throat.

She paused in the mouth of the open door with light from the hallway pouring over her shoulders. Like when she'd just walked in, her stranger sat in the chair. Now he was sprawled, thighs spread wide, the jeans yawning open and shoved down to make room for his sex.

He stirred in the dark, a slap of latex against metal as he threw the used condom in the trash. The darkness bathed his features, but she knew his complete attention was still focused on her.

"Thank you," she said and gently closed the door behind her.

Chapter 8

It didn't seem real. Yet it had been. The slight soreness between her thighs was proof. She had felt the man's heart beating against hers, felt him slamming into her body, pounding pleasure and sensation into her hungry center until she cried out. And there had been nothing attached to it. No promise of another date. No expectation of a call. Nothing.

And nothing remained from her hour with him, not even the sweat from their sex. It disappeared down the drain, swirling amid the bubbles and water, gone. She sighed in remembrance as the water flooded over her and steam hung heavy in the bathroom, thickening her air. It didn't seem real. Yet it had been. Silent and real and exactly what she needed.

Chapter 9

Mayson knew when Renee called on Saturday night to change the location of their Sunday brunch to a restaurant instead of her condo, something had happened. And she had a fairly good idea what that *something* was.

She got to the restaurant first and claimed a window booth, sitting in the full spill of the sun with her dark glasses on. The weekend had been a peaceful and meditative one so far. No women, no drama, just an early morning phone call from her giddy parents who were still renting a house in Jamaica while waiting for their own to be built. Mayson hadn't heard from them in almost a month and didn't realize how worried she was until a sigh of relief burst out of her at the sound of her mother's voice.

"May, you know that we're okay," her mother said in her deep, country voice.

"I know, Ma. But it's good to get a confirmation phone call once in a while, too. There's a lot in the papers about crime down there."

Her tone brought her father running to the phone with apologies, but she knew the same thing would happen again. After three months, her parents were still excited about the move. She'd called their house phone a few times but no one answered.

"It's okay, Papa." She had been the one reassuring them at

the end of the phone call. "I won't worry so. Next time I'll leave a message."

When the waitress stopped by the table with a glass of water and a smile, Mayson looked up with a smile of her own.

"What can I get for you today?" the girl asked.

By the time Renee breezed in wearing her pageboy hat, skinny jeans, and red stilettos, Mayson had already been through two glasses of lemon-flavored, room-temperature water and was working on a third.

"Don't you look well-fucked," she commented with a twist of her mouth as her best friend bent to give her a hug. Renee smelled like vanilla lotion.

Renee stuck out her tongue and sat down, dropping her handbag into the booth beside her. "Don't be jealous." She paused. "Not that *you'd* want any of what I had last night." Her eyes danced from under the brim of the charcoal-gray hat.

"So how was it?" Mayson asked, though the answer was fairly obvious from Renee's scrubbed and smiling face.

"It was good," Renee said with a smile, the dimples sinking deeper into her cheeks. "Very good."

"Thank God for that, at least. No murderer or guy with too-kinky tastes."

"Nope. It was perfect, like I went out and picked my own Christmas present."

Mayson couldn't hide her surprise at her friend's gushing tone. She raised an eyebrow. "Would you do it again?"

"Absolutely."

She decided to ask the question more plainly. "*Will* you do it again?"

"I think so. Wouldn't you?" Renee reached for Mayson's water and took a long drink.

Mayson nodded, not bothering to reach for a lie. "If it was half as good as that smile on your face says, hell yeah, I'd go back for more."

Renee leaned toward her, teeth flashing. "It was so intense, May. I had so much power in that room, more than I ever felt before with a lover." Her smile dimmed. "At one point I got a little scared, you know, but he backed off right away."

Mayson shook her head, wanting to know, but *not* wanting to know. More than anyone, Renee deserved all the happiness that a full sexual life could bring. Her sad marriage to Linc had closed her down to the possibilities of her body. Although he'd said he wanted to explore all of sex with her, toward the end of their relationship there was no sex. His impatience with her sexual inexperience coupled with his insistence on comparing her to previous partners turned Renee away from him, both physically and emotionally. When she'd shared these things, Mayson wanted to punch Linc in the stones until *he* was the one who cried.

If these encounters with strangers could repair the damage Linc had done to Renee, Mayson was all for them. But she couldn't stop the worry.

"What about the next guy, what if he won't back off?"

"Maybe I'll just keep going out with this guy. He's safe, not to mention a really hot lay." Renee grinned. She took a sip of her water, winking at Mayson above the rim of her glass.

"Whatever. I doubt you even make it to a bed with this guy to *lay* anything down."

Renee looked away, grin still firmly in place. She suspected that a scorching blush burned under her friend's cocoa skin. Mayson's phone vibrated just then and she slid it from her pocket. It was Iyla, a friend in LA she'd been playing phone tag with for the past few days. Mayson pressed "ignore" and put the phone back in her pocket.

"Ready for something more substantial than water?" The waitress materialized at Mayson's elbow.

Renee's dimples reappeared. "Absolutely!"

They shared a mound of wheat and nut pancakes, scrambled eggs, a plate of fresh fruit, and a pitcher of Bloody Marys between them, settling into their old Sunday afternoon rhythm, bantering back and forth about the previous week, life, and nothing at all. By tacit agreement, they let the topic of Renee's strangers go.

A couple walked by their booth with children in tow, heading for a nearby table. The woman, slim and brown in tight-fitting jeans and an off-the-shoulder T-shirt, caught Mayson's attention and held it.

"They need some condoms," Renee said, glancing briefly at the couple, young and barely past college with their three young children, the youngest a baby dangling from her father's hip.

"That wasn't quite what I was thinking." Mayson followed the twitching backside of the young mother. "But I'll go along with that too."

Renee gave her The Look, but quickly lost it when Mayson gave her lips an exaggerated LL Cool J lick and sank her teeth into a slice of pineapple. Renee fell back into her chair in a fit of giggles.

"I thought you didn't do straight girls."

"It doesn't hurt to look. There's no touching of that forbidden flesh in my future, you can believe that." She wiped the pineapple juice from her lips.

"I'll remember you said that," Renee murmured, still smiling.

"Please do," Mayson said and reached for her fork.

Chapter 10

Mayson slung her messenger bag over her shoulder and closed the door to the studio. Although it wasn't time yet for Dhyana Yoga to close, her last class was done for the day. She liked to have her sessions first thing in the morning—the first one at eight, the second at ten, and the last one at twelve-thirty—so she could have the rest of the day to herself. It rarely worked out that way, but today she got lucky.

She sighed in anticipation of her midafternoon bath and a session of solitary meditation in her sunroom. Smiling, she grabbed the railing and jogged down the sturdy wooden stairs toward the parking lot.

"That's a different outfit from the last one I saw you wearing."

A woman stood at the bottom of the stairs, blocking her way. She looked Mayson up and down, her eyes clearly appreciating the sight of Mayson in the black yoga pants and a snug gray tank top that bared her subtly muscled arms and clung to her tight belly.

Mayson stopped. An eyebrow rose in question.

"Do I know you?"

The woman was conventionally pretty, thin, with above-average-sized breasts pushing against her red T-shirt. Long black hair fell around her face in shiny waves like she'd just walked off the set of a shampoo commercial.

"It's Kendra," the woman said, her smile wilting around the edges. "We met at a party a week or so ago."

Mayson tilted her head in question, still not quite recalling.

"I spilled champagne all over your pretty tuxedo."

Ah. Yes. The pushy one. Mayson recalled in wincing detail the cool spill of the alcohol down her neck and the woman's insistence on paying the cleaning bill.

"Excuse us." Two women dressed in the yoga uniform of black tank, black pants, and sandals came up behind Kendra, heading for the stairs.

"Oh, sorry!" Kendra moved aside and the women walked up the stairs, greeting Mayson with identical white smiles. Their yoga mats, clutched under their arms, forged a path ahead of them as they moved past.

Mayson turned back to Kendra. "What can I do for you?"

"Not much. I found out you owned this place and thought I might luck out and catch you here."

"Well, here I am," Mayson said. "Now what?" She could have already been in her car and halfway to her bath by now.

"A couple of people I met at that party take classes here. I was hoping you'd talk to me about yoga. Maybe give me some advice on what classes to take. I can even start today."

But Kendra didn't look ready for yoga. If anything she looked set for a night at the club in a tight red T-shirt tied off at one hip, black Capri leggings, and gold sandals with straps that wound up her slender calves.

"My classes are done for the day," Mayson said. "You should come back tomorrow morning. My beginners' session starts at eight-thirty."

She came slowly the rest of the way down the stairs, her steps deliberately unhurried under the weight of Kendra's intense stare.

"Tomorrow sounds promising. But for right now, how about some coffee?"

"I'm not a coffee drinker." Mayson made her voice carefully neutral. If this woman was a potential client, she didn't want to piss her off. But if she was just hitting on her, Mayson wasn't in the mood.

"There's a great place I know that has the best tea and smoothies." Kendra smiled, leaning against the stairs. Her car keys jingled in her hand. "Caffeine-free."

There was something simultaneously inviting and secretive about the woman's smile. But again, Mayson wasn't in the mood.

"Listen, Kendra. I'm flattered but—" She stopped when her cell phone rang. "Excuse me."

She slid the phone out of her hip pocket and answered Renee's call. "Hey."

"I have to cancel on you tonight," her best friend said. "Can we do dinner tomorrow instead?"

"No 'hey, how you doing, how was your day'?" She took a few steps away from Kendra to claim some privacy.

Renee sighed. "How are you doing? How was your day?" she asked dutifully, then, "Are you okay with me canceling on you?"

"Yeah, sure. It's no problem. But if you're blowing me off for dick, just don't make a habit of it."

She could feel Renee's blush all the way through the phone and that made her laugh.

"It's nothing like that," Renee said. "I have to work late again tonight."

"Ugh. Even worse!"

Renee laughed. "Tomorrow night?"

"Yeah. See you then," Mayson said, still chuckling, and hung up the phone.

She turned and stumbled into Kendra's hopeful smile. Mayson sighed. She had been looking forward to the bath and her meditation and also to the long unwind of her midweek dinner ritual with Renee. The bath and meditation suddenly lost their appeal.

"Let's go grab that caffeine-free drink," she said. "But I'll take my own car."

Kendra grinned. "No problem, just follow me." She turned and Mayson's eyes dropped to the dip and rise of her ass as she walked across the parking lot.

Not bad.

At the coffee shop, Kendra parked her yellow Mustang near the front in the half-empty parking lot. Mayson followed, squeezing her convertible between two SUVs. Getting out of the car, she trailed behind Kendra's swinging backside into the cozy shop with its smell of roasting beans and heated milk.

At the counter, they got their drinks—a green tea for Mayson and some sort of latte for Kendra—which Kendra promptly paid for.

"I was the one who asked you out," she said.

Mayson didn't fight her for the privilege of paying.

By the time they got their drinks and moved to a table at the rear of the café, she'd had long enough to consider this woman and what it was that she really wanted.

"Am I wrong to feel a bit stalked by you?" she asked, cupping her hands around the warm paper cup.

Kendra's eyes went wide with surprise. "Absolutely wrong. I just know what I want. After seeing you at the party the other night, I definitely want you."

No more pretense about yoga, then.

Carefully, Mayson took a sip of her hot tea. She held the honeyed sweetness on her tongue for a moment before speaking. "You're very assertive."

"You say that like it's a bad thing."

"Everything in its time and place," Mayson said with a faint smile.

"Are you saying I shouldn't chase after you? Should I wait until you notice me, then bat my lashes to get you close?"

Kendra shook her head. "I don't work like that. And I'm not sorry about it." She took Mayson's hand and placed it on the table. With her eyes on Mayson's face, she traced long fingernails over the upturned palm. "A strong woman is nothing to be afraid of."

"Says who?" A shudder of delight bisected Mayson's body in the wake of Kendra's caress. She pondered the surprise of that reaction in silence. This Kendra woman was nice to look at but she wasn't the type Mayson usually went for. The long nails were a definite deal breaker, and she said as much.

"Then I'll cut them," Kendra said.

Mayson's lips twitched. *Ego stroke, check.* "Do you even know what you're running after with such enthusiasm?"

"Of course. A beautiful woman." Kendra shook her shampoo-commercial hair like she'd just given the correct answer to a million-dollar question.

Mayson sipped her tea and carefully scrutinized the other woman again, noticing the way she leaned back in the chair, breasts out, chin up, her leg a long, inviting line under their table. Especially when a man passed by.

"Have you ever been with a woman?"

Kendra looked down at her latte that she'd barely touched. "Not exactly." Her eyes flitted back up to Mayson's. "But there's a first time for everything."

"I'm not anyone's experiment," Mayson said, making her voice firm. "I *don't* do straight women." She didn't know why she was even entertaining Kendra's foolishness. This pushy woman wouldn't have gotten this far if it weren't for Mayson's reluctance to go home to an empty evening.

Kendra looked down into her cup again, swirling her finger into the lukewarm liquid. "I've wanted to be with a woman since I was eleven years old," she said without looking up.

"Then try this with someone else. There are a lot of women out there who'd love to take on a virgin. I'm just not one of them."

Kendra raised her eyes, peering up at Mayson through her lashes. Her hair rippled over her shoulders in a dark wave. Her lips parted to receive the finger that had been swirling through her coffee. She sucked the finger clean. "You can't honestly say that you don't want me."

"Oh, I never said that." Mayson couldn't lie about the unwelcome flicker of interest that flared in her belly. "No matter how hot they are, I don't fuck straight women. Period."

A smile shaped Kendra's lips as she slowly shook her head. "You're a hard nut, Mayson." She leaned in to touch her wet finger against Mayson's mouth. "But I'm going to crack you wide open. And you'll enjoy every moment of it."

Chapter 11

Kendra was making good on her promise. Any moment now, Mayson knew she would break under the straight woman's relentless pursuit. It wasn't that she needed sex—far from it. Mayson had gone months without it and was just fine. And it certainly wasn't because she found Kendra so overwhelmingly attractive that she had to have her.

It was simply that Kendra had good timing and good technique. She sent flowers to the studio, luscious and deep pink, with damp vulval petals and coyly hidden clitoral buds. Right after they were delivered, she called asking what the blooms reminded Mayson of. With a low laugh, Kendra shared that she had another floral delivery for her but this one she had to give in person. Like the flowers she already sent, it too was damp and Mayson would have to bring her nose very close to experience its unique scent.

In the late afternoon, she called when Mayson was still wet from the bath, her skin prickling from the water's heat.

"I wish I was there to dry you," Kendra said, her voice barely a whisper. "With my tongue."

Mayson was far from immune to the seduction.

"I don't think I've ever met anyone this persistent," she said to Renee over the phone after an exhausting day at the studio. Another day that hadn't gone quite as she planned.

One of Kendra's floral deliveries sat on her living room

table, already wilting under the burden of its third day in a vase.

"Are you sure you want to go there?" Renee asked.

"What do you mean?"

"I mean are you sure you want to have sex with her? Don't tell me that's not where your mind and your privates were going?"

Mayson shifted guiltily in the armchair even though her best friend wasn't there to see. "She isn't bad looking."

"If you say so. She's not really my type."

"Very funny."

"Poor May. The little straight girl has you all tied up in knots, huh?" Renee teased.

"Not yet."

They laughed.

A tone rang in Mayson's ear, another call coming in. "Hold on," she told Renee, then looked at the display. She didn't recognize the number.

"Hello?"

"Don't tell me you don't know my number by now."

Kendra's sultry voice on the other end of the line made her breath catch. What would the woman say this time? Mayson sank low into her chair and waited to find out.

"The point is, I know who's calling now," she said.

Kendra chuckled, her voice low and delicious, floating just so into Mayson's crotch.

"I'm not interrupting anything, am I?"

"Not a thing." Mayson's tongue floated over her lips. "What do you have in mind?"

"Just a little conversation, as usual. Nothing more."

But there was obviously much more on her mind. And although Mayson knew she should hang up, a part of her even *wanted* to hang up, she brought the phone closer to her ear.

"I'm listening," she said.

"I've been thinking about you." Kendra's voice dropped lower, creating an intimacy so immediate that Mayson readily imagined the woman unbuttoning her blouse to get more comfortable, easing it off her shoulders and leaving her breasts clad only in a lace bra. A red lace bra.

"I'm afraid to ask *what* you've been thinking."

"There's no reason to be afraid, Mayson. I'm just a girl, and you're a girl too. Isn't that perfect? It's like we belong together. Girl on girl." Kendra's wicked laugh came again, in adorable denial of her cheesy come-on.

Mayson pursed her mouth in amusement and surprise. She'd never been pursued this hard before and, although aggressive femmes weren't her thing, the blood thudded hard in her veins at the thought of what Kendra would do to her—what they could do to each other—when the straight woman finally caught her.

"Do you even know what to do with a girl? On a girl?"

"Not yet. But I can't imagine that it's anything different from what I've done before."

Mayson silently laughed. She was really starting to warm up to this situation.

"When I was little," Kendra breathed, "I played house with a bunch of neighbor girls. We'd grind on top of each other and pretend to make babies." Kendra made a low, sweet sound as if remembering those long-gone childhood days. "It felt so good." The sound came again. "I thought being with boys would be the same way, but it wasn't."

"Yeah, girls and boys definitely do it differently." *Don't say it. Don't say it.* But Mayson ignored the voice in her head. "I could show you how." And just like that, she took the bait.

"Really? I'd love it if you would." Kendra paused. "Tell me what you would do. Would you rub your juicy pussy all over mine until we both came?"

"Pussy," huh? Yeah, they were definitely on intimate terms now.

Mayson swallowed. "We can start with that if you like.

Ease in with the familiar since you've done that kind of thing before."

Even though Kendra said she'd never been with another woman before, Mayson didn't quite believe it. Her brain ran wild with images. Kendra in college playing dress-up. Hair in pigtails. Breasts a heavy handful as she crouched, naked from the waist down, over another half-naked girl. Holding her pussy lips apart. Grinding back and forth in wet friction, both girls panting, their mouths open in surprise at their marvelous discovery. Mayson's index finger nudged the seam of her pants.

Kendra's voice licked at Mayson through the phone. "You can fuck me with a strap-on, too. I've seen that in the pornos." Her voice held the tone of a confessional. "I could be that girl for you," she continued before Mayson could say anything. "The one who gets fucked by the big dildo. You can put it in my mouth first, get it wet. I promise not to gag on it."

Really?

Mayson's fingers slipped between the thin pants and her warm skin. The slightest pressure of her hand against her clit nudged her arousal higher.

"Go on," she murmured.

"I'll work it with my mouth, get my tongue all over it." The image of that pink tongue swirling around the head of her favorite dildo made Mayson's clit nearly jump out of her pants. She shoved the black cotton low enough on her hips to get better access. Her furred pussy peeked out, the hairs already damp with her excitement.

"When it's good and wet, you can ease it into my pussy, slowly. It's so big but I can take it. I'm pinching my nipples. You're getting ready to ream my pussy. My nipples are so sensitive. I want you to suck them and roll them around in your mouth—that fucking sexy mouth. Every time I see you, I just want to kiss you and smear my juice all over your mouth." Kendra moaned like Mayson was working a dick inside her, sliding it deep into that pink hole and strumming her thumb across Kendra's swollen clit.

Mayson hummed her appreciation, teasing herself as Kendra's words painted an image behind her closed eyelids.

Her hips moved in the chair, curling up toward her fingers.

"You can have that juice anytime you want, baby. I'm always wet for you. Always..." The word ended on a ragged groan.

Mayson was finished playing. She found her groaning place, thumb and fingers working her entrance and her clit. A tightening began in her belly. Her nipples hardened painfully under her shirt.

"I can't wait for you to fuck me with that big dick," Kendra gasped in her ear. "I'm ready for you. I'm ready!" Her panting groans stroked Mayson's senses. "My clit is so big thinking about what you'll do to me."

Mayson imagined sucking Kendra's clit held up to her mouth, the other woman on her back with her hips thrust up, holding herself apart with her fingers, baring her deep pink pussy to Mayson's ravenous mouth.

Ah. Yes. That would be very, very nice. Orgasm slammed into Mayson. She shivered in the chair, hips bucking as her juice ran between her fingers and soaked her thighs.

On the phone, Kendra's moans continued. Mayson waited until she heard what could have been an orgasmic wail.

"Damn," Mayson murmured appreciatively. She pulled up her pants, jerking as her fingers brushed her still-sensitive clit.

Kendra laughed. "Think about that until I see you next time."

The line clicked as she hung up. Leather pressed abruptly into the back of Mayson's head as she dropped back against the chair. She felt like purring. That was even better than the dream she had the other night about Kendra on her kitchen table. Renee would call her twenty kinds of—

"Shit!"

She grabbed the phone from where it had dropped into her lap and quickly hit "redial."

"I'm *so* sorry, honey," she said when Renee answered the phone.

"I can't believe you just did that. You ditched me to have phone sex with that...that person. Don't bother to deny it!"

"Sorry, Renee."

"You already said that."

"Am I forgiven?" Mayson asked, still cringing.

"Did you come?"

Mayson blushed, a fiery scorch of heat that blew across her face and squeezed her eyes tight with embarrassment. Even she hadn't been ready for that.

"That answers my question." Renee snickered. "You're a fast come. I'm surprised. At least with this preview, your little friend will know what to expect when she finally gets you into bed."

"I'm not always so quick, dammit. Not that you need to know that."

"I really don't." Her friend laughed again. "Seriously, though, Mayson. Be careful with this woman. She already seems too attached to you."

"I'm not going to do anything with this woman—"

"Aside from have a little more harmless phone sex? Before you know it you'll be asking her to come over for the sex in person. Then you won't be able to get rid of her."

"You think I'm that good?" Mayson had to laugh.

Renee didn't dignify that with a comment. "Chalk this one up to a loss, my friend. If you're so horny, go find yourself a real lesbian."

"Don't discriminate against Kendra because she wants to walk on the dyke side. If she wants to eat a little pussy and suck on my silicone dick, who am I to tell her no?"

Renee was quiet for a moment. "I see you've already made up your mind about this."

"Not really. I just like to fuck with you." *Although I'd honestly love to fuck little Miss Kendra too.*

"Whatever, May. Just take it easy. It's only sex. You don't have to take what she offers just because it's there."

"Don't worry, honey. No matter what happens, I'll be careful," Mayson said. But as she adjusted herself in the chair, her clit twitched with the memory of Kendra's words at her ear. "I will," she promised Renee again, not sure whom she was trying to convince.

Chapter 12

Renee hung up the phone and dropped it on the couch beside her. The uneasy feeling she'd had when Mayson met Kendra had only grown worse. The girl was too pushy. *And too trashy.*

She winced at the uncharacteristically spiteful thought. But Kendra *was* trashy. With that headful of weave and her tits practically shoved in Mayson's face, she reeked of desperation. And Mayson was soaking it all up with a damn biscuit.

Renee picked up the remote and turned on the TV. Oh, good. *Law & Order SVU.* It was an episode she'd already seen but she could never get enough of Mariska Hargitay. She drew the blanket over her legs and curled up on the couch.

Watching Elliot beat up a perp, Renee realized she'd become used to a mostly celibate Mayson. Over the years, there had been a few girls, but no one who occupied much of her friend's time or attention. Certainly no one she'd hung up on Renee for. In the bigger scheme of things, this woman, Kendra, meant nothing. Then why was her presence in Mayson's life so upsetting?

Chapter 13

The meeting had gone on far too long. Renee glanced at her watch. Half past six. Nine hours of her workday gone and nothing decided. She narrowed her eyes at Alonzo, who sat at the head of the conference table, laughing like a hyena at another one of Frank Delaney's weak jokes. The man next to him, Ranulf Skarsgard, smiled only occasionally, his teeth just another slash of paleness against his blond hair and his winter-white skin.

Frank apparently reached the punch line of his joke, because they all laughed, even Ranulf. In his mirth, Alonzo slapped the shoulder of the man near him, Ranulf's assistant, another blond, who looked uncomfortable but didn't move from the close circle of men, a circle into which Renee had clearly not been invited. Time and time again during the meeting, Alonzo had shoved aside or disregarded her ideas, downplaying her role in creating the campaign for Ranulf and his uniquely Norwegian chocolate company that was trying to break its way into the American market.

Frustration and resentment burned in her throat each time she swallowed. Like Mayson said, she needed to leave Banes Unlimited. But she couldn't find the courage to do it. Renee sighed heavily. *And so it goes.*

Everyone else not invited into Alonzo's circle had already filed out of the conference room, most looking tired and ready to find the comfort of their home or a lover. Renee just wanted to leave the damn building. With one last look at Alonzo's grinning face, she crammed her folders and slides into her briefcase and walked out.

There was no way she could go straight home tonight. She thought of calling Mayson to have a drink with her but remembered her friend had an all-day yoga conference in the Bay Area and wouldn't be home until almost midnight. At her desk, she grabbed her sketchbook and some files she wanted to look over at home. As she stuck the book and papers into her briefcase, her elbow nudged the mouse and gray light washed over her desk as the computer screen came to life. Renee paused.

Then she sat down at her desk and logged into her mailbox. There were so many men. But with the way she was feeling, she didn't have the luxury of studying her collection all night. Guiltily, she glanced up, but the narrow hallway in front of her cubicle remained empty. Making a quick decision, she sent an e-mail invitation. Within minutes she had an answer.

Renee got to the hotel first. With the room safely shrouded in darkness, she shrugged off her suit and pulled out the packet of condoms just as the door opened. A slim silhouette. The door closing. A smell of the outdoors and menthol cigarettes. The man came forward, saying nothing, maleness already pushing hard against Renee through the front of his pants. He didn't wait for her to crawl backward into the bed. Instead, with his breath coming fast and hard, he ambushed her by the chair, tilting her over it. Quickly rolled on a condom.

He braced his hands on both sides of the chair's back, his slim body eager against her bottom and shoulders. The chair pushed into her belly. He licked Renee's neck.

This one was young. She felt the youth in his excitement. In the way his hands trembled lifting up her skirt, parting her damp nether lips, and sliding slender fingers into the heart of her. *Ah, but the enthusiasm of youth.* She shuddered under those hands. He pressed his mouth against the back of her neck, his hands holding her breasts, stroking her nipples, while his hardness nudged at her bottom.

She arched into the pleasure.

For such a skinny boy, he had a big penis. It knocked, thick and full, at her entrance before he reached down to steady it, hold it. Slide it through her damp hairs. He teased her, nudged her eager center, working her nipples with the other hand. Teeth nibbled her ear.

And he slid in.

Renee gasped. A hot chill spilled through her body.

Yes, this was definitely a big boy. And he worked his tool like a puppy let out with a new toy, stroking her shallowly, then deeply, then the shallows of her again. Renee thrust back against him, helping her boy find his rhythm. At first he hesitated, then his breath quickened at her ear.

"Yes, that's it." She groaned her encouragement.

Behind her, he giggled and an answering laugh hiccupped in her belly. Soon, they were giggling and moving together, his manhood rocking luscious pleasure through her. A long moan fluttered in her throat. The slick friction worked its magic, and she laughed again.

"So good...," he gasped.

Renee reached back for him, to grab his butt and pull him closer, deeper. He felt smooth and round under her seeking fingers. Clenching and unclenching in quick rhythm as he fed her delight stroke by stroke. He grunted into her neck. Renee squeezed him again. Then her hand fumbled over something that didn't belong. A buckle. Leather straps. Smooth, hairless skin. Her hand dipped be-low the flesh still buried inside her. Nothing.

Renee gasped, shoved the slight figure back, and twisted away until they faced each other. She fumbled for a nearby light.

"What the hell?!"

The softness she had felt resolved itself into a woman. A girl. Smooth face. Short hair. A T-shirt pulled down over what looked like bandages strapping down her breasts. The girl's breath came quickly. She was still excited. Excited that she'd gotten caught.

"We can finish." The girl licked her lips and dropped her eyes low to devour Renee in the light. "Let me finish you off. It was real good, wasn't it?"

Renee backed away from her. Grabbed a pillow from the bed to cover herself. "Get out! This is not what I asked for."

"You wanted a dick." She grabbed the big black dildo that was covered with a condom and still ready for action. "I got a dick for you." The girl—and she had to be no older than twenty—wet her lips again, ate up Renee with her eyes. "I know you want it, too."

Renee's body was still flushed hot. Her thighs trembled and her clit was swollen and thick with the anticipation of orgasm. She squeezed her thighs together but shook her head.

"This is *not* okay. And this is not what you need either."

The girl drew herself up to her full height, which was still shorter than Renee. "You want these guys for their dicks. How different is that from me?" She grabbed the piece of silicone between her legs again. The jeans sagged at her knees, hobbling the steps she took toward Renee.

"No, sweetie. We can't do this. Go find yourself a girl who's going to want you for you."

The girl's eyes narrowed. "Well, fuck you then!" She yanked up her jeans, roughly arranging the dildo inside. The sound of her zipper was loud in the room.

She flung open the door, and Renee cowered back with the pillow still covering her nakedness. With a final, scornful glance, the girl stomped down the hall.

"Damn." Renee closed the door and sank into the bed.

Without lingering on the sheer strangeness of what just happened, she quickly gathered her things and left the room.

After paying her bill and avoiding the concerned questions of the front desk clerk, she went out to her car. The Saab chirped when she pressed the remote, headlights flickering twice. She reached for the door handle. Then stopped cold.

Etched in the otherwise spotless pale blue paint of her door were four large scratches, an interrupted W. Someone had keyed her car! Renee's eyes flickered around the parking lot to the rows of cars, the valet running past in his red shirt, a pale-skinned family of five unloading tiredly from their minivan.

Who could have done this? The marks hadn't been there when she left her office. The gouges in the car were as vicious as they were deliberate. Was it the girl with the plastic dick? No. That didn't make any sense. She wouldn't have known Renee's car.

Did anyone inside the hotel notice anything? She took a few hesitating steps toward the hotel, her heels tapping desolately against the pavement, before turning back to her car. As beautiful as the hotel was, it was also very private, very discreet. As long as no one got beaten up or killed, she doubted that the desk staff paid any attention to what happened in the parking lot.

"Damn it!"

Maybe this was a sign, she thought, sinking heavily into the driver's seat. Maybe she shouldn't do this anymore. A flash of the girl's angry, desperate face flickered in her mind's eye. The car keys slipped from her hands, thudding dully against the floor mat. Renee swallowed. It was a long time before she could put the key in the ignition and start on the lonely drive home.

Chapter 14

A small black and beige dog, a corgi, barked and took off across the grass, chasing a ball. Its owner, a long-legged twentysomething in cutoff shorts and a tight tank top, kept a firm hand on its leash as the dog dragged her all over the park.

"I wouldn't mind chasing after that bit of tail." Mayson's friend, Iyla, watched the woman with a halfhearted leer from her place on the lawn chair near Mayson.

Camille, another leggy femme but one who was in much closer, available proximity, gave Iyla a dirty look. Her long, curling dreads fell into her face.

Mayson stifled a laugh.

Their shaded canopy, a quickly erected insta-tent that Portia, Iyla's coworker, had wrestled from her truck, afforded them an uninterrupted view of the park and gave anyone who wanted to the opportunity to stare back as well. There were worse things to see, Mayson thought with a smug grin. She took a slow sip of her beer, savoring the Stella Artois' delicate bite at the back of her tongue.

The evening before, she had made the decision to drive to LA on a whim. An invitation from her college roommate, whom she hadn't seen in a few months, despite the fact that only a two-hour drive separated them.

"It's going to be a nice day in the park," Iyla had said, her voice gravel at seven o'clock in the evening, as if she were just crawling out of bed. "Lots of girls will be out for the Lesbian Film Festival this weekend. I'm bringing a friend from work, another pilot with the airline. Invite anyone you want."

Since it was set to be a day of girl-watching, Mayson didn't even think about inviting Renee. Instead she called up her best friend to let her know where she'd be and that she wouldn't drive back to San Diego until Sunday morning. Then she asked Tara to open the studio in the morning for classes. That taken care of, she jumped in her car with the top down and, with Tricky playing on the iPod, headed north.

Instead of hopping on the 5, she took the slow and scenic Pacific Coast Highway, tapping her fingers on the steering wheel to her music while the wind tugged at her loose hair and the Pacific shimmered like a silken veil at the edges of her sight. By the time she made it to Iyla's place in West Holly-wood, Camille was already there, lounging by the pool with a book.

"It's hot as fuck out here," Camille said, abruptly sweeping her tank top over her head.

Iyla and Mayson, used to foulmouthed declarations from the girl with wide eyes and soul-rocking body, only nodded in agreement. Portia, mesmerized by the sudden display of skin, stared like she'd never seen a nice-looking woman before.

"Did they just let you out of prison or something?" Mayson had to ask when Portia sat up in the lawn chair and continued staring at Camille.

"Prison? Shit, you'd have to be dead not to look at that." Portia smoothed a hand over her short hair, smiling, as Camille ignored her, squirting sunscreen into her palm and turning to Iyla for help rubbing it into her skin.

"I can do that for you, honey," Portia said, getting eagerly to her feet. But as she made her way over, Camille dipped her head Iyla's way. "I need those hands on me, honey. No other."

Mayson chuckled. Camille had been trying to get Iyla for years. They met back in the late '90s at one of those orgies Iyla liked to attend but not participate in. Ever since she caught sight of the ex–Air Force pilot, Camille was in a daze. It was common knowledge that when a house had become available in Iyla's ritzy neighborhood, Camille did everything in her power to move in, even though she could barely afford it on her magazine editor's salary. Ten years and not even one kiss later, Camille was still hooked.

Mayson often teased Iyla about breaking Camille off some but Iyla was adamant about *not* sleeping with her neighbor. She'd never given a reason but Mayson always suspected that Iyla was afraid. Camille had built up so much anticipation around a possible relationship, Mayson thought Iyla was terrified she wouldn't be able to live up to the other woman's fantasies. It was too bad. They would have made one sexy couple.

"Why *don't* you go chase that girl with the dog?" she asked Iyla despite Camille's sour look in her direction. "I'm sure she wouldn't mind being caught. One of us might as well get laid this weekend."

Iyla sat up to rummage in the cooler. She pulled out a Stella, popped the top, then poured a cup of sangria. Camille took the fruit-infused wine with a smile of thanks.

Beer in hand, Iyla eased back down on the lawn chair. "I'm feeling too lazy to chase anything today. If she came and sat on my face, now that I can do."

"That would be something to—" Mayson's phone sang out in her shorts pocket, the opening notes to Lionel Richie's "Dancing on the Ceiling."

"Gimme a sec," she said to Iyla, then opened the phone to answer Renee's call. "Miss me already?"

Mayson sat up on the blanket and, with the phone pressed

between her ear and shoulder, twisted her ponytail up and off her neck into a messy bun. Under the canopy, the burning Los Angeles sun couldn't touch her but the humidity had already spread a layer of sweat across her face and throat.

"Not hardly." Her best friend sounded agitated. "Where did you put my spare keys again? I locked myself out of the condo."

"Again?"

"Sue me. I'm having a space-cadet week."

"No shit." Mayson told her where to find the keys. "And put them back where you got them, otherwise next time you'll be shit out of luck."

"I love you, too." The smile in Renee's voice was unmistakable.

"Naturally."

Chuckling, Mayson hung up the phone.

"Let me guess, that was the lovely Renee?" Iyla tilted the beer from her mouth and looked at Mayson.

Before she could answer, Portia jumped in. "Who's Renee? Your girl?"

Iyla laughed. "No. Renee is a cutie who is the perfect girl for Mayson. The only thing is she's straight. And they're best friends."

"Seriously?" Portia looked at Mayson as if she were some sort of rare and mystifying creature risen from the sea with fish for brains. "That's gotta be weird, being best friends with a straight girl," she said.

"I don't see anything wrong with it." Camille rested the half-empty cup of sangria against her bare stomach. "Just because you couldn't handle that situation doesn't mean Mayson or someone else can't."

But Portia wasn't interested in the philosophy of cross-sexuality friendship. "Is she hot?" She turned to Mayson. "Do you fantasize about her?"

Mayson sipped her beer and swallowed, meeting Portia's

eyes with a hard stare. "That's a little personal, don't you think?"

Portia chortled. "That means yes." She looked at Iyla and Camille. "I told you, it's *impossible* to be best friends and *just* friends with a straight girl."

"How about an *ugly* straight girl?" Iyla raised an eyebrow.

The three women laughed. Mayson scowled.

Iyla nodded at Mayson. "I agree that sometimes it might be a little difficult, especially with a woman as damn fine as Renee—"

Camille twisted in her chair to look at Iyla. "Damn fine, huh?"

"Absolutely and you know it. That body of hers is heaven and when she looks at you all sweet, like the dirtiest thing she'd ever thought about doing was French kissing, well, it makes you want to just open up those—"

"Hey, hey!" Mayson held up her hands, definitely *not* ready to hear any more.

"All right!" Iyla grinned. "But like I was saying, if the friendship is worth it and the woman means more than any lover could, you fight to push whatever lustful feelings you have aside."

"Especially during those dry spells, I'm sure." Portia looked meaningfully at Mayson. "And I notice you didn't an-swer my question about jilling off to Renee fantasies."

"I'll ignore your trash talk since you don't know me and you sure don't know Renee." Mayson paused, thinking about the period of her life when Renee had walked through her fantasies on a regular basis, years ago when she was a teenager still learning the sexuality of her body. Even then, it had never occurred to Mayson to try and change the rela-tionship with her best friend into a sexual one. "Renee has been with me since the beginning. She's one of the few people in my life who've given me unconditional and complete love.

Our relationship is beyond blood and it's certainly beyond sex. I know it's hard to wrap your little brain around that."

Portia sucked her teeth, apparently intent on mischief. "No relationship is beyond sex, except those with blood ties."

Iyla made a dismissive motion. "I disagree. A lot of times in our community we tend to transition lovers easily to friends—"

"Exactly!" Portia burst out. "That's why so many dykes have a whole stable of exes who are now their *best friends in the whole world.*"

The sarcasm in her last words made Mayson's teeth hurt. She nodded. "That may be true, but it's hard to go the other way—from friends to lovers—then try to make it as friends again once you've fucked that up."

"That's not true. I've seen women who've done the shittiest, *shittiest* things to a girlfriend during a relationship turn around and become the new BFF after the relationship is over." Portia snorted. "I personally don't believe in that shit. I say once you've fucked them, let them go."

"Are you serious?" Camille drained her cup and wordlessly handed it to Iyla to refill.

"Do any of your exes even like you after they leave?" Mayson asked.

"Obviously not," Iyla said drily. "None of them stick around long enough to deal with her triflin' ass." She refilled Camille's cup and grabbed three more beers from the cooler. She passed the Stellas around.

"Whatever, honey." Portia snapped her fingers and swiveled her head in a fair gay-boy imitation. "Anyway, women are crazy, especially about each other. I don't see why you, Mayson, wouldn't see if things can work out between the two of you as lovers and if they don't you can go back to being friends again. Simple." She gave Iyla a pointed stare. "Despite some people's opinion, I think that's the perfect solution since this Renee chick is so amazing and you want to keep her in your life."

"You're always thinking with your clit, Portia," Iyla said. "But in this case you're forgetting the biggest part of the equation." She leaned toward her friend, laughter in her eyes. "Renee is *straight.*"

"Like spaghetti, only until she gets wet." Portia grinned.

"You're as bad as most straight men," Camille scoffed between sputters of laughter.

"Damn right you are," Mayson said. "Don't worry about me and Renee. We can handle what we have." She sipped her beer and shook her head, laughing.

All this was nothing new to her. Portia wasn't the first lesbian to question her relationship with Renee. Even Iyla at one time had been convinced that Mayson was having her best friend on the side. But that was back in college when bisexuality was the campus thing and Iyla herself was fucking every girl who looked twice her way and some who just looked good, regardless of their previous preference.

"Forget the straight girls," Camille said with an airy wave. "Give me a full-on lesbian any day of the week, time of day, what*ever.*" She rolled over on her back to pull her shorts down and off, revealing the matching bottoms to her bikini. "Give me a girl who knows what she's doing and I'll be happy to let her do it—after I've had my turn." She giggled, turning to watch a woman, muscular and slim with curly hair spilling over narrow shoulders, walk past. "Like that one. Damn, she fills out those jeans real nice!" Camille tossed another flirtatious look over her shoulder at Iyla.

Mayson watched Iyla struggle not to look at what was being offered. The pretty, full-lipped face. Soft handfuls of breasts, plump and spilling from the rainbow bikini top. Ten years of unshaken devotion.

Iyla cleared her throat and looked beyond their small shelter to the girl Camille had been leering at. "Is that really your style? Mayson looks kinda like that, and better too."

Three pairs of eyes swung to Mayson. Camille seemed amused but happy to play along just the same.

"You're right, Mayson is much cuter. A little softer looking. But I don't mind Twinkies." Camille giggled again.

"Don't you people have anything better to talk about?" Mayson scowled at them, annoyed at this new turn in the conversation. She shifted under their stares.

"What could be better than talking about you, sweetie?" Camille asked. "We know you, we love you, and you're hot."

Iyla laughed, her face easy again now that she no longer had the thorny issue of her neighbor to deal with. At least for now.

"She's absolutely right, Mayson. You have that soft butch thing going on, the strut with that long hair down your back. You don't wear makeup but with that clear skin and those pretty red lips, why would you want to? Getting you is like a two-for-one deal."

Portia jumped in. "Two for one, huh?" she smirked at Mayson. "I'll flip you for the top."

At the woman's comment, Mayson's eyes were drawn to her once again. In her arrogance, the other woman was irresistible. On a normal day, this kind of overconfidence would make Mayson want to either take Portia down a notch or ignore her. But today, with the sun soaking into her skin through the thin material of her shirt and pressing fiery little bites into her flesh, Mayson was getting…interested.

She looked the woman up and down from beneath discreetly lowered lashes. Portia wasn't bad at all. Lying on the chair, her tall and spare form invited an appreciative mouth and hands even as her confident gaze assured anyone who cared to look that any sexual transaction that took place would not go one way.

Beside her, Iyla chuckled softly and leaned close. "Don't even think about it."

"Why not? It wouldn't be anything serious. Someone like her would appreciate that."

"You think so? Maybe. But in my experience, the ones who say that the sex is nothing serious are the hardest ones to get rid of."

"What are you two whispering about over there?" Portia's gaze interrogated them.

Mayson stared back. "You."

"I hope you're saying something interesting."

The two women looked at each other, their lust out in the open.

"I was telling Iyla that I was interested in fucking you tonight, maybe for the weekend." Mayson moistened her dry throat with the beer.

"Iyla doesn't have anything to do with this," Portia said. "Why don't you ask me yourself?"

Mayson distantly heard Camille's hum of amusement, felt Iyla's curious eyes on them.

"Are you free for some casual, no-strings sex this weekend?" she asked.

"Hm." Portia tapped a finger against her jaw. "Let me think about it and get back to you." But her dark brown eyes twinkled as she got to her feet. Mayson waited for her to come close, to sink to her knees in the grass. Portia leaned over to straddle her. Her mouth hovered over Mayson's a moment before making full and firm contact.

Mayson heard a low moan; it might have been hers but she wasn't certain of anything but her need to drink Portia in. She grabbed Portia's short hair to pull her mouth more firmly against hers. The body followed until they were tangled together on the blanket and Mayson became a heated and sticky mess under her clothes.

"If you're fucking your friend, I guess it's not an exclusive thing." Portia breathed the hot whisper against her mouth.

"You're the only person I'm interested in fucking right now."

"Sounds good to me."

Their mouths met halfway. This time it was definitely

Mayson who made a noise. The slow, deep strokes of Portia's tongue widened her thighs and nudged her hips into motion. They rocked against the grass.

"Unless you two plan to give us and the entire park a show, I suggest you break it up." Iyla cleared her throat. "And I don't think any of us would mind necessarily, but any future political careers would definitely be at stake."

Mayson pressed her thigh against Portia through the loose shorts, then reluctantly pulled away. "You might have a point there."

She directed the words Iyla's way, not trying to disguise the roughness of her voice. Portia was a good kisser and she looked forward to seeing what else her mouth could do.

That night, while Iyla and Camille headed back to West Hollywood, Mayson hopped in Portia's truck and allowed the other woman to drive her out to the two-bedroom apartment in Monterey Park.

"Take off your clothes," she said, pulling off her shirt as soon as they walked into the spacious, well-lit living room. She didn't wear a bra. Didn't need to. Her breasts were small and firm, their tips already hard.

"Your bedroom, please." Mayson chuckled at Portia's eagerness but shook her head. "Those windows of yours are too wide and too damn open. I didn't come prepared to perform for an audience. Maybe some other time."

"Really?" Portia grinned. She looked intrigued.

"Let's fuck now and worry about those possibilities later." Mayson grabbed the waistband of Portia's shorts, flicking the button open. "Where's your room?"

It was like wrestling. Rough. Slippery. Unpredictable as to who would land on her back and when. Portia was stronger than she looked and Mayson had been told the same thing many times. With her hand buried deep in Portia's pussy from behind, she grunted and gasped. Surprise. Pleasure. The suck-kiss sound of fingers plunging into her again and again, teasing Portia's G-spot, kissing her pussy from the inside.

"Yes." Portia gritted her teeth and spread her thighs wider. Her legs trembled.

It had been a long time since Mayson had been with someone as strong as she was, and she enjoyed not having to hold back, not worrying about hurting a smaller or more delicate body.

Portia howled her orgasm, her cunt squeezing Mayson's fingers tight as she came. Portia panted, hanging on to the headboard like her body would fly away.

"Fuck," she gasped.

Mayson slowly eased out of her, careful and tender. Portia shuddered but pulled herself up to her knees. She licked her lips, wiped the sweat from her face. She was gorgeous.

"And now that you've had your fun," she said, her words tumbling over each other. She pounced and flipped Mayson over in the bed. "My turn."

She dove between Mayson's thighs, pushing them apart, her breath a moment's tease on Mayson's clit before she got to work. Pleasure ignited in Mayson's belly.

She was ferocious in her search for all the spots that made Mayson moan. A finger probed wetly at Mayson's ass while her tongue lapped at Mayson's clit, circled it, flickered like dragonfly wings. Sensation uncurled in her lap. Portia really knew what she was—

Abruptly someone, a woman, appeared in the entrance to the bedroom. With the flames tearing at her, Mayson only noticed the waist-length black hair, caramel skin, a hand diving into jeans. The woman seemed anything but surprised to see Mayson and Portia in there. Their sex noises had probably warned her before she'd come looking. Her fall of jet-black hair barely rippled as she stared at Portia's ass and spread legs, then at where Portia was joined with Mayson.

"I think—" Mayson gasped, for a moment unable to continue. "I think your roommate is home!" She curled her fingers hard into Portia's shoulder, not sure whether she wanted the woman to stop or for fuck's sake *not* stop until she came.

At her words, Portia's excitement seemed to grow. Her tongue curled and thrummed harder. Mayson gasped again, squeezing her eyes shut to keep the pleasure close. When she opened her eyes, the woman was gone.

But Portia's mouth was unstoppable. She delved in and retreated, sucked hard on Mayson's clit, then pulled back, slid fingers into her ass and her pussy, fucking her quickly, then slowly. Frantically then languidly. Portia clambered up on her knees but kept up her relentless pace.

"Stop being such a fucking tease," Mayson growled, but the woman only laughed. And kept up her unpredictable fuck-and-retreat pace.

Mayson's body arched, prepared for orgasm, felt the lightning flashes of the peak lick at her skin. She groaned, but clenched her teeth against begging. She panted and clenched her hands into the sheets so she wouldn't hurt Portia. But *fuck*, it was hard.

She looked down her body, past her sweat-slicked breasts, down her tight and damp belly to Portia's fierce face, to the mouth moving hungrily against her furred pussy, Portia's closed eyes, hands urging Mayson's thighs wide.

"God!" Mayson threw her head back. She hadn't had it this good in months! Not since Nuria and her endless appetite for pussy.

With each dive of Portia's mouth against her flesh, Mayson shoved her hips up, fucking Portia's mouth, rushing after the promised pleasure.

A flash of movement whipped her gaze away from Portia. The roommate stood at the foot of the bed with a red dildo strapped to her naked hips. She climbed into the bed, smoothing lube over the dildo's thick head and down the shaft. Without pausing, she gripped Portia's already upraised ass with one hand, the other dipping low to stroke the obviously dripping pussy. Portia groaned against Mayson. The roommate smiled, relishing the sound Portia made, and shook the dark curtain of hair back from her face. Mayson couldn't help but notice the way her small breasts shimmied with the movement. Then she sank her big red dick into Portia's pussy.

Portia surged against Mayson with a deep, guttural sound. But she didn't stop what she was doing. Her mouth opened even more on Mayson, lapping and sucking, tongue-fucking, and vibrating with her moans as the woman fucked her, shoving her face deeper into Mayson's cunt with each stroke.

The additional stimulation, the groans of the two women, Portia's obvious pleasure in her roommate joining in, sent Mayson, finally, screaming into her orgasm. With her heart still thudding loudly in her chest, her breath huffing like she'd just run the most intense sprint of her life, she jerked away from the rhythmic push of Portia's face into her. The other woman still lapped at her, intent on keeping her mouth busy as her roommate slammed intently into her from behind.

The woman's bottom lip was clenched between her teeth, sweat dripping down her sleek torso, her tight breasts. Her hips pistoned forward, relentless, as Portia gasped and grunted into Mayson's cunt. Mayson pulled away.

"No, stay!" Portia gasped.

The woman must have done something, moved her hips just the right way or stroked Portia's clit, because Portia reared up in the bed on her hands and knees, crying out. Portia's eyes rolled back in her head. Her roommate grinned in triumph, eyes flashing at Mayson.

"You can have her, honey," Mayson said. "I'm just passing through."

"Stay with us," Portia insisted.

But the roommate would have none of it. She moved quickly from behind and brought Portia down into the sheets, licking and kissing her face, her throat, her breasts. Portia purred deep in her throat as the woman, crouched over her like a jungle cat that had gotten its prey, sucked on her nipples and worked her hands between Portia's damp thighs.

Mayson enjoyed a threesome as much as anyone, but this was a little bit much. When she slid from the bed, neither of the women seemed to notice. She quickly pulled her clothes on and grabbed her shoes. On the bed, Portia flipped her roommate over and fiercely kissed her, pressing the wiry body into the mattress, spreading the slim thighs open with her own. The woman groaned and arched desperately to- ward Portia. Her short nails sank into the sweat-covered back. They both groaned.

This bed is way too crowded. Mayson turned and left.

Chapter 15

Renee slipped into the room and closed the door quietly behind her. Like most of the rooms in the two-story building that housed Mayson's yoga studio, this classroom was steeped in silence. The floor and the walls were the same pale gold wood, like the inside of a sauna, except the wood under her bare feet was shiny and cool. Large windows, naked and open, allowed in the faint breeze, a shadow-shrouded view of the meditation gardens below, and the evening's quiet. Renee sighed and sank onto the wooden bench at the back of the room. She put her canteen of cold water down beside her.

Wearing a pale green tank top and white tights, Mayson lay at the front of the room on her yoga mat, her lithe body bent backward in a tight triangle, stomach arched toward the ceiling, ribs a graceful slope toward the floor, the top of her head resting against the bottoms of her feet. Her black braid spilled onto the mat.

"Expand your chest with each inhale," Mayson instructed in her low, carrying voice. "Soften your belly with each exhale."

Her pose was one of perfect relaxation. Absolute ease. And everyone in the class—except Renee—mirrored her, some with more skill than others. With her back pressed against the wooden wall, Renee felt the room's calm trickle into her until she was as relaxed as Mayson looked.

A gong sounded, deep and low, and Mayson slowly uncurled from her pose, braided hair slithering from the floor to rest against her shoulders, body moving upright to sit with her legs straight and facing the class.

"Bharadvajasana I," she murmured and the entire room moved, shifting to mirror her body's new position.

A wink, lightning quick, was Renee's only clue that Mayson had seen her. Her friend's face remained peaceful, untroubled, relaxed. Although she wanted to smile, Renee's face tightened in envy. There were times when she felt so close to achieving personal peace that she could almost taste it. But she was the one holding herself back from the feast.

Watching Mayson, it was easy to imagine all of her life's dreams coming true. Her photography would become more than a hobby. Her heart would be healed from Linc's unthinking abuse. She would walk out of the darkness.

The gong boomed again.

"Uttanasana." Mayson bent forward in a graceful arch. A simple stretch, with her chest tight against her thighs. Her braid tumbled from her back and swept the floor, black silk against blond wood.

Renee's hands itched for a camera. They itched all the time now, especially when she was at work. A sure sign. But she was too afraid to give up the job that paid her mortgage and kept the lights on. Unlike her, Mayson had been fearless. Why couldn't she be the same? Her best friend had been a lawyer and a good one, but after getting burned out on backward justice, she turned away from a successful career to pursue a dream. Mayson had always been the strength to her weakness, following her passions while Renee only talked about hers.

She blinked at the sound of the gong. It rang out three times.

"Dhyana," Mayson instructed, and as one the class folded

into what looked like a Lotus position on their mats, their forearms crossed in front of their chests. They began chanting softly, touching a thumb to each finger of the same hand with each syllable of the chant.

Saa.

Taa.

Naa.

Maa.

The united sound rolled like a gentle wave through the room. Mayson lifted her head, connecting with each person in the class while her chest moved in rhythm to the chant. Renee found her smile when their eyes met. The peace came back to her.

The gong sounded again. Mayson released a deeper breath and a smile.

"That's it for today, everyone." She stood up, seeming suddenly taller, more approachable, and walked out into the class.

Renee stayed at the back of the room as Mayson talked with her students, smiled her encouragement at their words, gave a nervous-looking girl a squeeze on the shoulder. Here, in the studio, she was a different version of herself, quiet and calm, the very essence of peace and strength and the power to do anything.

Only when everyone was gone did she join Renee on the bench. Her body radiated warmth and she smelled pleasantly of sweat and her eucalyptus body oil.

"You know"—she reached for the canteen of water held loosely in Renee's fist—"you actually have to participate in the class to benefit from this yoga thing." She took a deep drink of the water and passed it back.

Renee accepted the silver canteen and sipped before twisting the cap to close it. She shook her head, already smiling in anticipation of the old conversation. "I don't have that much flexibility in me."

"I could teach you."

Smiling, Renee rested her head on Mayson's shoulder. A steady, intense heat emanated from her friend's body. "I know but I wouldn't learn." She sighed and rolled her head back to look up at Mayson.

The warmth in Mayson's eyes almost made her forget... everything.

"What's on your mind, dimples?"

She smiled again at the old nickname. "There's absolutely nothing on my mind, May. I'm blank right now."

"And why is that? Usually there's *too much* going on up there." A warm finger tapped gently at the middle of Renee's forehead.

Despite her best intentions, a sigh huffed past Renee's lips. "I—you were right, Mayson. I had no business meeting up with these men. It was stupid."

Mayson's body stiffened against hers.

"Did something bad happen?"

"Not bad, just..." She thought about the girl who had pretended to be a man for her. She thought about the scratches in her car's paint that needed to be repaired. "Something *annoying* happened," she finally said.

"Well, are you going to tell me or just leave me wondering?"

"There's nothing—"

Quiet footsteps sounded just outside the doors. A woman walked in.

"Oh, there you are." Linette, the studio's manager, looked relieved to see Mayson. "Tara said you must have left for the night, but I saw your office door was still open."

"I'm leaving soon," Mayson said. "Do you need me for anything?"

"Nope. We locked up the rest of the studio for the night and everyone except me and Tara is gone."

"Go on home then. I'll finish locking up."

"You sure?"

"I'm sure you wouldn't like it if I changed my mind and asked you to stay." Mayson's mouth twitched.

Linette backed out of the room, laughing. "Say no more, boss. See you in the morning."

Still smiling, Mayson turned back to Renee. "You were saying?"

She shook her head. "I'll help you lock up the building. We can talk and work."

It didn't take long to close up for the night—shut all the windows, set the a/c for the early morning classes, turn off everything that wasn't being used—even though Mayson had to deal with some minor paperwork in her office. As they worked, Renee told her everything, every sad and boring annoyance of the past few days.

"So you're telling me that you fucked a girl this week?" The file drawer hung open, ready for the papers in Mayson's hand. But she wasn't paying any attention to it. She was completely focused on Renee.

"Of all the things I told you, why are you concentrating on that?" She squirmed under her friend's scrutiny.

"Because it's weird. Don't you think it's weird?" A frown and something else lingered on Mayson's face.

Renee shook her head. At the time, it had been a fly in her ointment. The thing that she wanted, the thing she'd arranged her entire evening around—a hard and heavy session with a *man*—had been denied to her. She felt sad for the girl but there was nothing "weird" about their encounter.

"No. She was just a kid who needed to find other gay kids to play with."

Mayson looked at her again for a long moment. Then her shoulder hitched in a shrug before she turned away to tuck the papers into the file cabinet and slide the heavy wooden drawer shut. "I think it's a little weird but if you don't, then..."

She plucked her keys from a hook on the wall and picked up her messenger bag. Her hand lifted to the light switch.

"Ready?"

Renee nodded and moved toward the door.

Outside, they walked toward Renee's car. "We can take yours," Mayson said. "I'll hop on the trolley to get back here tomorrow."

Instead of getting into the passenger seat when Renee opened the car with the remote, Mayson followed her to the driver's side. She traced the scratches on the door with a long finger, her face thoughtful.

"If it's that little girl who tried to have you for dessert, I don't think you have anything else to worry about from her. She's long gone." Mayson traced the interrupted *W* again. "But it wouldn't hurt for you to be more careful next time."

"There isn't going to be a next time." Renee opened the door and got into the car, forcing her friend to step out of the way.

When she moved to close the door, Mayson grabbed it. Light from the parking lot haloed her tall body as she stood there looking down at Renee. "Why?"

"Was I just talking to myself in there?"

Mayson snorted. "Some girl was playing games, so what? The first time was..." She paused. "It was everything you thought it would be. This last time shouldn't be *the* last time if being with these men gives you something you need."

"But..." Renee's legs spilled out of the car, shoes lightly slapping the concrete. She didn't know what the "but" was. There was frustration in her. There was yearning. All mixed up into something unnamed that had been lying in her for a long time. The situation that she'd set up with these strangers quieted all that. Her eyes met Mayson's. In that moment, she felt as if her best friend knew everything.

She sighed. "Oh, Mayson."

Mayson crouched to look in her face. She took Renee's hand.

"I know you're afraid but I also know that you want this." Mayson's voice was low and soft, the same silken tones she used in class. "Take it. It's sex. It doesn't hurt anybody. Maybe having this simple thing will help you realize that it's possible to have more."

Heat flared under Renee's skin. Why was Mayson reading her mind? "Life is just one big smorgasbord, huh?" She tried to make her tone light but failed.

"Exactly. If something doesn't taste good, put it aside and pick up something else." Mayson's eyes glimmered with the beginnings of a smile. "You get what I'm saying?"

"Yeah," she said slowly, an answering smile on her lips. "It's kind of hard to miss."

"Good. Now let's get out of here. All this talk about food is making me hungry." Mayson stood up and closed the door. When she came around to the other side and sank into the passenger seat, she flashed Renee a satisfied grin. "So, is it your turn to cook or mine?"

Chapter 16

Mayson rolled over in the bed that was as familiar as her own. The windows were open, the ceiling fan whirled above her head, and the room was absolutely dark, just the way she liked it. But she couldn't sleep. In the room across the hall, she knew that Renee was knocked out, lulled into oblivion by her half of the bottle of pinot noir they'd shared after dinner.

Although she'd taken care to reassure Renee about her choice to sleep with strangers, the potential danger of it still bothered Mayson. Well, that and other things, but it seemed safer to dwell on the physically dangerous aspects of this adventure than anything else stirring up in her subconscious.

The sheets rustled again as she moved restlessly in the bed. She plumped the pillow under her head. There had to be something—Mayson sat up. There *was* something she could do. Or at least she could try. With the beginnings of an idea forming in her head, Mayson reached for her cell phone.

Chapter 17

Renee laced up her corset and turned to look at herself in the mirror. Her newly long hair lay in shimmering waves around her shoulders and down to her breasts. A tiny voice lingered at the corner of her mind. *Are you sure you want to do this?* But she ignored the voice. Pushed out her breasts, sighed at the press of the thong against her freshly shaved and oiled skin, against her clit. The laces of the corset brushed against the rounded globes of her bottom. She was absolutely sure.

After her talk with Mayson, she felt renewed.

"There's nothing wrong with pleasure," Mayson told her last night while she hand-grated a nutmeg for the Argentinean baked fish Renee was making. And Renee held on to those words, needing to believe there was nothing wrong with wanting passion from a man without the prison of a relationship with one. Needing to believe there was nothing wrong with *her.*

So she moved eagerly forward. At the beauty salon, she replaced her normal short, sleek haircut with a luxurious headful of long, silky black hair. A fresh manicure and pedicure left her nails gleaming a Hellbent Red. As she was on the way to the car with her feet slipped into high-heeled sandals and the new hair bouncing around her shoulders, a corseted mannequin in a window caught her eye. It only made sense to buy the simple and simply sexy black corset with the matching thong and stockings.

The purchase had been a good one. In the mirror, she looked very much the determined seductress. Renee stared at the picture she made—her breasts overflowing the tightly laced corset, the bare vulnerability of her throat, the hyper-feminine fall of hair—until she felt like how she looked. Alluring. Confident. She grabbed the black wrap dress from the back of the chair and slipped it on.

Tremors of nervousness gripped her fingers but she clasped them tightly together, breathing deeply. *Everything will go great tonight. It has to.* Although he had not included a picture in his profile, tonight's man was exactly what she wanted. The description said he was big, over six feet tall and muscular. In his e-mail, he had been very specific about what he wanted from her. His words had drawn her in effortlessly, quickly.

It was a different hotel from the last one. She'd never been there before but it was close to the restaurant where she and Mayson had brunch. Like before, she booked the room over the phone and checked it out by doing a quick drive-by after work. It was acceptable, a nondescript bleached brick building in the middle of Old Town. Pretty and intimate. She hoped her lover of the night would appreciate that.

He wanted to arrive after she did. He wanted to come into the hotel room and know that she was there waiting for him.

"I want to smell you when I walk in," he'd written.

Renee was wet at the thought of those words. She made it clear in her response that she could do that, only for him, but he couldn't talk. *They* couldn't talk.

She slipped into the anonymous hotel room, pulled the shades, trailed her hand over the bedspread as she walked past. A delicate shudder moved over her skin at the thought of what would happen in that bed when he arrived. He would erase her doubts, make her feel pleasure, take her beyond herself.

In the bathroom, she turned on the light, then closed the door to let out just the tiniest sliver of illumination. Nothing more. As she made her way around the room, the dress whispered against her almost bare skin, her stockinged legs, her nipples shielded in velvet.

6:17. The digital clock flashed the time. Thirteen more minutes. Her swollen nether lips rubbed wetly together with each step.

6:19.

The bed sighed and took her weight at its very edge. She imagined this new one. Strong, according to his self-supplied description. And used to command by the way he had asked her to make herself and the room ready for him. Well, she was ready for him now. Renee's thighs fell open. Her fingers climbed under the dress, slithering over her stockings, the voluptuously stretched garter. She sighed as finger met wet flesh. The muscles in her neck stretched, relaxed. Renee fell back into the sheets.

She stroked herself with the lightest of touches, the outer lips. Wet. The moisture up to her clit. A low gasp from her own throat like the touch had been unexpected. Her fingers dipped inside, teased the parted flesh, sending delicate shockwaves of sensation tripping through her body.

The door clicked open. Her body clutched around her fingers. The dark figure in the doorway drew in a lungful of air. A rumble of appreciation from a masculine throat. Renee's head fell back against the sheets. She could smell him, a mixture of mint and soap.

Light from the door only flooded across her lap, across the edge of the bed where she held herself open, widened her thighs for him to see more of her. His big body filled the doorway for a moment longer before he stepped into the room and closed the door.

His eyes on her were hungry, intent. Her skin tingled as he

stood there, tasting her with his eyes, his back pressed against the door, all of him clothed in darkness.

Thick waves of lust moved over her skin as he stood taking in the smell of her femaleness in the closed-in room. Her fingers moved deeper inside her the longer he stayed still and unmoving, his silence preserving the sanctity of the moment.

She knew he could see her face in that moment, stretched across the bed, her mouth open to release the moans she couldn't keep to herself. Renee felt his arousal. Felt it in the way he crept closer, as if he couldn't help himself. Big hands gripped her knees. Denim-clad hips moved between her thighs.

He shoved her hands away, quickly, violently. And fell to his knees, groaning, to bury his face in her heat. Renee's breath caught. It had been so long since someone had done that to her. So long. She shuddered as his mouth covered her weeping flesh. When he licked her from the puckered rosebud of her bottom to her clit, slid his tongue deeply inside her, she bucked against the sheets, gasping.

It only got better when he gripped her, pulling her to the edge of the bed, spreading her wider to the seduction of his tongue. He grunted, loving her slowly with his tongue, filling her, before withdrawing, pulling back to lavish her clit with hot, sucking kisses. Renee couldn't have kept quiet if she wanted to. Panting gasps left her throat as her fingers twisted in the sheets, twisted in his hair.

He knew exactly what he was doing, what would drive her out of her mind. Sliding his tongue in and out, playing at her entrance before diving back into her like his life depended on pleasing her. His greedy noises spurred her on. She could feel him pumping against the bed, provoking tiny squeaks from the springs. The hot spot in her belly tightened even more. Her body flushed blood red.

Gasping, she grabbed at his shirt, urging him to come up, to bury himself inside her. He shoved her hands away again. Deepened his sensual assault on her dripping womanhood.

His groans made the flesh under his mouth vibrate, pushing her arousal even higher. Deeper.

"God!"

He seemed intent on making her come. Caressing, licking her until the fireball inside her burst wide open.

Renee called out again. The rising flash dropped her, panting, gasping, exploding again and again, backward into the bed. Still, he continued, lavishing her with gentle kisses and licks, pulling her down for her orgasm while simultaneously pushing her toward another.

Gasping, Renee turned over onto her belly, twisting away from him and the too-intense stimulation. Her dress fell back around her thighs to shield her sex. Behind her, he groaned. Hands slid under the dress, squeezing her thighs. He pulled her up to her knees. Her face pressed into the sheets. Then his fingers were at her entrance again, playing in her wetness, sliding over lips and over her clit. Renee groaned. The drum deep inside her began to beat again. *Oh, he's good.*

She turned over to look at him. Or at least she tried. But a firm hand settled into the small of her back. Holding her still. She heard the faint crinkle of a condom wrapper, then felt movement behind her.

"This isn't exactly how I wanted it," he rasped from behind her, his voice deep and guttural, "but it'll do for now."

Then he filled her, his mint-infused scent overwhelming.

Hands gripping her hips, thickness buried inside her. Renee sighed. This was what she knew. Until her lover gave her what she had expected, Renee didn't fully realize how uneasy she had been. Lost in her pleasure but not lost enough to wonder why he gave her his mouth, her pleasure first.

He began to move. And she opened up. Thrusting back. Sighing. Then breath shivered in her throat when his fingers found her clit again, making lazy circles in time with his thrusts, pouring molten delight into her with each languid movement of his shaft. She raised herself up on her hands, getting enough leverage to push back harder into him, letting him know that this was nice, but she wanted more. He grunted a laugh.

"All night, remember?" He pushed more firmly into her clit to send the point home.

Renee shuddered. In his e-mail, he'd said he wanted to take his time with her and she should come only if she was ready to devote the night to pleasure. But at the time she'd taken him just for another man boastful about his staying power. She figured as long as she got one orgasm out of the deal she was happy and he would be too.

But this lover was as good as his word. He was large and strong inside her, slamming into her with sure strokes that angled perfectly each and every time. She moaned. His fingers stroked her clit and squeezed nipples through the lace corset. She arched her neck, threw her head back. Strands of hair caught in her mouth, clung to her damp neck and shoulders. Her body tingled and ran with sweat that caught in the lace of her corset.

His deep grunts punctuated the lustful quiet. The slap of his thighs against her thighs. In the storm of his attentions, she became sharply aware of everything. The pinch of her thong into her hips from where he'd pulled the panties aside to take her past the thin silk. Traffic's whispering hush beyond the open window. The dark smell of her lover behind her, a combination of their sex and crushed mint.

Renee reached back, touching him where they were joined, reaching back until his heavy seed swung into her palm with each thrust. He made an urgent sound. Gripped her hips tighter, and began moving more deeply, more purposely inside her. She gritted her teeth against the needful sounds that rose in her throat, digging her fingers into the bed as he pushed into her and she shoved back into him. Renee rolled her hips, squeezed herself tightly around him. The explosive give and take of his body slamming against hers and his grunts rising harder and faster in the air. Sweet heat twisted through her body, rising and falling, waxing and waning. Orgasm teased her, tugging at her with golden fingers.

"Fuck," he gasped, bending hard over her.

Fire burst inside Renee when his teeth sank into her shoulder. He groaned something loudly, something muffled into the flesh of her shoulder. Grabbing her hips, he thrust deeply, once, twice, three times, and shuddered against her, explosively emptying himself. He gasped. Her body still tingled, tiny points of sensation, electric shocks tripping over her skin. Waiting to be brought over to the other side of her desire. She writhed between him and the sheets.

Almost. Almost. Renee touched herself, squeezed her clit between trembling fingers.

"You didn't come," he rasped.

Her lover bit into her shoulder again, more gently this time. "You didn't come." He kissed a path down her back, tugging at the corset as he went. Her breasts fell free of the velvet and lace. *What—?*

Renee barely got over her astonishment that he knew how to get the thing off before a groan split her apart. His tongue licking its way down her bottom. Tiny bites on the soft flesh. His fingers sliding between her cleft, over her clit, separating her juiced lips. A tremor raced through her at his expert handling. This was a man who knew women. Knew how to please them and didn't rely on his penis to do all the work. Cool breath blew against her superheated center. He teased her apart and she trembled, body quaking as he slid inside her. *Ah!* She pushed back to swallow more of the fingers.

She bit her lip. The fire rolled through her again. Insistent, undeniable, with each motion of his fingers inside her plumped and juiced flesh. *Oh, God.* He took her. Deeply. Hard, then harder.

His fingers played her clit, circled, stroked, flicked until she was bucking in the bed, trembling, coming around his fingers. Renee trembled when his lips found her back again, pressing into her damp flesh as he brought her gently down from her orgasm. Her arms and knees failed her. She crumpled into the bed, face pushed into the sheets, gasping.

Clothes rustled. The click of the bathroom door closing and that small sliver of light extinguished. Renee rolled over on her back, blinking into the complete darkness. Cool sheets settled into the damp hollows of her skin. The sensation made her tremble. Or was it from the silent regard of the man who stood over her, naked now, just as she was?

"All night." His low voice scraped over her sensitized nerve endings.

She shook her head and sat up, but he kneeled on the mattress, his knee sinking into the space between her thighs, into the thick bedding.

His hands gripped her arms.

Renee tried to find his features in the dark but only found more darkness and the certainty that he could see every curve and hollow of her face. He wanted them to have the entire night and, suddenly with the cool fire of his gaze on her, she wanted it too. There was work waiting for her at home, but it could wait some more.

Renee reached for her purse on the nightstand and fumbled inside for the phone. She sent a quick text to Mayson. Her hand emerged with a pack of condoms that she dropped on the bed beside her. His approval at her actions was as loud as the silence.

"Wear this." Without waiting for a reply, he picked up something from the nearby debris of discarded clothes. He pressed it against her cheek. A piece of velvet cloth. Renee felt it with her hands. A blindfold. She shook her head.

"Afraid?" His whispered question rasped against her skin and she shivered. His voice was low, unreal, the sound of a man being deliberately seductive. A generic voice. He was like every man she'd ever heard, but also like no one she'd ever heard.

"*Should* I be afraid?" she asked softly.

"No."

Renee shook her head again, sending the hair rustling over her shoulders and back. She *was* afraid. Mayson's warning words rang in her head. She didn't know this man. Why should she trust him to blindfold her and not take advantage in some way that she didn't want?

Her hands knew what she wanted before she did. They took the blindfold and slipped it over her head. A smell of familiar spices clung to the cloth, an immediate comfort.

He came closer. "Now, about tonight." His whisper tickled her mouth.

His body was hot against hers. Everything about him felt immediate. His unrelenting stare. The firm insistence of his muscled chest mere inches from her mouth. His penis was still slack but already halfway to hardness against her stomach.

Her body prickled with awareness of him. The blindfold heightened every feeling, every breath that passed her lips. He cupped her jaw and brought her mouth up to his. Mouth settling lightly on hers, not taking as she'd expected, not plundering, but a sweetly worded question, seeking permission for more. This was so different from before that she nearly pulled away. But he held her jaw firmly, brushing his lips against hers. Again and again, lightly seeking entrance.

Wild butterflies danced in her belly. She closed her eyes and allowed him to be gentle. Their mouths slid together, then their bodies, meshing, falling back into the bed. He rolled over until she lay on top, her hair falling around her face and his in a thick curtain. In the midst of kisses, his soft mouth and hard body, the warmth of him that raised the answering heat inside her slowly, there was her awareness of the cloth on her face. Its smell. He nipped at her throat. Gave her the unrelenting suction of his lips, the press of his teeth. She opened her mouth to tell him "no marks," but his fingers floated over her clit and she gasped instead.

"You're perfect," he whispered into her throat, his voice muffled by her skin. "I knew you would be."

Don't speak.

She wanted to cover his mouth but her body had other ideas of what it wanted to do. She flung her head back as she balanced over him, the tips of her breasts grazing his lightly furred chest, threading needles of sensation through her skin. He played her clit again, still feasting on her neck. His fingers slid into the wetness, then back to play at her rear entrance. A surprised gasp tore loose from her. Renee pushed back against his fingers.

The blindfold gave her and him perfect anonymity. Renee felt bolder with it on, even with him being able to feel and hold and taste her, knowing her face while she knew nothing of him. It gave her a new and welcome sensation: freedom.

"Again," she demanded, abandoning her rule of silence.

Renee spread her legs wider for him. Felt herself become even more drenched for him. "Again."

He chuckled deep in his throat and proceeded to give her everything she asked for.

Chapter 18

She was nearly comatose from satisfaction. Limbs heavy. A luscious wetness between her legs. Renee sighed, opening her eyes, but it was dark. Too dark. With a start, she realized she still wore the blindfold. Renee raised her hands to take it off.

"Keep it on."

His whisper came from across the room. The chair. He wasn't in bed beside her.

She ripped the velvet mask off her face. It was still dark, but shaded with gray now, a shadowy hint of things in the room. The edge of the bed. A chair. The sprawl of masculine thighs, clothed in denim, his big hands carefully balanced on his knees. His pose reminded her of another man. Another night. The first man. But this man's face lay in perfect shadow.

His anonymity was comforting, but it had been more so when she'd anticipated his touch and even when he finally touched her. Now she just wanted him gone.

He had given her the hard facelessness of sex. Now it was intimacy that she craved and there was only one person who could give that to her. She sat up in the bed, pushing her lethargy away. "I thought you'd be gone," she said.

When he didn't reply, she swung her legs off the bed and began pulling on her clothes.

"You should go." She didn't look at him.

He hissed. A dangerous noise.

Renee finished dressing. Although a new silence was building in the room, she ignored it. The other had been the tense, hungry silence of sex. What she felt now was anger. Why? Hadn't they both come here for anonymous sex? That part was over now. It was back to their respective worlds.

In her high heels, she was nearly as tall as he was. She walked past him, or at least she tried to. She half anticipated a movement from him and when he made one, reaching out for her, she thought, Renee flung herself back from him and toward the door, fear and anger twisting her stomach in knots. Too late, she realized he had only been taking a breath. Not moving to interfere with her leaving the room. Embarrassment heated her face.

He made the dangerous noise again and this time, he did touch her. One moment, she was dashing for the door, and the next he had her shoulders against the wall, his massive bulk held away from her. He vibrated with anger.

Oh my God! Mayson was right. I'm going to die for sex. The thought scraped through her, sudden and terrifying.

They were both in shadow. She couldn't see his face. She doubted he could see hers. Renee only felt him and his anger. But she remembered his kisses and thought suddenly, stupidly, that someone who kissed her the way he had could not possibly hurt her. Renee covered his mouth with her hand.

"Don't ruin this," she said.

He bit her.

"Ow!" Renee snatched her burning hand away from his mouth, cradling it in her other hand. Tears of startled pain pricked her eyes.

"*You* ruined this," he growled, the words an ominous rumble deep in his chest.

He released her and she stumbled away from the wall. *You bit me!* She stared down at her hand in disbelief like she could see through the darkness the imprint of his teeth in her skin. Was there blood?

A slash of light pierced the room. She winced and turned away from the sudden brightness. The door slammed shut. Her hand throbbed dully and she held it against her chest, staring at the vague after-image, a big man's silhouette in a bright doorway. She replayed the last few minutes' events in her mind once, twice, then three times, each time feeling more and more the fool for how she'd acted. She had dismissed him like a whore and then flinched from him as if he would turn into the murderer of her nightmares.

It had been good. And *she* had ruined it.

Chapter 19

When the call came from Kendra, Mayson wasn't surprised.

"Have lunch with me," the other woman purred in her ear. Mayson hesitated.

"It's only lunch." Kendra laughed. "What am I going to do, throw my pussy in your face at the table and force you to fuck me? Come on!"

Her low-throated chuckles trickled goose bumps down Mayson's arms. Tempted. She was *so* tempted. That night on the phone was still a blazing memory that she often took to bed with her at night. One moment it was Renee on the phone with her and the next it was Kendra, purring and wicked in her ear. The straight woman had caught her in just the right circumstances and now Mayson was hooked.

"Sure." *Why not?* "Where?"

The "where" turned out to be a familiar restaurant down the street from her house. They had thrown open the windows of the usually dark and intimate restaurant to let in the afternoon sun and the smell of the recent rain. In the garden just beyond the windows, thickly green Elephant Ears wagged lazily under the lulled heat. Rows of pink and white roses released their strong scent while light winked in the beaded drops of rain still lingering on their leaves.

It would have been a good day to take her bike out to

Point Loma, cycle along the coast toward the lighthouse, and feel the burn in her calves as the sun beat down on her neck and shoulders.

She sat down at the table, stretching her sandaled feet under the crisp white tablecloth, and opened the menu.

"My lunch date will be here soon," she told the hovering waitress, though she had no idea when "soon" was. They had arranged to meet at one and it was already ten past.

A flutter of conversation brought Mayson's eyes up from the menu to somewhere near the front of the restaurant.

Damn.

She carefully put down the menu, clenching her teeth to make sure her mouth wasn't hanging open. The Kendra bouncing toward her wasn't the same one she saw two weeks ago. This Kendra was a feast.

Her breasts, offered up in a sheer black blouse and dark red bra, were the first things that Mayson noticed. Those luscious mounds of flesh rippled like Mayson's dessert with each step that drew her closer. A short black skirt hugged her hips and thighs. Her lips glimmered the same shade of red as her bra. Dark, tempting, and wet.

"I think your date is here." The waitress grinned, her artfully messy dark hair moving like a cloud around her face as she looked from Mayson to Kendra, then back again. "I'll come back to get your drink orders." She went off to another table.

"Mayson."

Kendra leaned down to kiss her cheek.

Her clit jumped inside her jeans.

Kendra smelled like pussy. Like she'd played with herself, fucked herself with all ten fingers, one after the other, and then smeared cum all over her neck and behind her ears. From the smell of her, Kendra might have even licked her own fingers, feeding hungrily on the taste of herself before coming out to play with Mayson.

When Kendra made to withdraw, she kissed her neck, capturing the musky salt flavor on her tongue. This lunch was definitely more than lunch.

"Please, sit."

Kendra dropped into Mayson's lap and tossed her bag into the chair Mayson had intended for her. With a sly smile, she spread her fingers wide. Like before, the nails were colored a vivid red, but they were cut down to the quick.

"For you." Kendra stroked her naked fingertips against Mayson's cheek.

Mayson chuckled, clasping the errant fingers. "You know this is a family place." But the other people in the restaurant barely paid them any attention. A few eyes wandered their way, but in Hillcrest, the sight of two women in the same chair was nothing new. Still...

"I'm sure they've seen more scandalous things in this neighborhood."

"But not from me." Mayson consciously held her hands away from Kendra, though the press of the other woman into her thighs and against her chest made her palms itch to touch.

"Was this your plan all along, to lure me into a restaurant and seduce me in front of everyone?" Mayson asked, only half joking.

"Not quite, but I have to start somewhere." Kendra slipped her hand around Mayson's neck, under her braid. "Are you going to start with me? And for real this time, not just over the phone." Mayson's breath hitched when the other woman's lips hovered close to her ear. "I come real good in person too."

I bet you do. She put her hands at Kendra's waist and lifted her from her lap into the neighboring chair. "Let's see about lunch, huh?"

They managed to order, then eat their lunch in peace with Mayson only occasionally having to push Kendra's hand off her thigh. The woman grinned back at her every time, leaning back in her chair to innocently nibble at her crab cakes.

"If you're not really interested, I'd like to apologize then," Kendra said. She dabbed at her mouth with a napkin. "I'm not the type to keep chasing when the other party isn't interested, so"—she shrugged—"if you don't want me, I'll move on. It's as simple as that."

But it wasn't that simple. There was the memory of that night between them, when Kendra had called and the two of them had phone-fucked so good that Mayson had forgotten about Renee waiting on the other line. Or almost forgotten. She wanted the woman, but her rule against fucking straight girls was strict. It was drama she didn't need at all. Ever since college when she'd gone out with her dorm neighbor and ended up the third in an unsatisfying threesome, she'd sworn off straight women.

So Mayson didn't want her, didn't need her. It *was* as simple as that.

"Here's the refill on your mimosas," their waitress chirped as she wrestled a full pitcher onto the table.

"I didn't order this," Mayson said but the waitress only shrugged as she took away the empty pitcher.

"I ordered it," Kendra murmured. "Lunch is on me. You can have anything on the menu." The smile said that *she* was definitely on the menu and Mayson was more than welcome to nibble. Or swallow her whole.

Mayson's mouth began to water.

She blamed the second pitcher of mimosas for being unable to stop herself from reaching for Kendra as they walked out to the parking lot. Her hands roamed over the transparent blouse to reach for what her eyes had been full of all afternoon. She ignored the other woman's look of triumph just before her mouth swooped down to taste Kendra's, diving in to lick the taste of rum-flavored bread pudding from her lips.

Kendra's hand tangled into the back of her shirt, slipping under it to grip Mayson's skin as she backed Kendra against somebody's car partially sheltered by an overhanging tree.

Mayson lifted Kendra up and onto the car. Long legs clasped her waist and her naked pussy arched into Mayson's hand.

"You were expecting this, weren't you?" Mayson gasped against her mouth, sliding her thumb over the hard, slippery clit.

"I hoped." Kendra's laugh became a groan.

"You're so fucking wet!" Mayson's pants already felt too tight against her clit as she dove again, knuckle-deep, into the liquid pussy.

The car shuddered under their bodies, heaving with each thrust of Mayson's fingers, each time Kendra's hips rose up to meet her hand.

Kendra licked her mouth, her rum-scented breath huffing against Mayson's bared teeth. "This can be so much better—ah!—at my place."

But here was so good. The feel of the hot cunt around her fingers. The breasts heaving, nearly overflowing from the red bra. Almost as if to prove her point, Kendra dropped back against the car, bracing herself on her palms, legs falling away from their grip around Mayson's waist.

She thrust hard against Mayson's fingers, liquid and tight. Her neck arched back. She panted. Her wide-open pussy, with its thin strip of hair wetly swallowing Mayson's fingers, was a forbidden pleasure in the sunlit parking lot. Sudden footsteps—voices—sounded from nearby, coming closer. *Fuck.*

"My place is closer," Mayson said. She didn't want to move away from the sweet pussy. "Fuck..." She thrust her fingers deep into the heated cunt one more time, relishing the liquid fucking sound, the answering curl in her belly, before pulling Kendra up from the car hood. "Come on."

Kendra hit Mayson's bed with a gasp. Her legs fell open and Mayson fell onto her, one hand unbuckling her belt, the other reaching to push the slim thighs even farther apart. She pushed her pants and shoes off, shoved against Kendra's steaming center, and groaned her relief at finally, *finally* having full flesh-to-flesh contact with the pussy. She smelled hot, musky. Suddenly it felt like it had been a long time since she'd had pussy in her mouth. Mayson licked her lips.

"Do you—do you have—anything?" Kendra gasped the question, uncertain.

"I don't need a rubber, honey," she chuckled. "You won't get knocked up fucking with me."

"No, a—you know—a dildo."

Straight girls. Always with dick on the brain. Mayson slid luxuriously against her again, groaning silently again at the sensation. Electric tongues of delight. "We'll get to that later. I want to sample you for myself without the aid of any...external devices."

Still, that was a good reminder about other things. With their legs tangled together and still pushing her dripping cunt against Kendra's, Mayson felt around in the bedside drawer for the package of dental dams she knew was in there somewhere.

Ah. Here we go.

She eased up from Kendra's body and watched her, the fog of her drunkenness finally beginning to disappear. Their recent evening of phone sex had fired Mayson's imagination to the point where she almost believed those scenarios had all actually happened. They were so vivid in her mind, Kendra's panting, the way her pussy had easily swallowed the impossibly large dick, she could have easily fooled herself into thinking they'd come to this point—her in the bedroom—and beyond. But she wasn't so far gone that she mistook fantasy for reality. Kendra's words, though, had given her a very clear idea of what the woman liked or expected in bed. A man with breasts.

Kendra arched her back against the bed, her legs spread wide. She fingered her nipples, licking her lips. Long hair fanned around her head. An actress starring in a porn fantasy.

"I'm ready for you, baby," Kendra purred, sliding fingers down and between wet and swollen lips. "Give it to me."

A red-tipped finger slid into her pussy, lazy and arousing. Despite the crudeness of the action, an answering wetness flooded between Mayson's legs.

Kendra fucked herself with two fingers now. "I'm ready," she said again.

Mayson shook her head and laughed softly. Did Kendra even know what she was ready for? Another dyke to use her dick on her, just like her last boyfriend or husband did?

"First," she said, "we'll do a bit of what I like, although I'm sure you'll get into it too. And then—" Mayson shrugged. Humor bubbled pleasantly through her. "We'll just see."

She gently took the exploring fingers. "Let me do that for you." Her voice sat low and deep in her chest. Kendra watched her, hands stilled, as if hypnotized.

Mayson took the wet fingers into her mouth, licked them, settling the salty pussy flavor against her palate. "You taste like you need a good fuck," she said.

Kendra answered with a dazed smile.

"Are you going to give it to me?"

Although the damage was already done with the sample from Kendra's fingers, Mayson brought a dental dam into play, pressing the lavender latex against Kendra's pussy with a slow, firm pressure that made the woman gasp. Her eyes were still focused on Mayson and not on the thumb stroking her clit through the rubber.

Mayson didn't bother to answer her question. "Suck the rest of your pussy juice off your fingers," she commanded. "Lick your fingers like you did this afternoon, before you got to the restaurant."

Kendra grinned, in familiar territory again. Before she did as Mayson demanded, she moved the rubber aside, swirled her finger in the wetness gathered at her entrance, and then put the finger to her mouth. She treated it like an ice cream cone, licking kittenish at the base of her fingers, gradually moving with each lick to the next knuckle, wrapped her tongue around the width of one finger, pulled away, then licked again.

Mayson flashed to their phone sex again and the image that Kendra had poured into her ear. Her mouth wide around a big dildo. Mayson couldn't deny it. This was sexy as hell to watch. She pushed into the bed, groaning softly. But as good as the show was, there were other things she wanted to get started on. Like this pretty pussy getting wetter under the rubber with each passing moment. Mayson reached back into the bedside drawer and pulled out rubber gloves, quickly pulling them on.

Spreading out before the feast on her belly, she dipped her head and licked at the latex-covered clit. Kendra hummed softly, an encouragement. Not as satisfying as getting her mouth wet and deep into the real thing, but she'd take it. Mayson deliberately shook herself from her thoughts, focusing fully on the aroused woman in front of her.

"Your mouth is so soft," Kendra gasped in wonder.

Mayson felt the body under hers shiver. She reached up for the hard nipples, squeezing them in time with the slow strokes of her tongue, flicking her thumb across them until low chanting moans curled from Kendra. Her name.

Mayson. Mayson. Mayson.

She wasn't going to rush this. After all, Kendra had chased her for nearly two months, being alternately patient and underhanded. If this was the surrender, Mayson was going to make it last for them both.

She followed the graceful winglike pussy lips with her tongue, light butterfly strokes, then a delicate finger at her entrance. Alternating soft and hard strokes, she explored every surface of Kendra's pussy with her tongue, bringing her to the edge, then pulling back, fucking her deeply with her tongue, then shallowly with her fingers, stroking the puckered asshole with a tease of what could be, until the woman was twisting her hips on the bed with frustrated need. Kendra dug her fingers into Mayson's neck to make her go faster, but Mayson had her own agenda. Kendra sobbed and clawed at the sheets, called her name.

"Please!"

Only when the wet spot under Kendra was nearly a puddle did she relent. The sun burned against her back through the open windows, spreading its golden glow over her skin, into her veins, through every limb, and into her overflowing cunt. She fucked Kendra. Stroking and licking and sucking, thrusting and humming and laughing. Kendra screamed with frustration. The sound, vibrating through Mayson's body, pushed into her center like a firm tongue.

Mayson trembled and pushed her pussy into the sheets, into the bed. She felt the molten cum rising, helpless to it as it exploded inside her. She burned with it. Her body moved mindlessly, thrusting against the bed in the hot mercy of her release. She trembled again, ready to share that mercy with Kendra.

She gripped the woman's thighs, spreading them to lap at the wet pussy through the latex, to suck on that fat clit until the sounds from Kendra's mouth changed. Until she was shouting with pleasure, not frustration. Kendra's pussy clutched at her gloved fingers, again and again, squeezing, gushing thickness over Mayson's fingers.

Kendra jerked in the bed as if shot through with a bolt of lightning. Her hips bucked hard. Through it all, Mayson carefully held her teeth back from the delicate flesh.

Hm. She pushed her pussy into the bed again, rolling her body in the delicious aftershocks. She was ready to go again. With a hungry smile, she peeled away the dental dam and stripped off the rubber gloves.

Kendra flinched from the glancing touch. "Oh my God!" she panted. "Were you trying to kill me?"

"Uh-uh." Mayson shook her head. "We're just getting started."

"I can't." She pushed at her weakly, her hand sliding in the sweat on Mayson's belly.

"You can and you will." She teased Kendra with a light kiss on the mouth. "Come on."

Half carrying, half pushing the other woman, she guided her up the stairs to the third level of her townhouse. Her studio. The light was brighter up there. On some days it seemed like light was all there was to the uppermost level of her house. Just after she'd moved in, she put in skylights, a sliding series of glass panels that, depending on which button she pushed, let in all the light or shaded most of it with a dark UV filter. Now, light poured down through the unfiltered panels, illuminating blond hardwood and the thick white pallet she used as a yoga mat or a bed, depending on her mood.

Other than the pallet and the crowded built-in bookshelves on two walls, the room was empty. She guided Kendra down to the pallet. The woman spread out against the white cotton on a space big enough for three people, her limp body turned up to absorb the sun. With her damp-skinned nakedness and her hair a wild mess around her head, Kendra looked sexy enough to fuck again. She blinked at Mayson.

"Where are you going?" Kendra asked.

"Relax. I'll be back in a few minutes."

True to her word, she was back less than fifteen minutes later with a tray of water and a bowl of yellow watermelon slices.

"Are you going to feed that to me?" Kendra asked, a slow smile lighting her face.

"I was actually hoping we'd feed each other," Mayson said. "You know, reciprocity."

She set the tray down near the pallet. While downstairs, she'd taken off the shirt she'd been in too much of a hurry to discard when getting her hands on Kendra. Kneeling at the edge of the pallet, she felt Kendra's eyes finally begin to take her in, evaluating—Mayson thought—the slender hardness of her entire body. The eyes lingered on breasts that Mayson

sometimes thought were too big for practical purposes but
something none of her lovers ever complained about. They
were high and firm with nerves that triggered all the right responses. That was all that counted.

Kendra's gaze continued its journey up until she met
Mayson's eyes.

"You like what you see?" Mayson asked.

"I'd be stupid not to."

Mayson allowed her smile to show. That didn't exactly answer her question, but she'd accept it for now.

Kendra sat up and reached out to touch the tight, smooth
braid that ended just below Mayson's shoulder blades. "You
remind me of someone," she said. "Especially with your hair
like this."

They sat face to face on the pallet with barely a foot of
space separating them. Mayson held herself still as Kendra
caressed her hair, tracing the black strands that connected her
to the woman or man from the past.

"I hope it's a good memory," Mayson said.

"It is." Her lashes flickered but she didn't break eye contact. There was pain behind that steady brown gaze but
Mayson didn't pursue it.

If Kendra wanted to tell her something about this person—male or female—whom she reminded her of, she would.
She had been fucked as a substitute before. It wasn't a great
feeling but it was a side of the equation that everyone had to
be on at one time or another.

"Does that mean you've been with women before?" Mayson
asked.

Kendra shook her head, preoccupied with staring at May-
son's body again. She seemed absolutely fascinated with
Mayson's physicality in a way she had not been before. "No.
Never."

Mm. "So now that you've felt another woman's mouth on
you, where do you want to go from here?"

"I want to make you feel as good as you made me feel."

Kendra chuckled ruefully. "Although that might be impossible. The way you touched me was so damn intense. When I came, I thought I was dying."

"It wasn't that bad, was it?"

"Oh, it was that good! It was so powerful." Her eyes slid over Mayson's body again, lingering long enough for the dormant heat to begin rising again. "But I want to try."

Mayson grinned. "Good."

Maybe she'd known what the straight girl wanted to do all along. Maybe she'd just been hoping. But when Kendra suggested in an oddly shy voice that Mayson lie down, spread her legs, and put her arms above her head, a devilish imp inside her jumped for joy. Kendra also wanted her to close her eyes. *Okay.*

She lay back, at ease in her body, eager for what would come next. A sigh of hedonistic delight slowly eased past her lips.

Anticipation rose gooseflesh over her skin even with the sun's heat washing over her from above. The first touch of cold made her eyes leap open. She hissed. Kendra leaned over her with a piece of watermelon in her hand, watching the cold juice drip to Mayson's chest.

"Relax." Kendra threw the word back at her, bringing the fruit closer to Mayson's skin. The cold dribbled over her breasts, puckering her nipples even more. A thin golden slice painted a line of wet on Mayson's chest, just above the breast, then circled the nipple without touching it.

"You're so beautiful," Kendra breathed.

She painted the other breast languorously, again avoiding the nipple, then down to Mayson's belly. The fruit wasn't as cold now. Kendra lifted the thin slice up and dropped it into her mouth. Her slender throat rippled as she swallowed.

Mayson kept her eyes open long enough to watch her reach for another slice. The touch of the cold on her nipple was a shock, then a delight. She purred from the sensation of the fruit painting one nipple and Kendra's mouth engulfing the other. Teeth skimmed her skin but avoided pain.

Kendra alternated between the cold juice and her hot mouth, sometimes applying both at the same time, stirring Mayson's legs restlessly against the pallet. The heat of the sun, the wet of Kendra's mouth, the cold of the watermelon, and hard nipples skimming her body as Kendra moved lower, dipping down her belly, along her sides, lips delivering sweet little kisses that reminded Mayson of her first sleepover when she was fifteen. She could feel the juice dripping from her body to the white pallet but she was beyond caring.

At Mayson's hips, Kendra hesitated. She could feel the hovering presence, the juice dripping between her legs. Cold, cold drops on her bared clit, Kendra's hand on her thigh.

Her belly clenched with each drop of the juice against her clit. She wanted to shove Kendra's mouth there. But she restrained herself and stayed very still.

This is why you don't fuck straight—

Mayson hissed at the mouth on her clit. The heated mouth that engulfed her and shoved every thought out of her head but *thank you*. She opened her legs wider, put a guiding hand on the back of Kendra's head as the woman sucked her clit.

"Ah—that's nice." She groaned the encouragement while the pleasure spiraled up from her core. "That's very, *very* nice. A little more tongue. Yes, work your tongue under the hood of my clit. Yes. Get my clit out and play with it. She's not shy; you shouldn't be either."

A long, luxurious moan floated from her lips when Kendra followed her directions. The timid explorations became more adventurous. Mayson panted as the tongue moved faster and firmer against her. She was close, *so* close. She gripped the back of Kendra's head, shoving her pussy hard against the woman's mouth. Harder. Kendra's tongue slowed down. Stopped.

Mayson groaned in heartfelt annoyance. "I hope you're

not trying to pay me back for earlier." Then she felt the jaw tremble against her.

Kendra pulled away and sat up, her mouth and chin smeared with Mayson's wetness.

"My jaw is getting tired," she said. "And I can't really breathe." This last was said in a disappointed wail.

This is what you get when you give your pussy to someone who can't handle it. Dammit!

"It's fine," Mayson said even though it damn well wasn't. She wanted to shove Kendra backward on the bed, shove her pussy back on her face, and grind against the straight woman's mouth until she came. But Kendra wouldn't enjoy it very much and although a come would feel fantastic right now, afterward she'd feel like shit.

"Let me take care of this myself, then we can talk."

"Can I do anything for you?" Kendra looked so earnest that Mayson nearly laughed.

"Yes, as a matter of fact, you can."

After Mayson told her what she needed, Kendra hopped up like a good little helper. She leaned over to suck and bite Mayson's nipples, her eyes watching Mayson to make sure she was doing it right. At the nods of encouragement, she continued, sucking, licking as Mayson strummed her own clit and fucked herself with two fingers. Heat flared quickly and the fires soon consumed her. She came with a hoarse shout, panting in Kendra's hair.

Kittenish and warm, the woman still licked her breasts. Mayson gently nudged her mouth away.

Her body shivered, deliciously tingling. "Come talk to me."

Kendra blinked. She drew away. "Don't bullshit me. Just tell me what I was doing wrong."

"You weren't doing anything wrong. It's natural for your jaw to get tired." Mayson rolled to her stomach and propped herself up on her elbows, looking down at Kendra.

"But yours didn't." Kendra's voice fell into a soft whisper.

"You just kept going until smoke was coming out of me."
Her eyes closed and she reached blindly up for Mayson.

Mayson grinned, unable to prevent a burst of pride. *But straight girls are always so easy to impress,* her inner voice said, stomping firmly on her ego. "It takes practice. And even when your jaw gets tired or your tongue hurts, use your fingers until your lover comes or until you feel you can get back into things."

"But I'm sure a hand doesn't feel as good."

"Most times that's true. But I've gotten some pretty amazing hand jobs in my life." Mayson teased her with a smile. Her body simmered on "low" now despite her recent orgasm. "Do you want to try it with your hands this time? We can do each other at the same time." Her smile widened. "Once I think you've had enough practice, I'll let you try your mouth again and we'll go from there."

The light in Kendra's eyes grew brighter. Her smile emerged to play with Mayson's. "Can we try it now?"

Kendra was a fast learner. And Mayson reaped the rewards of her quick study eight times before they both fell into a deep sleep on the pallet. Sex buzzed through Mayson's veins, sang in her head, twitched her muscles, and made her want to crawl through her sleep to gorge herself on Kendra again, to fuck until her skin rubbed off and all her conscious thoughts disappeared in a haze of satisfied lust. Which was pretty much what happened. Desire tore relentlessly at her, and something about it was so familiar that she nearly cautioned herself against it and sent Kendra home. But the tide was too strong for rational thoughts.

At one point, she heard the house phone ringing, then her cell phone. She wasn't interested enough to go searching for either. They rang in tandem before finally dying off into silence.

The sky had turned pink while they took turns sleeping

and fucking. Soft light poured from above, bathing the stark room and their damp bodies in a roseate glow.

"This moment is so perfect." Kendra sighed.

She stretched against the pallet and watched Mayson with contentment oozing from her pores. "If I'd known that being with a woman felt like this I would have crossed over years ago."

"We don't all fuck alike, you know."

"I didn't think that. The men I've slept with certainly all didn't make me feel the same way." She paused. "The way you know my body and what to do with it has to be a female thing."

"Again, my little neophyte, not all of us fuck or eat pussy the same."

Mayson was getting bored with the gushing enthusiasm for the uniqueness of lesbian sex. The next time a big dick came along, she'd forget all about the way Mayson made her feel. Speaking of which...

Mayson trailed a hand up Kendra's arm, watching as the woman closed her eyes and trembled delicately. "I've been so caught up in enjoying you that I almost forgot about what you keep asking for."

Kendra didn't open her eyes. "What have I been asking for?"

"My dick."

The dark eyes popped open. They moved to Mayson's crotch as if expecting to see a penis, full-grown and hard, already magically attached there. Mayson chuckled and rose to her feet. She cupped Kendra's cheek, tracing the slightly parted lips with her thumb.

"I'll be right back."

In the bedroom, she grabbed the necessities and turned to go back upstairs. Then she remembered the phone. It was Renee who had called. She listened to the message.

"I figured you're hibernating with your usual round of this time of the month insanity but I wanted to remind you about our trip to Dana Point this weekend."

Time of the month? Mayson tilted her head. Then it suddenly hit her. She was ovulating. Ovulating and nearly sex obsessed.

Every month before her period, she became blindly horny. Most months, she meditated through those two or three days until the pulsing between her legs returned to something like normal. Other months, if there was an acceptable and willing woman, she would fuck for nearly three days straight without coming up for air. During those days, everything was sex. When the air brushed her nipples through layers of cotton it felt like someone had pulled her breast into their mouth. She tended to not have classes those days. Even the feel of panties gently hugging her clit was unbearable.

Why was it that Renee knew when she'd forgotten? *Because you've been distracted, that's why*. With an irritated sigh, she tuned in to the rest of Renee's message.

"If you need me to bring you anything just let me know. In the meantime, play safe and I'll see you soon."

Mayson checked the time on the caller ID and made a mental note to call Renee in the morning. *Ovulating. Jesus.* Upstairs, Kendra was waiting right where she'd left her. The woman's intent gaze focused on the cloth bag she carried, although something in that look sagged with disappointment that Mayson hadn't appeared wearing the whole setup. She grinned.

"I'm going to need some help with this," she told Kendra. "Hope you're up for it."

If possible, Kendra looked even more intrigued. She bit her lip, eyes shining and expectant as Mayson came closer. She nodded.

"Get on your knees." Mayson meant the words to be gentle, a suggestion, but they growled past her lips instead and she was instantly wet when Kendra's knees hit the pallet without hesitation. Maybe she wouldn't need the help after all.

"Should I get it wet for you?" Kendra asked, her excitement making the words nearly a pant.

"No. I want you to get *me* wet for it." At Kendra's uncomprehending expression, Mayson spoke again. "Put your mouth on me."

Again, there was no hesitation. Kendra slid her hands up Mayson's thighs, slowly, savoring her task. She licked her lips and scooted inside the pyramid of Mayson's legs. Her fingers trailed down Mayson's ass.

The warm breath eased closer and closer, heightening her arousal. Her tongue probed delicately between Mayson's thighs, tasting the wetness already there, then curled up to stroke Mayson's clit, first with light, then broad, heavy strokes. She seemed eager to show what she had learned. Mayson sighed her approval.

Her thighs widened. Kendra covered her with hot, sucking kisses. It was tempting, oh so tempting, to let Kendra finish her off with her newly acquired skills.

She gasped at a particularly delicious stroke. "Hmm, let's—ahh—let's put that on hold for a while."

Kendra snaked her head, following her retreating hips. Mayson laughed breathlessly, pushing a restraining hand on Kendra's shoulder.

"I promise you can have more of that later."

With a slightly shaking hand, she pulled the dildo and the small bottle of lube out of the cloth bag. She let the bottle drop to the pallet.

"That's interesting." Kendra's eyes fastened on the graceful curve of the deep purple silicone in Mayson's hand.

The double-headed dildo had been a sight for Mayson too when she'd seen her first one years ago. It was quite a sight for the uninitiated, with its odd shape that looked like two jutting cocks fused together at the base, thrusting in opposite directions, one end curved high and thick, the opposite end straighter, longer, like an arrow heading directly for a target.

Now, there was no other way she liked to fly if she was going to use anything other than her hands and mouth. No trading off on pleasure. If the timing was on and if Mayson was doing it right, they both got what they wanted and at the same time.

"It *is* interesting." Standing with her legs braced apart, Mayson stroked herself with the shorter, more upright end of the dildo. "That part feels really, really"—she groaned softly as she slid the dildo between her wet lips, over her clit, and into her pussy that Kendra had made wet—"really interesting."

The silicone was light and firm in her hands. It had been a while since she'd used it and even now it stretched her more than was quite comfortable. But she persisted, working the dildo in by inches. She stroked her clit, calling up more wetness to make the journey deep inside easier. Kendra watched with interested eyes, rocking back and forth on her knees, touching her nipples to the sight of Mayson easing the big purple dildo into her pussy.

Finally it was in and Mayson squeezed her internal muscles around the intrusion, flexed, gratified by the spark that licked at her from the inside. Kendra's eyes bulged at the sight of her ready, the long purple phallus thrusting out into the air, stiff and ready. The head was thick and bulbous, the shaft ridged and firm.

Mayson went to her knees on the pallet beside Kendra, cupping her face and drawing her in for a kiss. "Now," she murmured against the woman's parted lips, "we both get what we want."

She kissed her. Kissed her to taste herself on that mobile and slick tongue, the salt of her own pussy already washing away. Their mouths moved hungrily together. The sight of the long purple dick had ignited something in Kendra. She squeezed Mayson's arms, her back, her ass, soft needful whimpers at the back of her throat. Her thighs were already wide to take the dick and it slid between her thighs, moving back and forth between the skin, already damp with sweat and pussy juice. Her pussy was wet, soaking. Mayson slid her fingers through the wet hairs, the lips, full and pursed like they were waiting for a kiss.

She squeezed the dick inside her, sighing into Kendra's mouth as little bolts of pleasure darted through her. She wanted to share that feeling. She wanted to push that feeling higher.

On her back. Mayson was on her back and Kendra moved into position to straddle her before she could process that was what they needed, wanted to do. Kendra's wide-open pussy hovered over the thick purple head of the dick. She held herself open for it, then slowly slid down its long length, the juice already trickling down her thighs, making it a slow and easy glide. Kendra sat down heavily on the dick, on Mayson. They both gasped.

"I know it's presumptuous of me, but I thought you might like to ride," Mayson said through teeth clenched against the hot waves licking at her body. Kendra's weight and the ridges of the dick against her clit made it hard to think. Or talk. Her pussy was so wet it was a small miracle the dildo didn't just slide right out. But she did her Kegel exercises every day like a good little girl and her internal grip was strong.

Kendra sighed and moved her hips to test out her new power. She groaned. "I like this."

Answering sensation rippled though Mayson. "That makes two of us."

It was her turn to sigh when Kendra moved again, a slow roll of her hips. The woman on top smiled. Kendra straddled her like she was born to ride, the long hair wild around her face, her naked body glowing faintly under the twilight sky. She cupped her breasts, playing with her small nipples, tugging them.

"I feel like I'm the one fucking you from up here," she gasped.

Mayson quivered. "That's right, baby. Control your fuck.

You wanted this dick. Ride it like you know what to do with it."

"I definitely know what to do with it." Her heavy breasts bounced above Mayson as she moved on the dildo.

Although she'd given Kendra permission to pace the fuck, Mayson was impatient to move. The sight of the woman above her, now licking her own nipples, steadily but slowly moving her hips, was almost more than she could take.

Enough of this spectator shit. Mayson grabbed her hips and pushed up. She felt the echo of the action in her body.

Kendra gasped and stopped touching herself. Mayson thrust up lazily into her, enjoying the bounce of breasts above her, the way pleasure moved without guile across the woman's face.

Ah. Hands-free fucking. Sometimes she forgot how much she loved it until she was in the middle of it, twisting her hips up, gripping tightly with her internal muscles. She grunted with the force of each thrust. *Yes.* She loved this. Absolutely loved this. Sparks flew inside her when Kendra leaned down to caress her breasts, moving her hips in counterpoint to Mayson's, becoming involved in that blind search for the place to make them both sing. They moved together, rippling against each other like waves in a churning sea.

As she fucked Kendra, the dick fucked her, pounding wetly against her clit, stroking her deeply on the inside, nuzzling her sweet spot. Heat pulsed in her middle. She moved her hips faster. She reached up to squeeze the hard nipples in time to the movement of her hips. Their gasps chased each other, the sound of skin-to-skin slap, of dick in wet pussy. Kendra licked her lips as she hopped on the deep purple dick, her breasts jiggling, the dick wet with her juices, bits of purple appearing and disappearing at the entrance to her pussy as their bodies moved together.

"I love how you feel inside me," she moaned.

Mayson threw her head back, thrusting her breasts up into

Kendra's pinching fingers. Her breath came fast, drying her mouth. Her hips jerked.

"You feel so good!"

Yes, it was good. So good that Mayson wanted to keep going. She wanted to fuck forever. But already she could feel it coming to its inevitable close. Her skin prickled with electricity. Sweat marched down her chest into the heaving valley leading to her pussy. Her muscles tensed. Fire and lust and pleasure and desire and joy uncurled in her belly.

"Yes," she hissed at the ceiling. And the light exploded behind her clenched eyes. It washed through her entire body, incinerating everything that had been there before. "Yes!"

On top of her, Kendra was frantic, breasts jumping, her hips surging against Mayson's dick. "Oh my God, Mayson. Oh my God!"

Mayson didn't want to move anymore. At the tail of her orgasm, her body was too sensitive from the overload of stimulation. But she didn't stop. She had never been that kind of lover. Mayson gripped Kendra's hips and thrust deeper, harder, moving despite the shudders of rejection rippling through her body from the cock that now felt too thick, too hard inside her.

She panted along with Kendra, gasping when she gasped, encouraging the orgasm rising just under the woman's skin. "Come for me, baby." Her hips were unrelenting. She pulled at the already hard nipples. "Come."

Finally, she got her reward. A guttural scream tore through Kendra. She flung herself hard one final time against Mayson, undulating against her in her orgasm. Beautiful and fierce, her eyes wide open, almost frightened as she trembled. Her tremors eased and she stopped moving on Mayson's lap. Panting, she climbed off the dildo and sagged into the pallet.

Mayson tugged the dildo free from her body. It slid out with the sound of a liquid kiss, leaving her muscles clutching at the newly empty space inside. The purple silicone toy thudded against the hardwood when she threw it. On her back, she sighed into the ripples of satisfied desire still moving through her. She closed her eyes.

Except for her ragged breaths, Kendra was silent beside her. The house was silent, her body was still, its hungers satisfied for now. It was night in the room. Without opening her eyes, she felt the dark and the silence and the satisfaction.

"Thank you." Kendra sighed beside her.

Mayson opened her eyes. Starlight winked down at them through the skylight, pale and inconsequential in their scatter around the brighter half-moon. The Big Dipper sparkled, a cup of diamonds. Kendra's pretty brown face glowed in that faint light, peaceful and serene. For the first time, Mayson was seeing her as a person, not just another body that insisted on throwing itself in her way.

She traced the silver-etched cheek with one finger and Kendra closed her eyes, smiling.

"My pleasure," Mayson said. She meant it.

Chapter 20

With a low groan, Mayson rolled over in her bed, squeezing her eyes tightly against the sunlight. The first thing Mayson noticed when her body shifted awake was the heavy smell of another body in her bed. *Kendra*. Memories of the day emerged as if from a fog. The lunch date. Drinks. The ecstatic hours afterward. Renee's phone call reminding her how at her hormones' mercy she was.

A light touch landed on her belly.

"You awake?"

Since she didn't trust her voice yet, she turned her head to face the woman in her bed, not quite knowing what to expect after the excesses of the night before.

Kendra's hair spilled black and abundant around her face and against the pillows. Their eyes met and comprehension dawned on her face at Mayson's lukewarm response.

She touched Mayson's arm. "This doesn't have to mean anything, you know."

Mayson couldn't ignore the rush of relief that made her nearly light-headed.

"You're hot, I'm hot," Kendra continued, her hand moving lower on Mayson's belly. "We were just being hot together."

Mayson stilled the wandering hand. "Don't you have to go to work? It *is* Monday morning."

She had to be at the yoga studio herself by eight-thirty.

"It's no big deal if I'm a few minutes late. It's not like they don't get their money's worth out of me at the office."

Kendra sat up in the bed, hair falling around her shoulders and framing the firm brown breasts. Her nipples pouted in the warm air. They were still swollen from the night before, and Mayson was warm-blooded enough to allow her eyes their meander over the tempting peaks of flesh, down the flat belly to the neatly trimmed bush that did nothing to hide the thick pussy lips.

Kendra pulled the hair away from one shoulder, exposing one side of her neck and the lace of hickeys Mayson had left there. She trailed fingertips through the long hair, down her breast and the tongue-moistening line of her belly.

"Thanks for yesterday, Mayson. It was the most—the most *incredible* experience I've ever had. The things you made me feel"—Kendra drew in a slow sigh, lifting her breasts even more, then released it—"I didn't realize that it could be like that between women. When you fucked me, it wasn't just my legs that shook. It was my whole world."

Her hand fell into the V of her thighs as if to recapture the feeling from the night before. She looked at Mayson, head slightly bent, the waterfall of hair falling down one side of her face, leaving her heavy-lidded gaze bare. "I don't expect any kind of commitment from you, but I hope we can do this again. Soon."

"Soon, huh?" Mayson felt reeled in, flattered, her body awake enough to be interested.

The sex had been good. And after each orgasm, Kendra had gotten better and better at pleasing. Mayson had certainly enjoyed herself, feasting on Kendra's very willing and responsive flesh. For her, it hadn't been the earthshaking experience Kendra described but she'd had worse.

Her first time had been a disaster of miscommunication and fumbling hands. It was only the certainty that she could never allow a man into her bed that allowed her to try sex again. Even back then, though, in the attic bedroom of the high school track star who had only wanted to finger Mayson for a few quick minutes before squatting over her face, there had been a few moments of expansive pleasure, where the anticipation of it, the nearness of the girl's skin, made her feel like she'd shot to the surface of a bright green ocean after struggling to breathe underneath its murky depths.

"I'm sure we can arrange something," she said in response to Kendra's wish to see her again.

Mayson took in Kendra's body one more time before pulling away from the clinging fingers. She rolled out of bed. Stretched. "For now, the day calls."

From the bed, her new lover watched her with appreciative eyes. "Want to share the shower with me?" Kendra asked, her mouth a dark, wet curve.

"Sure. Why not?"

Of course, that turned out to be a bad idea. What started off as a shower became a teasing game that became a fucking game that became serious business completed on the cold bathroom floor. As new as she was, Kendra also had a very adventurous spirit and by the time Mayson walked out her door, she was sure she had tile squares imprinted on her back and ass, and each time she took a step she swore she felt the press of Kendra's mouth between her legs.

She got to the studio late, of course, cursing herself for forgetting that Tara didn't have a key and Linette didn't get in until ten. And although Tara didn't complain too loudly, the people waiting to take her class did, throwing Mayson annoyed looks and making comments about "respecting other people's time."

Only Fatimah, the woman she'd had a very satisfying one-night stand with weeks before, flashed Mayson a teasing smile.

"Lucky girl," she murmured for Mayson's ears only.

Embarrassed heat climbed into her cheeks as she twisted the key in the lock and pushed the building's red doors open. The dozen or so people swarmed in behind her and headed directly for Tara's intermediate Tantric yoga session. The lanky redhead gave her an amused look but said nothing. Only when Mayson got into her office, shifting the piles of paperwork on her desk to begin the day of business, did she catch a look at herself in the mirrored Quan Yin altar by the door.

She looked well and thoroughly fucked. The color sat high in her face. Her mouth looked naked and red. Eyes slumberous and bed-bound, as if she couldn't lift them high enough to look beyond the lover who had been in her sights not too long ago. No wonder the students heading into the yoga class hadn't wanted to hear her excuses. She might as well have had pussy juice smeared across her face.

"Jesus." Mayson dropped her face in her hands.

Two hours later, she was back in her office, unwinding from her first class and catching up on the monthly paperwork.

"Mayson."

Linette, the studio's manager, stood in the doorway. "These just came for you," she said, holding out an armload of red roses bursting from a tall rectangular vase.

Without waiting for Mayson to respond, she came into the office and arranged the delivery on the desk. She plucked out the card and dropped it in front of Mayson.

"Is this what bad girls get when they stay out late on a work night?"

Mayson shot her an irritated look. "Only if they're very good the next morning."

Linette laughed and let herself out the door.

The flowers were overpoweringly sweet. Mayson picked up the note, already knowing whom the roses came from, and tucked it in her pocket. She sighed. Kendra may have said she understood that their new relationship was a casual one, but she wasn't acting like it.

Mayson threw open the windows to let some fresh air in and the too-sweet smell of the roses out.

Chapter 21

"**A**re you joking?" The dimples deepened in Renee's cheeks as she laughed. "I would have totally cussed you out if I was Tara. She could have lost some students. Hell, *you* could have lost students." Renee looked at her significantly over her teacup.

Mayson shrugged. *I know, I know.* The words went unsaid but she sighed, admitting guilt. "You would have cussed me out, regardless. Remember when I forgot you were on the phone that night Kendra called?"

"How could I forget, you horny little"—Renee sputtered—"worm?"

"Do worms even get horny?"

"Don't try to deflect."

"I'm not trying to deflect. You brought up the horny worms." Mayson grinned, glancing sideways at her friend. "Did I tell you she sent me flowers that same day?"

"What? You did *not* tell me that." Renee's eyebrow rose. "Were you that good?"

"Of course." Mayson waggled her eyebrows. "The girls can never get enough of this hard candy."

Laughter exploded from Renee, abrupt and loud. "You are so damn cheesy!" She laughed again, ignoring the glances she attracted from other patrons of the teahouse.

At half past noon on a Wednesday, Ms. Tuffets was crowded

with the lunch-hour business crowd, Renee included, running in for a bite to eat before dashing back to their corporate prisons. Mayson didn't quite put it in those terms, but her raised eyebrow at Renee's grim gray suit spoke volumes.

Mayson joined in Renee's laughter although she wasn't at all serious about this thing with Kendra. The clarity of Renee's questions made her see that. The girl—the *straight* girl—was a nice distraction but wasn't worth any potential headache when there were plenty of willing lesbians she could occupy herself with instead. Although apart from this aberration, she didn't really have the energy, or the urge, to seriously pursue any women.

"Hard candy. Okay." Renee's eyes twinkled. "I understand about good sex, honey. Just make sure you keep a balance." Then Renee made a face like something just occurred to her. She shook her head. "And maybe I should be taking my own advice too."

"What do you mean? Were you able to hook up with that last guy again? You seemed pretty into him." Mayson took a careful bite of her veggie sandwich.

Her friend pursed her lips. "I've been too much of a chicken to contact him again. I feel so bad about what happened afterward."

"He's a man. Contact him. If the sex was as good as you say, he's not going to turn down another date."

"You think so?"

"Hell, yeah," Mayson said. "They think with their dicks. If his dick likes you, then whatever bad feelings he might have left over from the other night won't matter."

Renee forked the spinach from one side of her plate to the other. "I hope you're right. Before I screwed things up, that night with him was the best I've ever had."

Which was quite a statement since she'd been married to Linc for over four years and the great sex had been the reason Renee gave for staying with him for so long.

"It was perfect with him, you know." Renee's gaze bounced

back to Mayson's face. "In the dark, I felt desirable again and free from someone else's demands."

Mayson nodded. They were both thinking about Renee's ex. Mayson knew that the marriage to Linc had been far from perfect. As handsome as the guy was, he was also needy and controlling, using his supposed love to back Renee into an emotional corner. And he'd never liked their friendship.

At the beginning of their involvement, before asking Renee to marry him, he'd tried to isolate her from Mayson, claiming Mayson would try to seduce Renee away from him. That amateur move hadn't worked, of course, but from that point on Mayson had written off the relationship as a failure and impatiently waited for Renee to come to her senses enough to see it as a failure too. It took four years, but that moment finally came.

"Linc is in the past, honey. Just make sure you keep him there."

"That's one thing you don't have to worry about with me," Renee said.

Mayson heard the false note in her voice, but she didn't force the issue. Instead she reached for her glass of pineapple juice and took a sip.

Renee could tell herself—and Mayson—whatever she wanted to about Linc. That she was over him. That the decisions she made now had nothing to do with how broken he had left her. Mayson knew better, and she would be there to catch Renee when the realization sent her tumbling.

Chapter 22

A *pologies for the first time. Meet me again for a*
better second time?

Renee finished the e-mail and hit "send."

Sitting at her kitchen table, she frowned at her laptop. If she were in the stranger's place, she'd ignore that message. Aside from the fact that their bodies had connected, there was nothing in it for him. Still, she hit the "refresh" button to her Internet browser to hurry any new messages into her inbox. Just in case.

On the television, yet another commercial for a trade school went off, making way for the late-morning judge with her slash of bright lipstick and an eyebrow raised in amazement at her scandalous plaintiff trying to sue his two wives for alimony. These shows were her guilty pleasure, Jerry Springer–light, whenever she took the day off from what Mayson called "sucking corporate dick."

She shoved the new abundance of hair out of her face and back over her shoulder. A window popped up at the bottom of her screen. New e-mail. A hand flew to her mouth.

Yes. Same place? I promise not to bite this time.

A breath of relieved laughter leaked past her fingers. Anticipation raced through her, quick and heady. She could barely coordinate her fingers enough to type a reply.

Same place. Seven tonight?

His response came back immediately.

Yes.

Tonight. Seven o'clock. The phantom scent of his skin came to her then, of mint and the outdoors and sweat. She jumped up from the kitchen table. No use moping around the house. There was a beautiful day out there to enjoy.

The blindfold was on the bed when she came into the room. Black velvet against the pale floral sheets. The bedside lamp radiated a faint glow. Was this to be their usual, then? The fabric of the blindfold licked the sensitive skin of her hands, sending a shudder through her body. She put it on.

The velvet, fragrant with a faint but familiar scent, settled against her cheeks. Its smell was—she jumped when hands clasped her waist from behind.

"Yes?" He breathed the simple question against her ear.

Renee let her body speak for her, sinking back into him with a sigh. He took the sigh into him, holding her more tightly for a moment before tugging her across the carpet, pushing her down onto the bed. She lay there for a moment, under his intent regard, feeling *something* from him, although she wasn't sure what it was. There was one certainty: He wanted her. That was enough.

She lay still while he stripped her body naked. His hands stroked her breasts. The heavy heat of him sank between her thighs. Renee sighed. Sensation slithered under her skin.

In the bed, they came together, not like before but still good. His big body overwhelmed her with its taste and its sweat and its immediate and hard length inside her body. The drive to pleasure was slow and easy. It took Renee away from herself, kept her in the dark with the faint nutmeg scent of the blindfold, the scrape of her smooth legs against his furred ones, her body open and wet and moving like a dream against the sheets.

He grunted.

She gasped.

The bed shook.

Afterward, he pressed a kiss into her throat that blossomed into a line of kisses down her body. His damp lips brushed the bottom of her foot, then nothing. A rustle of cloth. Him getting dressed. Startled, she sat up in the bed, reaching for the blindfold.

A hand stroked her foot and her hands fell away. *This isn't the last time.* She felt the words as surely as if he'd spoken them.

Renee stretched out on the bed, pulling the pillow tight against her face and inhaling the smell of mint, of nutmeg, of their sex. When the door opened, she didn't turn around to watch him leave.

Chapter 23

"**S**ometimes I forget how pretty this place is." Mayson guided the open convertible through the winding streets of her old neighborhood, away from the harbor and the boats littering the crystal-blue ocean behind her. From the passenger seat, Renee nodded in agreement.

"It's a quiet beauty that you just can't find in San Diego," Renee said. "Everything here is like a memory of something good."

They cruised past a tri-level glass house, its yard strewn with the startling red of ginger plants. The house next door was nearly hidden by the tall fan of a jacaranda tree with its explosion of purple blossoms. A scattering of pale petals lay on the deep green grass.

"How could Mama and Daddy leave this behind?"

Mayson paused at a crosswalk to allow three bare-chested boys with Boogie Boards to pass in front of the car.

As usual, she had been thinking about her parents on and off during the drive up to Dana Point. Like Renee said once, it seemed strange to come up here, to come *home,* and not see her parents. And she couldn't stop the spasm of jealousy at the ready accessibility of Renee's parents. The Matthewses, retired and reliable, were always there for their daughter and whatever drama that brought her rushing back home to them.

Mayson's life had been relatively drama-free, but that wasn't the point.

"They just wanted a slower life, you know that," Renee said.

"What the hell is slower than Dana Point?" Mayson muttered.

"Stop it. They always wanted to go back to Jamaica, you know that." Renee's voice turned teasing. "May, you're all grown up now. If you want to see them, buy a plane ticket. They'll be happy to see you. Unless you show up whining like a baby who needs her titty."

"Shut up."

Renee chortled. Then she turned to Mayson with her serious face. "I know you miss them. Just remember that before they left, you were the one urging your mother to live her dream. Life is too short. Isn't that what you're always telling us?"

"Shit. One day I'll learn to keep my mouth shut." Mayson pouted.

"Poor baby." Renee giggled.

They pulled up into the Matthewses' empty driveway. By the time Mayson put the car in Park, the front door opened.

"Renee. Mayson. You're just in time to watch us leave." Renee's father chuckled heartily like he'd just told the biggest joke.

"Oh, Daddy!" Laughing, Renee jumped from the car and threw her arms around her father's neck.

"We came up a little early in case you needed any help making dinner." Mayson climbed out of the car and hugged Renee's parents, then kissed Mrs. Matthews on her powdered cheek.

"You didn't have to do that." Renee's mother threw a thin scarf around her shoulders. "We were actually heading to the market for some dessert."

"What are you going to get?" Renee slipped between her

parents, slinging an arm around each of their waists. "Ice cream?"

Her mother laughed. "Sure, if that's what you want."

"You could get bread pudding," Mayson suggested hopefully.

"Or both." This from Renee's father. His wife shot him an aggrieved look.

"You two should come with us," she said. "Pull your car into the garage."

Renee and Mayson looked at each other and shrugged. No one had to ask them twice to go shopping for something sweet.

Chapter 24

The trip took longer than they had planned, diverging at the seafood market and then Trader Joe's, where Mayson and Renee sampled everything there was to be sampled, frustrating Mr. and Mrs. Matthews just like when they were kids. But they eventually left the store with bread pudding, ice cream, and nearly full bellies.

"We can skip dinner after all that," Mayson said, swallowing the last of a mini quiche as they walked through the parking lot to the car.

"I wouldn't go that far," Renee's father muttered.

Although he was as skinny as a fence post, her father had never met a meal he didn't like. Renee often wondered if he had worms.

"Let's get home, then," she said. "We don't want to eat dinner too late."

The sun was already stale in the sky, casting long shadows that were a prelude to evening.

At the house, they divided up tasks by habit of their long years together. Renee and Mayson set the table and retrieved the bottle of chilled white wine from the fridge. Renee's father pulled the pot of brown rice from the oven, spooned some into a serving bowl, and took the bowl to the table. Her mother emerged from the kitchen with two platters with clear glass covers fogged up from the steam they trapped inside. One platter held tofu, the other thinly sliced curls of beef, both still simmering among segments of red, green, and yellow peppers in a sweet-smelling sauce.

"The food smells great, Daddy."

"I helped too, you know," her mother said with laughter in her voice as she slid the platters onto the table.

While her father had cooked most of the meals Renee remembered eating at home, it was her mother who made their drinks—everything from lemonade to any of the more complex concoctions she'd only had to taste once in a bar or restaurant to duplicate.

"This is a lot of food," Mayson said.

She lifted the glass cover to peek at the tofu. A plume of scented steam lazily wound its way toward the ceiling.

"It is, isn't it?" Her mother looked down at the food, then over at her husband. "We should invite Grant over. He loves your peppered steak."

Renee winced. "I'm sure he has other stuff to do," she said quickly. The last thing she wanted to do tonight was put up with more of her parents' matchmaking. When were they going to get it through their heads that Grant—no matter how "settled" and "sweet" he was—would not be the next one to put a ring on her finger?

"But you don't know that, darling," her mother said.

Just then a cell phone rang. Mayson's. She glanced at it before pressing the "ignore" button. Renee looked away from her parents, worried by the shuttered look on her best friend's face. She raised an eyebrow in question.

Kendra. Mayson mouthed the woman's name and Renee felt her face freeze in disapproval. Although they'd slept together only once, the woman kept on calling Mayson, acting as if their sexual relationship were more than that. Renee squeezed Mayson's shoulder as she passed to lay out the last of the silverware. *Leave that mess until we get back down to San Diego.*

Mayson nodded.

Renee turned her attention back to her parents but her father had walked away. He left the dining room and came back with a small manila envelope. "Go ask Grant if he wants to join us, and give him this." He dropped the envelope in Renee's hand.

"Daddy!"

"Quit whining." Mayson snickered.

Renee flipped her the bird and flounced out of the kitchen.

As she walked across the quiet street partially shrouded in evening, it occurred to Renee that Grant had always been here. Ever since she could remember, his family had lived across the street, three houses down, in the light gray Spanish-style house with the tall border of deep purple myrtle trees always in bloom. The house hadn't changed but the family had.

Over the years, all three of the Chambers boys had left home. When Mr. and Mrs. Chambers had decided to move to Florida, Grant moved back into the house, becoming a fixture in Dana Point. Was that the reason she, despite her parents' gentle prodding, could never see him as anything more than that neighborhood guy? Whenever she came to see her parents, he was always around. Such reluctance to leave home and hearth made him a coward in her eyes at worst, a boring mama's boy at best.

She looked at the envelope her father had given her to pass on to Grant. Should she just put it in the mailbox? No. If the envelope never made it into his hands, she would feel terrible.

Renee rang the doorbell. When no one answered, she peeked through the windows. Knocked. Then she remembered the old workshop at the back of the house where Mr. Chambers had spent so many of his evenings and weekends. She followed the pretty stone path flanked by thick vines of creeping honeysuckle. The privacy gate was closed but not locked. Once in the low-grassed backyard, she heard a low mechanical buzz.

The sound led her to the wide-open doors of the workshop. In the gray evening light, all the colors were muted. Red dimmed to pink; the green and purple of the irises had become pale shadows of their daytime selves. But the light in the workshop was bright and it showed everything clearly, sharply.

Grant stood with his back to her, leaning over an unfinished boat. It was turned upside down, resting on some sort of wooden stand while Grant, shirtless, moved a sander—she remembered that tool from her father's shed—over its sweeping brown curve.

The muscles in his bare arms flexed. And his back was a mesmerizing landscape of ridges and hills. Faded jeans sat low enough on his hips to suggest he was that beautiful all the way down.

"Grant," she called out, reluctant to get closer.

The sander droned on. He didn't turn. Renee walked closer. Not toward him but to the front of the boat he paid such loving attention to. She called his name again. This time he did turn.

"Renee." He turned off the sander, a smile ready for her. "I was just thinking about you."

Sawdust and bits of wood speckled his sculpted chest and belly. He took quick inventory of her, so quick that she might have imagined it if she hadn't been used to that particular look of his. Like he was making sure everything on her was exactly the way he saw it last.

"Here." She shoved the envelope at him. "This is from Daddy."

He stepped close to take the envelope, bringing the scent of sweat and cedar with him.

"Thanks."

He shoved the envelope into his back pocket without

opening it. The muscles in his chest jumped in that small motion and suddenly, Renee again was anxious to look anywhere but at him. Because all she wanted to do *was* look at him. At his sweat-gilded body, his slight but knowing smile.

She bit her lip. "Daddy also wanted me to invite you to have dinner with us tonight. He made one of your favorites." *Please, please, please say no.*

Grant looked at her for a moment before slowly shaking his head. "Tell your father I appreciate the invitation but I already ate."

Renee nodded, relieved. She wanted to hurry back across the street and away from the awkwardness his nearness caused. But her mama hadn't raised a rude child.

"Looks like you'll be able to get her in the water soon." She gestured to the boat, almost wincing at the inane comment.

Grant's smile widened. "She won't ever get wet," he said. "I just come out here to be with her when I need to think. I don't trust my boat-making skills enough to take her out on the water."

"Oh, okay." Her eyes flickered to his chest, then to his broad hand draped across the boat. His thumb brushed against the wood. Back. And forth. Back and forth.

"You don't have to stay here out of politeness, Renee."

She flushed. "It's not that." At least not completely. A bit of blue plaid caught her eye. She grabbed the shirt. "Put this on, please."

He looked at her for a moment, then chuckled, shaking his head. Slowly he did what she asked, taking his time snapping each button of the long-sleeved shirt into place. In laughter, his eyes sparkled like dark wine.

"Better?"

"Much," she muttered. "Listen, it's not you. Not that there's anything wrong with how you look, but my boyfriend"—his eyebrows rose at that—"I haven't seen him"—*ever*—"and it's a little difficult for me right now."

His wordless look begged for an explanation but she only shrugged. That had to be the only explanation. He had a beautiful body and she would have reacted to any beautiful body.

"Anyway, do you have anything to drink in this place? Or a cold shower I could use?"

He chuckled. "In the house."

After turning off the light and locking up the workshop, he guided her through the now darkened backyard and into his house. Although the outside of the house hadn't changed since his parents had left, Grant had completely overhauled the interior. The slightly worn but comfortable furniture and beige walls had been replaced by deep copper walls, a set of brown leather chairs, and gleaming dark hardwood. He had knocked out a wall, creating an open space that invited in every source of natural light.

Instead of the old prints of generic tropical destinations his parents once had, the walls held two large, canvas-mounted photos of the Chamberses. The first photo was of the three brothers, looking nearly identical with their close-cropped hair, brown skin, and white smiles. Another was of their parents, sitting back to back, facing the camera without the required smiles. They looked happy.

"What would you like first, something to drink or that cold shower?"

His eyes were laughing at her again. They invited her to laugh too.

"Let's start with the drink and see what happens," she said.

"The safer option." He led her into the kitchen.

When he showed her all the choices—orange juice, beer, wine, soda—she shook her head and just asked for water.

"So, Renee..." He took down two glasses and pressed them, one after the other, against the fridge's water dispenser. "Tell me about this boyfriend of yours. Is he as good-looking as me?" His teasing smile flirted with her.

She blushed again, reaching for the glass of cold water he held out to her.

"Boyfriend? Is that what I called him?"

At Grant's low hum of agreement—she still couldn't look at him—she said, "We're not that official. Far from it. He's just a man I enjoy spending time with."

"And you haven't seen him in...?"

It would sound too strange if she confessed to Grant that she'd never seen his face and barely seen his body. "I haven't seen him in a while."

"But you want to."

"Sometimes," she said, feeling a smile beginning to take over her face. "But I *always* want to feel him."

After too long of a silence, she turned to look at Grant. His smile had disappeared and the water still sat on the counter, untouched.

She tore her eyes from him. Before he could say anything, she walked out of the kitchen.

"The house looks good. I like the new touches you made."

He cleared his throat. "Thanks. I had to change something if this was going to be more than my parents' house."

She jumped, startled at the nearness of his voice. Renee moved more quickly toward the living room and sat on the sofa. When he sat across from her instead of beside her, she breathed a quiet sigh of relief.

"I couldn't live with the same stuff that I did when I was a kid. Besides"—he grinned—"my parents took most of the furniture with them to Florida."

A reluctant smile warmed Renee's face. "You know, even if my parents gave me their house, I don't think I could live in Dana Point again."

"Why? Not pretty enough up here for you?" The views in Dana Point were legendary.

"I don't know what it is. It just feels stifling up here to me. After a couple of days, I want—no, I *need* to run back to the city."

He shook his head. "I lived in LA for almost six years. It was fun but after a while the shallowness of all my relationships got to me. Here is a better place to be than most." He shrugged and managed to look worldly and domestic at once. "Guess I'm just a small-town boy."

Renee was starting to doubt that.

"Maybe you weren't willing to form deeper relationships in Los Angeles," she said.

He looked at her for a long moment. "Maybe you're right. Maybe I thought there was something better here waiting for me."

"Good things don't wait," she said, deliberately rejecting his loaded words. "You either grab them or they're gone."

"You really believe that—?"

The phone rang. It jangled loudly, twice, before he got up to answer it. "Excuse me."

As he passed the bar, her eyes noticed the clock on the wall. Was that the real time? From the darkness settling firmly against the windows outside, it undeniably was. She'd spent over an hour with Grant and hadn't even noticed the time passing.

At the bar, she leaned toward him to catch his eye from his prop against the refrigerator.

"I have to go," she mouthed.

"Hold on," he said to the person on the other end of the phone before covering up the mouthpiece. "Come and see me before you head back to San Diego. We can have a proper, uninterrupted conversation. I'll even keep my clothes on."

She rolled her eyes. "I'll drop by if I have time."

The smile reached his eyes before his mouth caught it. "If that's what you're giving, I'll take it." He started to leave the kitchen. "I'll walk you out."

"No. Go ahead and finish your call. After all these years, I know where your front door is. You haven't changed the place *that* much." She threw him a wave and left.

*   *   *

Everyone was sitting at the dinner table when she walked in. The pitcher of her mother's homemade pineapple juice was already half empty.

"Sorry." She went to the kitchen sink to wash her hands. "I started talking with Grant and lost track of time."

"That's a good sign," her mother said, leaning over to scoop brown rice onto a plate for her.

"Mom, stop. It's not like he and I were making mad love on his living room floor."

"But you thought about it." Her mother watched her carefully.

Renee turned away from her mother's perceptive stare and sat down.

"Good," her father said as if she'd answered the question. "We like him. You could do much worse."

"You *have* done much worse," Mayson chimed in.

Renee cut her eyes at Mayson. Her friend lifted a fork and deliberately speared a piece of golden brown tofu and a bite of zucchini and yellow pepper. She lifted the food to her mouth, smiling.

"So tell us, then, what did you and Grant talk about for a whole hour? I thought you didn't find him very interesting."

"Renee probably spent the entire time staring at his body and finding excuses to linger and stare some more." Her mother laughed. "If every policeman was that fit, I bet there would be fewer complaints about being pulled over."

"Dad! Do something about this!" Renee stared at her mother. Although she was used to her mother's plain speaking about most things—sex included—it seemed somehow wrong to talk about Grant that way. He was like the son they never had, for heaven's sake!

Her father only shrugged.

"It's only normal to appreciate Grant's obvious physical gifts, if that's what you were doing." Her father wagged his fork at her. "He's been here for a while and you've never shown any interest in him before. That's interesting. Was he lounging around his house naked or something?"

"You were the one who sent me over there, Dad. I was just being neighborly."

Her parents looked at each other.

"There you have it, darling," her father said to his wife. "She was only being neighborly."

Despite her father's serious look, she couldn't let go of the feeling that he was laughing at her. Mayson watched her with a crooked smile. Renee glanced down at her plate and resolved to say nothing else about Grant Chambers for the rest of the time she was in Dana Point.

Chapter 25

The visit home had left Renee frazzled. Grant. She had been attracted to *Grant?* Away from him, the absurdity of it would have made her laugh if her libido hadn't been shoved into overdrive after her visit. Sex crawled through her mind on its belly, coating everything with its viscous perfume.

With Grant as the catalyst, she couldn't *not* think of her lover. It was like he stood near her. All the time. Everywhere. In her cubicle at work, she felt him, his gravelly whisper at her ear telling her to slip on the blindfold, to touch herself until *he* came. Her lips plumped and grew damp against her panties. A throbbing settled low in her belly. Renee squeezed her legs together, barely stopping herself from running to the bathroom and touching herself hot and fast with her fingers while reliving the night with him behind tightly clenched eyelids. Her mind wouldn't let him go.

Chapter 26

Renee clenched her teeth so hard her jaw hurt.

It had been a long and unsatisfying day in the cubicle farm with Alonzo breathing so hard down her neck that she wanted to turn around and punch him. No matter what she showed him for their newest client, he hated it, demanding that she start over and create "something sexy." Is this what she had gone to art school for, to sketch sexy ads for a guy who used the Victoria's Secret catalog as his jerk-off rag?

Darn it. She clenched her teeth in frustration. Then winced when her cell phone rang.

"Yes?"

"Why don't you just quit and put yourself out of your misery?" Mayson's dry voice on the other end of the line resurrected her smile.

"Because I have bills to pay." She dropped the pencil on her desk and leaned back in the chair. "Unless you want to support me while I set up my little studio in La Jolla and go broke waiting for the revenue to come in."

"I would, you know," Mayson said, her tone flip and serious at the same time. "I would support you."

She sighed. "I know. But I'm not ready."

"Pussy."

"I thought that's what you liked about me," Renee murmured. She twirled in her chair to the music of her friend's laughter.

"When I see you tomorrow you better be in a better mood," Mayson said. "Go blow off some steam. That job's got you wound way too tight."

"Tell me about it."

"Only one cure for that kind of tension." She could practically see Mayson's dancing eyebrows as she made her suggestion.

"Thanks, doctor. I'll take your prescription under advisement."

Mayson laughed. "Whatever, gorgeous. I'll see you tomorrow night at my place. It's my turn to cook."

Renee put the phone on her desk after Mayson hung up, staring at her kaleidoscope screen saver. The tension in her body was bearable. Once she walked out of the office it would disappear. But...

The idea of sex was tempting. With a low sigh, she massaged the muscles in her neck, dropping her head tiredly forward. A round of uncomplicated sex would be the perfect way to wrap up this beast of a day. Damn Mayson for putting that suggestion in her head.

But despite her protests, her skin flushed at just the thought of being with him again. The perfect way he handled her body, how he was willing to do anything to please her, and how those things had pleased him. And afterward he hadn't clung. After the last devastating orgasm that dropped her into a brief and deep sleep, she'd woken up to an empty room. There was no trace that he had been there. No clothes, no note, even the blindfold he'd given her to put on was gone. If it hadn't been for the used condoms in the trash and the pleasant soreness between her legs, she would've been convinced that the whole night had been a dream. An intensely erotic and fulfilling dream.

Her hands made the decision for her, logging into her e-mail, reaching out to him.

Meet me tonight at the Old Town Inn?

With the message sent, she sat in nervous anticipation, knowing he'd say yes, until his reply came in. Renee opened the e-mail, her clit tingling at just the thought of him at the other end of that message.

Eight o'clock?

Yes.

With the e-mail sent, she felt better. Now there was something to look forward to beyond seeing the back of Alonzo until tomorrow morning. Maybe now she would be able to concentrate on work.

But concentrating wasn't the problem. Every time she thought she had made some headway on the design, Alonzo took a look at it, decided there was a problem, and demanded that she start again with a different idea, in a different direction. At half past five she was at the same place with the project as she had been at nine o'clock in the morning.

Alonzo popped over the top of her cubicle, his eyes pinned to her computer.

"Much better," he said. "Get me a complete draft on my desk first thing tomorrow. I want to have this thing ready for Monday morning's meeting."

Before she had a chance to protest, Alonzo was gone. The pencil in her hand snapped, flying across her desk in two clattering pieces.

"Damn. It." Her jaw ached from clenching her teeth.

He was leaving for the day, that smug prick, while she had

to work late to get this project in decent enough shape for him to see on Friday. Tomorrow. She wanted to hit something. She looked up at her computer screen. There was no way she would make it out of the office in time to meet her stranger at eight o'clock.

"Darn it!"

If Mayson heard her now, she would laugh her butt off. The thought didn't lessen her irritation in the least. With a sigh, she sent a quick e-mail to her date, telling him she was stuck at work and maybe they could do it again some other time. Renee turned back to the sketches spread out on her desk. After a few minutes bent over the desk, she hissed another sigh of irritation. *I need different scenery.* Gathering her sketches, laptop, and bottle of water in hand, she swept out of her cubicle and headed down the hall to the drafting room. There, at least, she could spread out. And not look at her computer, a constant reminder of the lover she would be missing tonight.

She leaned over the drafting table, cursing Alonzo and every hair on top of his stupid, pointy head. It was almost nine o'clock and she was finished. Finally. The mock-ups were neat, clearly presented, and ready for the client's closest scrutiny. She dared Alonzo to find something to criticize about the presentation.

To her surprise, he'd come back into the office a few minutes past eight, talking loudly on his cell phone. The few people who'd been working when Renee moved to the drafting room were long gone, so until Alonzo had come back it was just her in the office, slightly warm now since the a/c had turned itself off at six o'clock.

Hands settled on her hips from behind and she jumped. Anger flared in her belly.

"If you think this is funny, Alonzo—!" But the hands wouldn't let her turn around. She tensed to elbow her boss in the belly but a familiar scent washed over her. Gun oil. Mint. The outdoors. Firm thighs pressed against hers and her arm fell slackly back to her side.

"Shh," her lover urged unnecessarily.

Renee shuddered. Heat, immediate and undeniable, replaced the anger in her belly. Her head swam with the swift shift in emotion and she sagged against him. Just like that, her panties were soaking wet.

"What are you doing here?" She hated that her voice trembled. And she knew, just like he must have known too, that it was from excitement. And fear.

Instead of answering her question, he pushed his hips against hers again and she felt him hot and hard, rising against her backside. *I'm here for you,* his body said.

But how did you find me here? She was stiff and unresponsive, needing an answer to the question, even as inside she was melting to the slow movement of his hips against hers. At last, he seemed to understand. She felt him shift behind her, then a small piece of rectangle landed on the table bearing some of her weight. A business card. Hers.

But where had she...?

His tongue stroked her ear and she trembled. *That's not enough of an answer for you?* he seemed to ask. Insanely, it was. Her body loosened against him, relaxed enough to push back against his maleness.

"I'm not alone here. There's at least"—she gasped—"one other person." But he was pushing her past the point of caring. Alonzo's office was far down the hall and around the corner. That wasn't close enough for him to hear. Right?

He kissed behind her ear, down the side of her neck, stubble rough against her skin. Breathing low and deep, he licked her throat and she opened up for him like a sprung jewelry box. Renee moaned. Then bit her lip at the thought that someone might hear.

Purposefully, his fingertips brushed her thighs, lifting up her skirt. He kissed the back of her neck and her head fell forward, arms still braced against the table. Cool air brushed against her ass and she was abruptly glad of the sudden urge from the morning to put on the lace panties, white, that came halfway down her cheeks, the rounded globes of brown skin peeking enticingly through the lace. At least that's what she'd thought when she looked at herself in the mirror and imagined him looking at her, wanting her.

He groaned low in his throat. His big hand palmed her bottom, slid down between her thighs, pushed her legs apart. His breath fanned against her behind, hot through the lace. He tongued her through the lace. She gasped, cocking her butt in the air to give him more to taste. He chuckled against her, pressing his mouth into the lace, his tongue finding her wet and ready for him. She bit her lip against rising moans as he slid his tongue past the panties, between her swollen lips, lapping at her up-tilted femininity while his hands played with her swollen clit. She pushed back even more into his face, lips parted, eyes closed.

Pleasure fizzed through her, sparkled in her veins as if she were a shaken bottle of Perrier. He eased a finger just inside and she bit her lip, swamped in the delight of his big body, his agile tongue at her rear entrance, probing. Eager for more, she pushed back against him, but he withdrew. As always, he never rushed.

His fingers sank into the skin of her bottom. She felt each print clearly as he lifted her, parted her to his gaze. The crotch of the panties slid between her soaked lips, rubbing against her clit. Renee bit back a moan. The air moved behind her. He must have stood up. She clenched her eyes tightly shut to feel even more of him.

His belt. His zipper. His—ah!

The crinkle of plastic. His heavy maleness at her entrance.

"Yes," she gasped and pushed back to take him inside her.

But he held her still. Brushed the head of his hardness against the panties and her dripping heat.

"Please." A gasp. He gripped her hips and shoved into her. And his pulse was inside her. Her pulse around him.

"Yes." She swallowed. "Yes."

The edge of the table bit into her palms, a ratcheting pain. She pushed back into him; he pulled back, shoved into her again, firmly connecting his flesh with her flesh. It was like someone had replaced her blood with molasses. Every part of her ran hot and sweet.

"Oh!"

He touched her clit, circling and caressing it in time with his thrusts. Renee bit her lip against the sounds spilling from her lips. He moved deeper, firmer, but did not speed up. She sobbed quietly. Her grip tightened on the table as tears of heightened desire pricked her lids.

"More!" she gasped softly.

His laughter vibrated against her neck.

He gave her more. His hips moved faster, maleness pounding firmly into her, his fingers moving slickly over her clit, sliding over the excited flesh, delving under the hood where she was most sensitive. He grunted with each slam of his body inside hers. His fingers squeezed her nipple through the thin shirt and bra.

A flash of heat roared through Renee, lashing her hips, into her core, radiating up to her breasts, into her nipples. The tight pain in her nipples made her cry out.

"Oh!" *Ohmyohmyohmyohmy!*

"I'm going to tell her to do that. It shouldn't be a big difference in cost, right?"

Renee jerked at the alien voice. It came closer, saying something else.

Dammit. Dammit. Dammit! "That's my boss!"

Panicked sweat exploded on her skin. She tried to pull away from her lover. Or at least she thought she did, only her body pushed back into him again, desperately trying to hold on to the shimmering heat beginning to slip away.

"My boss is coming!" she gasped.

But her lover didn't slow down, he didn't stop. He covered her mouth with his hand and she gasped, inhaling the scent of her own body in his big palm.

She clenched hard around him. He made a low noise, cupping her breasts, kneading them, squeezing her nipples as he moved inside her, leisurely, firmly like they had all night and Alonzo wasn't coming down the hallway. Coming closer.

"Please," she gasped softly. Not knowing if she was asking him to stop or to finish what he started. She bit his palm hard. He bucked inside her. She clutched around him again, excitement and panic fighting inside her body. He moved faster, fingers strumming her clit. And she was gasping quietly again. The fire lashed her again. And she was trembling, trembling, trembling where she stood, orgasm shaking her like a tree caught in a hurricane.

She felt him too. He shuddered inside her with his face buried in the back of her neck. In apology, Renee licked his palm that was still over her mouth. He released her and stepped back, pulling his body from hers. Renee sagged against the table, her knees weak, eyes tightly shut. But quickly, with shaking fingers, she tugged her skirt back down, smoothed it, and rebuttoned her blouse. She swallowed thickly. Pleasure sang a lower note inside her body now, but it was no less sweet.

She did not turn to look at her lover.

"Just the woman I was looking for." Alonzo's voice boomed from the doorway.

Renee whirled to face him. Incredibly, she had forgotten about him. He looked at her in surprise.

"Your lipstick is smudged."

Renee's eyes flickered around the room. *Where is he?*

She cleared her throat and deliberately slowed her breathing. "Did you"—*see a half-naked man run out of here when my back was turned?*—"want something? I'm finished with the proposal and I was just about to put it on your desk and go home."

Alonzo walked deeper into the room, then paused as he

drew closer to her. His eyes held a question in them, studying her more closely.

He smells the sex in here, she thought.

Before he could say anything, she turned her back to him, gathering her originals. "I've already sent scanned copies of my sketches to you. Look them over tonight if you like, but I'll talk with you tomorrow."

"But I have a—"

"Tomorrow," she said firmly, then, with her sketches tucked under her arm, turned and left the office. Smiling.

Chapter 27

Mayson climbed out of the car with a groan and a long, vertebrae-popping stretch. It had been a long day at the studio. Long and worthwhile. But still her body ached from being pushed to its limits—four evening classes back to back plus an hour in the pool swimming laps until her body vibrated with exhaustion. Her hair, loose and still damp from her shower, lay heavily against her neck and down her back. With her bag slung over her shoulder, she walked into the house from the garage. A yawn nearly unhinged her jaw.

"I won't do *this* shit again," she muttered.

Exhaustion dragged at her body like lead weights. Thoughts of pulling her clothes off piece by piece, of the cool sheets, the pillow that would cradle her head, paraded behind her eyes like a luscious fantasy.

She locked the door to the garage and turned to head upstairs. A broad beam of light swept through her front windows, briefly illuminating her living room—the sofa, the pale walls, her hand on the banister. A car door slammed.

Who the hell?

She made it to the front door in time to hear the doorbell ring. Through the peephole, she saw Kendra on the front step, arms crossed, looking impatiently to the right, then to the left.

"What's up?" Mayson asked when she opened the door to Kendra's glad smile.

"Nothing. I thought I might stop by and see if you feel like some company tonight."

Mayson stared at her. "Kendra, it's late. I just got home from work."

Her smile disappeared. "Are you saying you don't want to see me?"

Where is this coming from? I thought this was supposed to be a casual thing.

"It's not that I don't want to see you, but I'm really tired." Even saying the words felt like too much effort. "I've had a long day and I have another one tomorrow."

"But we can just cuddle. You'll barely know I'm there." Kendra stepped closer, her smile reappearing.

Suddenly Mayson noticed the overnight bag at the other woman's feet. *Okay. No.*

"Not tonight, baby. I wish you had called first and saved yourself the trouble." She shoved the hair out of her eyes. "There's a lot I have to do early tomorrow. Maybe we can do something this weekend." Mayson made sure to put emphasis on the *maybe*. "I'll call you later in the week, okay?"

Kendra turned kohl-ringed eyes up at her, lashes heavy with disappointment. "Are you sure? I brought my own toothbrush."

Mayson shook her head. "I'll call you later."

Grudgingly, Kendra picked up her bag. "Okay. Go inside and get some rest." She slung the bag over her shoulder and cocked her hip like she was packing something dangerous. "Rest up for when I get you to myself again." She leaned in and Mayson allowed the kiss, a quick disconnection of lips. "Later."

Inwardly, Mayson cringed. But she nodded and stepped back from the door, locked it, and turned on the alarm. *Okay,* she thought, watching from behind the curtains as Kendra drove away. *That was different.* She pressed her forehead against the cool window frame for a moment. The curtain fell from her hand and back across the window as the exhaustion descended more firmly on her.

She tiredly climbed the stairs up to her bedroom, dropped her bag on the floor, and stripped off every stitch of clothing. The bed was just as good as she'd imagined. Firm, cool, and undemanding. Mayson closed her eyes.

An insistent ringing at her ear pulled Mayson out of a deep and luxurious sleep. The cell phone. Her hand fumbled for it on the bedside table.

"This better be good," she croaked.

"It's me. Can I come in?"

Mayson sat up, sleep instantly forgotten. "Did something happen?" The dim light on the radio announced that it was well past midnight. "Are you okay?"

A forced laugh came to her from the other end of the line. "I will be when you let me in."

She tried to clear her throat of its worry. "Use your key. The alarm is on. I'm in the bedroom."

"Alone?"

"Would it matter if I wasn't?"

"Shut up and quit playing with me. Are you alone or not?"

"Bring your ass up here, girl. There's nobody in this bed but me tonight." Mayson scrubbed a hand through her loose hair and hung up the phone. She reached over to snap on the bedside lamp.

By the time Renee walked through her bedroom door, she was awake enough to drag on a T-shirt and boxers.

"What's going on?" she demanded.

Renee still wore her work clothes, a skirt and matching jacket and a lavender blouse underneath. But they were badly wrinkled, like she'd thrown them in a corner and stepped on them before carelessly pulling them back on a long while later. Deep pink color suffused her swollen lips. Renee kicked off her shoes and climbed into the bed beside Mayson.

With the dim light from the small bedside lamp spilling over their linked fingers and the touch of Renee's shoulder against hers in the bed, it was like they were little girls again sharing their secrets at a sleepover. But Mayson could smell the sex on her.

"Have you ever had an experience that scared you?" She shook her head quickly when Mayson opened her mouth. "Not because of what some other person did, but what you've done?" Renee's voice was a low, ragged whisper.

"No, I haven't."

Pressed against her side, Renee shivered.

"Is it one of these men? Did something happen?"

Renee raised her large brown eyes to Mayson. There was still innocence in them, but a yearning for something else that they had only just recently seen.

"I've always been boring—no!" She raised her hand before Mayson could deny it. "But I never minded. I didn't care that I wanted a lover and the house and someone to drink hot chocolate and watch sunsets with. I was okay with being that ordinary. But after Linc I got soured on all that." She shook her head. "Now, I want something different. And with this ad that I've put out there, I'm getting it." A small smile shaped Renee's lips for a moment. "It's been nice." Her hand convulsively gripped Mayson's. "There's this one, he feels so dangerous to me, so bad—"

Mayson's heart began to thud in her chest. Her hand on Renee's tightened. "Did he do something to you?"

"No. Nothing like that." She blinked. And fat tears dripped from her eyes. "It's me. I've become this sex-obsessed person. Anything he asks me to do, I do it."

Mayson breathed a deep sigh of relief as she let go of the images of a madman wielding a whip at a terrified Renee. "Oh, honey, I think that's natural. You're just growing as a sexual being. It's okay."

Renee looked at her with wide, dawning eyes. "You can't even imagine the things—" Then she looked away. "Maybe you can." She sighed. "Sometimes I think I'm so naive, even though I've been married before."

Tears fell on the back of Renee's hand, darkening the skin. Mayson rubbed at the moisture with her thumb, tracing the veins under her friend's delicate skin. "I'm not saying that I know what the full range of sexuality is, but as long as it's consensual and safe, I don't think you have anything to worry about." Mayson raised an eyebrow. "You know I'm dying to ask what you've done but I'm not sure my poor little heart could take the details."

Renee's smile emerged slowly from behind the veil of tears. "Jesus, Mayson. If you think what I'm doing is normal then I—"

"Don't go there, honey." Mayson relaxed in the bed, slowly unwinding her tense limbs in relief. She shoved the heavy fall of wavy hair from her face, tucking it behind her neck. "We both know you've always been a prude—which has always been somewhat of a relief, to tell you the truth. I've never had to go back to Dana Point and lie to your parents after finding you in a crack house with some trick's pus-swollen dick up your ass."

"Ew!" Renee choked on outraged laughter. She shoved not-so-gently at Mayson until they were giggling and rocking back and forth in the queen-size bed.

"You really think it's normal?" Renee asked when she could talk again without succumbing to an attack of the giggles.

"Well"—Mayson smiled—"until you tell me exactly what you and this stud are doing"—she waggled her eyebrows—"I can't be too sure." She dipped her head close. "Whisper it in my ear."

At first she didn't think Renee was going to say anything, then she felt the brush of her best friend's lips against her ear. Smelled again that scent of old sex and new excitement on Renee's skin. The almond oil from her hair.

"He put his tongue in my...behind."

Mayson's eyebrow rose again. Pretty bold for a straight man. And a stranger to her ass at that. "Hm, I think I like this guy already."

They both chuckled, leaning into each other, again like little girls sharing their secrets at a sleepover.

Chapter 28

Mayson held the Downward-Facing Dog asana, emptying her mind deliberately of the extra matter threatening to distance her from her body. But the fluid feel of her body, the muscles stretched and pulled tight until that perfect ache sang through them, couldn't fully take away the thoughts of her conversation with Renee two nights before. As they had talked, everything seemed fine. She was there for Renee in the old ways, just like her friend was always there for her, but as the hours passed, regret swam to the surface of her feelings. Now, days later, Mayson found her thoughts returning to those hours with Renee. Even as she'd comforted and teased and reassured, jealousy twisted like a fanged snake in her belly. It was troubling. Irritating.

"This is something I could get used to seeing."

Mayson drew a deliberate breath at the sound of Kendra's voice, then released it. She hadn't seen the other woman since the night she appeared on her doorstep uninvited.

"You know that the studio is closed?" she murmured, not straightening from her asana.

"Is that all you have to say to me?" Kendra dropped to the floor in front of her mat, face only inches from Mayson's. Her skin looked freshly scrubbed and bare of makeup. When she didn't get an answer, she continued. "I know the studio is closed. I waited until almost everybody was gone, then I asked the last instructor—I think her name is Tara—to let me in and lock me in with you. I told her we were very good friends."

Mayson would have to talk to Tara about believing everything that pretty girls told her.

On her back, Kendra reached over to smooth a hand over Mayson's flexing jaw. The palm was hot, almost feverish. "Is it wrong to try and get you to myself sometimes?" Her voice dropped to a whisper although there was obviously no one nearby to hear. "Is it?" She spread herself out on the floor, thighs spread and lazily butterflying back and forth in the air.

Today she wore a long peach-colored dress, thin and gauzy. But with her back against the floor and her thighs spread, the dress fell back to pool at the top of Kendra's thighs. She wasn't wearing any underwear.

Mayson's body responded to the heat of Kendra's skin. The way the nipples stood out against the thin dress. Mayson wanted to reach inside the cotton top and scoop out the delicious handfuls of flesh and bring them to her lips. Threads of the haunting two-day-old conversation pulled tight, and snapped.

She stretched deeper into the pose, palms and feet flat against the mat, her spine lengthened and stretched, pushing back and down toward her thighs. Another kind of ache settled into her center. The smell of her own arousal, fresh and immediate, drifted to her nose.

Mayson gave up. She released her pose and dropped down to sit next to Kendra, flipping her ponytail back over her shoulders.

"I think I liked you better with your ass in the air and your mouth close enough for me to kiss." Kendra smiled.

"Hope you enjoyed it while you had the chance."

"Believe me, I did." She took Mayson's hand and pressed it between her legs. She was startlingly wet.

Mayson groaned low in her throat. Unable to prevent her

fingers from curling, sliding between the damp pussy lips and into the hot, inviting cavern. Kendra gasped.

She'd never fucked anyone at the studio before, not even close. But suddenly, with the smell of Kendra's cunt in her nose, that was the only thing she wanted to do.

"Did you lock the door after you came in here?" Mayson asked, her voice a low growl.

"Yes."

Mayson doubted she was telling the truth, but her pussy throbbed so fiercely, so immediately, that she didn't even care. She yanked down the top of Kendra's dress. The breasts, full and abundant, spilled onto her face. The nipples slid into her mouth, one after the other. Mayson shoved up the dress even higher, nearly drunk on the smell of Kendra's wet pussy that was thick and hot in the studio's small space.

She covered Kendra with her body, fingers moving between the spread thighs, a slow, slippery ride, while her mouth sucked the stiff nipples. Her arousal rose higher with each moan Kendra released.

"Just like that. Yessssssssssss!" Kendra clutched the back of her head, pushing Mayson's face deeper into her breasts. Her other hand sank into Mayson's ass, her hips arching up to swallow more of the fingers gliding into her. Thighs spread wide, pussy so hungry Mayson thought it would swallow *her.*

Kendra looked triumphant. Teeth bared like a woman who'd gotten a chance to ride the tiger and was enjoying every dangerous moment of it. Mayson felt her everywhere, squeezing wet and fast around her fingers. Nails digging into her back and shoulders. Her breath smelled like strawberry candy.

"Baby, you're the best!" Kendra panted in Mayson's ear. "The best."

The words became a chant, rolling over and over into Mayson's ear. "The best. The best!"

Kendra twisted her mouth toward her for a kiss. But

Mayson buried her face in the damp neck instead, focusing on the powerful and immediate motion of her body. The muscles of her arm burned with the fucking effort. Sweat skimmed down her face, down her back. She grunted. Kendra's melting pussy sucked at her hand, harder and wetter with each thrust, with each pass of her thumb over Kendra's clit.

She heaved her hips against Kendra's thigh. The sweat, the electricity, the exhilarated burn all rolled inside her, belly-deep. Her toes curled. Her arm burned and ached. Kendra's pussy was melting good-God-how-sweet around her fingers. Her body tumbled toward its destination, but she held out a little while longer. Her entire being shook with the effort to hold herself away from the precipice.

Kendra jerked against her and cried out sharply, "Mayson!"

She let go. Orgasm rocked powerfully through her. Mayson flung her head back in the delicious agony of it, plucking all her nerves into one howling song. Her body dissolved on top of Kendra. Boneless. In the lap of ecstasy.

But the feelings didn't last long. Already, the frenzied heat of her body was fading to allow reason and a slow sense of mortification to surface.

Well, that wasn't the best idea you ever had. She shoved strands of loosened hair out of her face and focused on her breath. Slowing it, smoothing its ragged edges. Fucking to forget was never a good idea. Even now, the threads of her conversation with Renee reattached themselves, wound through her consciousness, unable to be ignored.

She drew in a deep, purposeful breath and released it. Kendra sat up beside her, the dress still pooled at her waist and pulled up to her naked thighs. A ripple of faint arousal moved through Mayson. She still itched. The sex had been like a thin film of lotion over an exposure of poison ivy. To avoid, to ignore, to not think. That was the true temptation that left her body weak and liquid under the other woman's touch. Kendra trailed a hand over her chest. Even through the thin tank top, her skin reacted. Her nipples hardened.

Mayson grabbed Kendra's hand, keeping the breath running evenly through her lungs. She released the woman's hand and stood up.

"I think that was enough," she said.

"Really? I can see that you still want me."

Sitting at her feet, Kendra was temptation incarnate, the peach dress only a slash at her middle, complementing her luscious cinnamon skin. Heavy breasts and small nipples that puckered like summer-ripened raisins under her tongue. Mayson licked her lips. Kendra only had to lean a few inches for her mouth to brush the damp spot in the V of Mayson's pants.

It would be so easy, so easy to push down her pants and invite Kendra's mouth closer, to cover her pussy, already wet and tingling with new arousal. Kendra wound her hands up Mayson's thigh, like the model on the cover of a paperback romance. Mayson would have laughed if Kendra hadn't looked so fuckable doing it. Silently, the woman's mouth said, "Fill me." Her body panted, "Touch, I'm yours." Mayson clenched her hands into fists and deliberately stepped away, forcing Kendra to drop her hands.

She yanked at the elastic tie holding her ponytail together. The hair crackled with each jerk of her fingers through it. With quick and efficient movements, she tucked the long strands into a braid and tied it off with the elastic band, all the while walking away from Kendra.

"I have to lock up. Do you—" She forced the words past her lips. "Do you want to grab some coffee?" After all, they'd just fucked. It was the decent thing to do.

Kendra seemed surprised by the invitation. "Only if I promise to keep my hands to myself?" Smiling, she raised an eyebrow to make it a question.

"Can you?"

"Have you looked in the mirror at yourself lately?"

Mayson reluctantly laughed and shook her head. "So does that mean you—" She stopped when her cell phone rang, playing Renee's theme song. "Excuse me." She turned away from Kendra and crouched to pick up her towel and water bottle.

Mayson opened the phone. "Hey. What's up?"

"Are you done at the studio yet?"

"Just about." She watched Kendra slowly pull up the straps of her dress, arranging the cloth just so on her shoulders. "I'm wrapping up a few last-minute things."

"Good. I made us a late dinner. Come over."

She turned away from Kendra. Despite everything—the questions, that damn late-night conversation in her bed—seeing Renee was the only thing she wanted to do. It had been a long day. The perfect antidote for it was to sit across from her friend in her bright kitchen and share the events of their day, share their laughter, over a meal.

"That sounds pretty good, actually," Mayson said.

"Can you be here in an hour?"

"Absolutely, and I won't even have to speed."

Renee laughed. "Great. See you soon."

Mayson pursed her lips and turned to Kendra, taking care to tuck an apology into her gaze. "Can you take a rain check on that coffee?"

The smile cracked and fell off the other woman's face. "You made another date that fast?"

"Not exactly." Mayson didn't say anything else.

"Oh well, I guess I didn't act fast enough." She tried to smile again but it was a pale attempt. Bare feet slid into sandals. "When will I see you again?"

"Soon," Mayson said, not sure if she meant it.

"Okay, soon." Kendra unlocked the door and pulled it open. She stared at Mayson, the longing naked in her gaze. "I'll hold you to that," she said.

Chapter 29

Mayson stretched her full length out on the sofa and sighed against the plumped cushions. The day had been beautiful. Perfect. Three morning classes, home for a long bath, then a cleansing meditation under the skylights while the sun poured down on her naked body. Absolutely perfect. Now, at almost three in the afternoon, she was bonelessly relaxed. Content.

She reached for the book she had been pecking through for the past few days, a recently published how-to on Tantric lesbian sex, and flipped it open to her bookmark. So far, it had offered up no great insights but she was willing to see where the writer was going. Before she could move aside the bookmark, the cell phone rang.

"If you called to ask me out to lunch, it's too late. I already ate."

Renee snorted in her ear. "You *do* know that it's three o'clock, right?"

"It's lunchtime somewhere." A loud announcement blared through the phone, garbling whatever Renee said.

"Where the hell are you?"

"The airport." The words were like a confession.

"Ah. Rough day?" Mayson turned the book upside down on her lap and adjusted the phone more comfortably against her ear.

"I'm thinking about quitting the firm."

"Why just *thinking?*"

Renee laughed but the sound wasn't very convincing. "It's not that easy, May. I'm not as strong as you."

Mayson frowned. "Strength? Come on now."

"Yes, strength. And I just don't have it." Renee's voice was low, heavy with the weight of unnamed feelings. Something was wrong. The book slid from Mayson's lap as she stood up. Jacket. Keys. Wallet. At the door, she slipped on her shoes, ratty black Converse sneakers she'd had since college, and headed out.

"It's not about strength, love, it's about faith," she said into the phone.

"Oh, is that all?" The humorless chuckle came again. "Maybe I just don't have any faith in myself at the moment."

"Then have faith that your world won't let you fail. If you want this other career as badly as you say, then jump for it. You were meant to succeed, Renee. I can't believe you don't see that."

Her car coasted through the quiet side street, then out onto Sixth Street. The cyclists were out this afternoon. They wove fearlessly through the light traffic, bodies sailing into the wind on their two-wheeled machines. A small crowd gathered along the edge of Balboa Park. Women in shorts and bathing-suit tops. Bare-chested men. They tossed Frisbees through the air, laughing, running across the green grass.

Mayson cruised past, the breeze batting at her braid.

"I know I've been twenty times blessed," Renee said through the phone. "After all I have you in my life. But it doesn't stop me from feeling like a big steaming pile of poop right now."

"Baby..."

A low sound of distress hummed back at her through the phone. What the fuck had Alonzo done to Renee now? Her hands tightened on the steering wheel as the car tilted down Laurel, hood pointed toward the harbor and the airport. Behind her sunglasses, she narrowed her eyes against the sun's glare and the sidewalks that sparkled fresh from the morning's rain.

"Should I come with my pooper scooper?"

Renee laughed. A real one this time. "If you did, I'd adore you more than I already do."

"I thank whatever gods out there that you're so easy to please."

"I love you too, May."

"Only because I loved you first."

Renee laughed again, although it was an old joke. Old but never stale.

At the airport, she took the ticket to pay the parking machine, parked the car, and joined the steady stream of people striding across the pedestrian crossing and into the airport.

The double doors slid open, releasing a cool rush of air over Mayson's skin, the sound of a thousand conversations, a woman's voice on the PA system. Mayson never quite understood why her friend loved airports so much. They were noisy places filled with frantic activity, panic, and misplaced luggage. Whatever the reason, Renee found calm and security in them. Whenever her mind was turned inside out, whenever she was frustrated, she came to the airport to sit and absorb the chaos and twisting energy. In that chaos, Renee found her own calm.

"So did you just walk out and tell Alonzo you weren't coming back?"

"No." Another sigh. "I turned up my yellow belly and said I had a client meeting and wouldn't be back until tomorrow."

Mayson chuckled. "Did he ask you which client?"

"Even he knows better than to try that micromanaging crap with me."

Mayson heard a wooden creak in the background and another, fuller exhalation.

"Keep that up and you're going to start hyperventilating."

"Shut up," Renee muttered, but Mayson heard the smile

in her voice. "Why do I get the feeling you're not taking me seriously?"

"I do, honey. I do."

Standing in the middle of the light-filled terminal with people rolling their luggage briskly past, with children nearby crying and tugging at their mothers' skirts, Mayson looked up. A pair of bare feet resting next to black stilettos immediately caught her eye. Then she saw long legs, thighs covered in a pale green skirt, and an elegant but lonely looking hand.

Renee sat in one of the wooden rocking chairs near the railing that led away from the departure gates. She wasn't supposed to be up there without a boarding pass. Her pretty smile must have worked on the right person. But as Mayson approached the stairs, the uniformed woman who was supposed to be allowing only downward traffic stared listlessly off into space. Mayson jogged quietly up the stairs before the woman could turn around and notice her.

"Somehow, I don't believe you," Renee was saying into the phone as Mayson approached. The words echoed back at Mayson through the earpiece.

Since she'd last seen her two nights before, Renee had gotten rid of the fake hair, leaving her small head covered in buds of short, natural curls.

"And whose fault is that?" Mayson asked the question from just behind Renee's chair. Her friend turned with a surprised gasp, a pleased smile.

"You sneak!" She shot to her feet and smothered Mayson in her scent, the familiar softness of her body. "What are you doing here?"

"The obvious," Mayson said, grinning at her friend's surprise. She trailed fingers down the back of Renee's neck before releasing her from their hug. "I like your hair short." Her phone closed with a snap and she dropped it into her jacket pocket.

"Me too, actually." Renee touched her neck.

"You know me, I prefer short hair on women, but that has to do with my own predilections rather than aesthetics."

Renee gave her a sharp look. "Are you saying I don't look pretty with my hair short?" She cocked her head, showing off the flirtatious line of her throat.

"I'm not catering to your vanity today, darling. Try me again tomorrow." Mayson pulled a nearby rocking chair closer and sat down.

Below them, the airport bustled on in organized madness. The muted shout of hundreds of voices. From far away the squeak of an ancient luggage carousel. A brilliant day shining outside the glass doors, California bright with palm trees rippling in the breeze. A line of yellow taxis trickled past.

"This is the nicest surprise." Renee slipped her bare feet onto the edge of Mayson's chair.

Her red-painted toes wriggled. Even in her work clothes— the tucked-in white blouse, pale green skirt, the jacket lying on the back of her chair—she seemed childlike. Wicked.

"You haven't come to the airport with me in a long time." She smiled, and Mayson was relieved to see the sadness receding behind her eyes.

"It's been a long time since *you* came," Mayson said.

Renee shook her head. "I was here three months ago. Not so long ago."

Thinking back, Mayson narrowed her eyes. *Ah.* When Linc called her the last time.

"If it's not Linc, it's Alonzo or somebody. One day"—she pinched Renee's bare toe—"you'll learn that men are nothing but trouble."

"One day I will, but for now I guess I'm just a slow learner."

"It's okay. One of us has to fuck to preserve the species. It might as well be you."

Her friend wrinkled her nose.

"What?" Mayson demanded.

"I don't know why, but I thought once you got more into yoga and the spirituality behind it, then you wouldn't curse as much."

"I don't know why you'd think that either." Mayson grinned lazily, rocking back in her chair. It *was* relaxing sitting here above it all, allowing the chaos to happen while being apart from it. "Since we were kids I've had this dirty mouth. Why would I change now?"

But she knew it wasn't really about her. Renee's dissatisfaction with the things in her life—her job, her relationship with her ex-husband—was starting to spread. On a normal day, she wouldn't give a shit about Mayson's language.

"There is something to be said for a well-placed 'fuck,'" Mayson continued, watching her friend's face. "With all the action you've been getting these days, you should understand that now more than ever."

Renee snorted. "Making love is one thing, saying *that* word is another."

"You are not *making love* with these men, Renee Matthews. What you're doing is fucking, and there's nothing wrong with that. It makes us animal but it makes us human too." Mayson unsuccessfully fought against the irritation in her voice. Renee didn't do prissy and hypocritical often, but when she did... Mayson clenched her back teeth.

"I didn't say there was anything wrong with it." Renee's tone hardened in response to hers. "Don't judge me like that—"

"What's this, a lovers' quarrel?"

The bitter voice turned them quickly around in their chairs. Mayson's eyes narrowed. A tall man stood just behind them, self-consciously fashionable in his sneakers, designer jeans, and Marcus Garvey T-shirt. A laptop bag hung from one shoulder. The sunglasses didn't disguise the scorn on his face.

Renee's mouth shut with an audible snap. Her face tightened, and the eyes that had been crackling before with the beginnings of her anger were suddenly dead, flat brown in her frozen face.

"What this is, is none of your business, Linc," Renee said.

Mayson stood up so fast that her chair rocketed backward. Here was a much better target for her irritation. "I swear to heaven, if you don't keep your ass moving away from us, you're going to make me do something I won't regret." Her chair creaked angrily back and forth in the air.

At a few inches above six feet, he was taller than Mayson but it gave her a vicious pleasure to see him back away from her. As people passed by, a few glances flickered their way but no one stopped to pay them any lasting attention.

Linc's gaze moved from her to Renee, contemptuous and sad. "Nothing's changed, has it? There's no room in your world for anyone but the two of you."

He gripped the strap of his laptop bag. "The last time, all you could do was talk about her. Now, I finally see you after almost six months and you're *with* her." He shook his head. "You two deserve each other. The pathetic thing is, you don't even see it." His shaded gaze focused on Renee. "No wonder you couldn't love me. You've been in love with Mayson your whole damn life."

Renee shrank back in her chair.

Is this the kind of dumb shit the asshole is beating her down with every time they have a conversation? A red mist flashed behind Mayson's eyes. Her knee came up, connecting with a solid thump between his legs. He grunted, the air slipping from his mouth in a high squeak. Linc folded, cupping his balls, groaning. He fell to the ground. The bag slipped off his shoulder.

"You should have kept walking like I told you." She almost kicked him again for fun.

"Oh my God! Is he okay?" A woman in pink ran up to him, her two children trailing behind her with large, interested eyes. She dropped to her knees beside Linc's curled body.

"Fuck." Mayson looked around. "Security! This man needs some help."

On the floor, Linc panted, gasping and incoherent while the woman patted at him, asking if he needed anything. Her children hovered around them. The uniformed woman from the stairs stomped toward them in her heavy boots.

"I think he fell." Mayson jerked her head toward Linc.

The woman grabbed her radio and shouted into it.

"No!" Linc panted from the floor. "She—!" Another groan cut off whatever he was going to say.

"Time to go," Mayson muttered.

But Renee already had her shoes on and the jacket thrown over her arm. Wide-eyed but quick, she clutched at the hand Mayson held out and they walked swiftly away from Linc and the crowd growing around him.

"I can't believe you did that," Renee hissed.

They jogged down the stairs, weaving through the slow-moving crowds.

"I wish I'd done it years ago. That fucking prick." The breath moved easily through her lungs as she ran.

At her side, Renee clattered along on her high heels, panting. Pissed. They ran toward the automatic doors and the glass slid open, shoving them out into the warm day. Mayson swallowed hard to control the anger still surging through her veins.

"But it's the airport. They have cameras. He'll press charges." Renee's hands fluttered in agitation.

They slowed down, walking toward the pedestrian crossing and the parking lot.

"He doesn't have the balls to press charges." Mayson snorted. "And the cameras only saw me giving an old friend a hug. It's not my fault he went faint from my affections."

Renee sputtered with reluctant laughter, shoving at Mayson. "You!"

They moved with the stream of pedestrians, crossing in front of the cars waiting patiently for the light to turn back to green. As they walked toward the parking meter machines, Mayson squeezed Renee's hand that she still held in hers. "We need to talk."

Deep brown eyes flickered to her face. "Yes, we do."

She pulled Renee down beside her on a nearby bench. A man in a black shirt and white pants glanced at them briefly as he paced near the parking machines. His cigarette smoke left a trail of gray behind him.

On the bench shaded by the low overhang, they sat with their shoulders touching. Mayson took Renee's hand in hers. "You know I love you."

"Of course." Renee frowned.

"And you know I respect the person that you are."

"Yes." Renee drew out the word as her frown deepened, but she said nothing else.

"Good." She gave a tight smile. "This thing you have with the job is wearing both of us out."

"That's what—?"

"No, let me finish." Mayson held up a hand, resisting the initial urge to touch a finger to Renee's lips.

Renee folded her hands in her lap, rolling her eyes.

"Before Linc showed up, I was starting to get pissed and you were starting to get pissed." The skin around her eyes tightened at the remembered irritation. "I've never had a problem with you being a prude, and I know you've never cared whether I say 'fuck' or even who I fuck. But as work has been getting more annoying, things that didn't bother you before are driving you into bitch territory." She shook her head when Renee tried to talk. "This is the last time I'm going to say this: Fix this thing with your job before I do something drastic."

"Like what? Kick Alonzo in the balls?" Renee's mouth stretched in a thin smile.

"Sure. I'll try that." Mayson shrugged. "He'll fire you then for sure, and you'll have no choice but to move on."

Renee bit the inside of her cheek and looked away. For

once, it was hard for Mayson to decipher the look on Renee's face. There was something behind that half frown; she just didn't know what *it* was.

"Is that all you wanted us to talk about?" Renee finally asked. The line on her brow wavered.

"Yeah. Is there something else you think we should talk about?"

Renee pressed her lips together. "Linc..." But she didn't say anything else. She sighed and leaned into Mayson's shoulder. "God, I'm such a..." Again, she didn't finish.

"Baby, that turd isn't worth the piece of paper it would take to wipe him off your ass."

Renee chuckled weakly. "I know, but it's so hard to ignore him. The things he says, the way that he says them." She sighed again, her forehead on Mayson's shoulder. There was something desperate about the way she clung briefly to Mayson's arm before letting go. "I don't know why he hates me so much."

"You didn't become the person he tried to turn you into. That's all." She lightly stroked her friend's head, unable to help the shudder of pure sensual appreciation at the tight curls licking at her sensitive fingertips. "When men, and some women, see a girl like you, they want to turn her into a doll, something to play with and dress and show off. It doesn't matter what or who you were when they first met you. If you reject that transformation, they'll hate you for it." A fleeting smile moved across Mayson's lips when Renee snuggled even closer. "And that's just life."

Renee shuddered against her and said nothing.

Chapter 30

No wonder you couldn't love me. You've been in love with Mayson your whole life.

The words haunted Renee into the hotel, tumbling over and over in her head, an echo of a bad dream. When would she ever be free of Linc and the shadow he had cast over her life? Renee drew the thin coat tighter around her shoulders, shivering despite the day's relative warmth.

In the hotel lobby, she greeted the woman behind the desk with a bland smile and made her way to the stairs, the black overnight bag a comfortable weight on her shoulder. She had just pulled the room door closed when she heard the key card slide in from the other side. Her heart began a slow, hard thud in her chest. She turned away from the door just as his solid presence filled the room.

As always, the darkness was a comfort. He came behind her, smelling of the outdoors and mint, with something spicy-sweet on his breath. Ginger? The blindfold slipped over her eyes, that special darkness he brought with him meant for her alone.

She'd told him what she wanted. Written it confidently in the e-mail, as her thighs clenched together in anticipation, wondering if he would be able to do it. If it would bring the release it promised. And he'd said yes to her, just as he'd said yes to everything else that she'd suggested, bringing his yes and the blindfold and the stinging fulfillment of his body into their dark room.

With the blindfold on, she turned to him, eager to taste. Yes, it was ginger. Candy, spice edged with sugar. With pleasure, she uncovered tiny pieces of the root under his tongue, between his teeth. She sighed, drinking him in, losing herself in the sheer sensuality of the experience that he allowed, even encouraged with low sounds, unending kisses, sinuous movements of their tongues that mimicked what was to come. Groaning, Renee licked the corners of his mouth, sucked his full lips, tasted every part of his mouth until he was growling against her. He pulled her closer.

No wonder you couldn't love me.

She clung tighter to her stranger. *No. Please.*

Tonight was about forgetting. Tonight was something she'd asked for. She wanted to erase Linc and his words and her cowardice. And this would help her to forget, if only for a few moments. Renee shivered under the stranger's touch.

No wonder you couldn't love me.

He pulsed against her hand, an echo of her heartbeat, her lust. Abruptly, her world spun and she gasped. He lifted her and dropped her on the bed, settling his body against hers moments later. She sighed into his mouth. He pressed into the V of her thighs, his manhood rubbing at her center through his jeans, through her panties.

"Hmm." Her whole body vibrated with the sound.

He moved against her, pushing himself against her. She wriggled against him, pressing her clit against his hardness as he touched her breasts through her shirt. As they breathed each other's breaths.

Although he'd been inside her over a dozen times, it felt so dirty and forbidden to rub against him, nearly out of control with need for more sensation. Renee tightened her legs around him, locked her ankles, trying to climb up his body while desire climbed through her. Her wetness straining against his hardness. She couldn't get enough.

His tongue twined with hers, sliding, probing. Her stranger's kisses fanned the arousal higher and higher. The tiny orgasm caught her by surprise. Her eyes abruptly squeezed shut and she shivered deliciously in his arms. A breathless laugh broke the seal of their mouths. And she shivered again.

His fingers probed beyond the edge of her panties and for a moment he paused at her entrance, perhaps surprised at the unexpected flood of wetness there.

"I got one early." She giggled against his mouth, unable to keep quiet.

He chuckled. His fingers moved again, sliding easily inside her, teasing. He stroked her clit. Long, languid strokes that reignited her. Her breath caught when fingers dipped inside her again. She was ready for another one. This one she wanted them to reach for together. Renee fumbled for his belt buckle, loosened it. Peeled down his zipper. His thickness sprang into her hand. Wordlessly, he pushed a condom into her hand, then moved his body back, giving her enough room to put it on. Even with her blindfold, she managed it quickly. He panted with her hands on him.

When she released him, he reached down and dragged her panties off with a low noise of impatience. *I need to be inside you.* It was frightening sometimes how easily she could read his silences. But this one was obvious, a shout of his need.

He sank deeply, swiftly between her waiting thighs.

"God!"

They were both fully dressed. Just his jeans unzipped, her panties off, and her skirt flipped up. The sweat of arousal and sex slid under their clothes. She was as horny as a teenager in the backseat of a car. The zipper of his jeans dug into her thighs. She felt overheated under his heavy body, under her clothes. But it was also sinfully, unbelievably good. She twisted her arms around his neck, kissed the parts of his face she could reach, licked his mouth.

This lust she understood. It was physical and mindless and simple. There was nothing else. There was *no one* else.

His slow movements were exquisite torture. Slow, methodical strokes easing into her body, then pulling out almost completely before easing back again. The bed rocked with their weight. He breathed easily over her, effortlessly in his exertion, but she could smell his rising excitement, the clean sweat that rose off his skin mingling with the scent of mint.

Faster. She wanted him to move faster. But he was a man intent on a mission. A slow, torturous mission. Renee clamped down on him and he gasped. She sank fingers into his back and moved her hips faster, urging him on.

With his large body over and inside her, she was desperate again, skin clawing for satisfaction. Her nipples tingled and drew up tightly. She gripped his head and drew it down to her breasts. She sighed when he tongued her nipples through the cloth. Getting it wet. Getting her wetter.

Faster. He moved faster inside her. Renee arched her neck, gasping. The zipper bit into her thighs as he moved faster. Then she didn't feel the discomfort anymore. Only the friction and bubbling heat in her center, his mouth sucking her nipples, sending sensation deep into the heart of her. She bucked harder against him, reaching for more. The bedsprings squeaked, screamed as he pounded into her. He groaned something into her breasts.

"Yes," she gasped. Splaying her thighs wider, feeling her body drip, and weep, and sigh for more.

Something covered her face. Something thin. Her underwear. She could smell herself in the silk, feel the dampness from the crotch pressed into her nose. Renee shook her head and twisted away from the thin fabric, although she could still smell, although she could still breathe. He moved faster, his iron length slamming into her until she was gasping under the silk, overwhelmed by her own smell.

Then his hand clamped over her nose and mouth.

She struggled against him, trying to breathe. She couldn't. Spots of light danced behind her tightly clenched eyelids. A darkness reared up, threatening to swallow her. It retreated. Her head thrashed against the sheets as awareness came and went. The sensation was there, a conflagration, a steady pull of heat promising total oblivion. *There!* Just out of her reach. Renee stretched for it, her body arching in the sheets, thrashing up, desperate. Like a hungry fish, she leapt up for it. A thousand lights exploded inside her. Then darkness.

When she came back to herself, it was still dark. Not the darkness of the blindfold, but of a shuttered room. She drew in a long breath. That simple act she'd taken for granted was divine, the air moving easily in her lungs, her chest rising and falling without effort.

"Did it go all right?" she asked.

"You tell me." His voice was a hoarse whisper from very near. She turned, surprised to feel him so close to her in the bed.

"My orgasm was amazing," she whispered. The memory of it made her tingle still. Renee reached for his hand in the dark, took it, and brought it to her throat. "You were perfect."

Her trust in him had been spectacularly rewarded. She shuddered again at his strength when he'd stopped her breath. She'd felt the hesitation in him, but only briefly, then he dove into it as headlong as she had.

That long moment of breathlessness had been sublime. Amnesic. All of her body and her mind had been wiped clean in that surge for breath and pleasure. Nothing else had intruded. No one else had appeared behind her tightly closed lids to haunt her.

Breathplay was something she'd heard of in school. She'd even talked about it with Mayson but had never thought she could try it. Until him. When she asked him to choke her, he'd hesitated. Even in the e-mail she could sense that uncertainty. Then he had asked for time to do some research to make sure it could be done safely. His days of investigation led them here, finally, to this dark and full room.

His body shifted closer to her. He relaxed. Then for the first time she realized he'd been tense. With a smile she brought his hand to her lips.

"That was the last time," she said.

His damp kiss burned into her shoulder. "Good."

Chapter 31

Renee came to the surface slowly, becoming aware by degrees of the warm cocoon of blankets, sunlight across her eyelids, another body close to hers.

"Hmm." With a sigh of contentment, she peeled the blankets away from her shoulders. The room was cooler but not uncomfortably so, the mild touch of a San Diego spring.

"You plan to lie there all morning?"

"Maybe."

She opened her eyes to Mayson, propped up beside her in the bed, her hair loose around her shoulders, a thick folder spread across her lap.

"I already made and packed up our lunch. Breakfast is waiting on you." At Renee's blank look, she chuckled and poked at her ribs through the blankets. "The beach. We're spending the day at Mission Beach before heading up to see your parents, remember?"

"Of course I remember," she said. But she didn't.

When Mayson came over last night, they'd cooked together, talked, played a sleepy game of checkers in front of the dark fireplace before heading to bed. They hadn't discussed the next day.

"Liar." Mayson poked her again, but the smile still lingered around her mouth.

"I know. I suck." Renee sat up, yawning, scratched at her

head. She pushed the blankets away and left the bed for the bathroom. "But it's not as if I made other plans."

"I know. And even if you did, all you had to do was cancel them."

In the bathroom, Renee smiled. Mayson was right. She stood up and flushed the toilet, turned on the sink to wash her hands.

"What are you reading?" she asked, walking out of the bathroom and drying her hands. She tossed the damp towel in the hamper and clambered back into the bed.

"Your portfolio." Mayson shoved the heavy fall of hair out of her face and anchored it behind her shoulder. "You're getting better."

She looked at the studio photos, a series of photographs Renee had taken at Dhyana Yoga, mostly black-and-white shots of students, the building, the meditation garden.

Renee reached over and turned the page. "I could be better."

The photo she turned to was of Mayson, or at least her arm, its long curve of subtle musculature and dark skin, braced against a stone wall in the garden.

"Couldn't we all," Mayson said. She closed the portfolio, looking meaningfully at Renee. "Oh, I almost forgot." A grin shimmered across her face. "Three of your prints we had on display at the studio sold this week. I put the money in your bank account before I came over."

"Really? Are you sure you didn't buy them yourself just to make me feel good?" She took the heavy portfolio from Mayson's lap. It felt good to have its substantial weight in her hands. She hugged the portfolio to her chest.

"Why would I pay good money when I can get it for free?" Mayson tickled her through the nightshirt.

She yelped, pushing her away.

Mayson fell back against the pillows, watching her with a lazy smile. "I'll even tell you who bought the pieces if it makes you believe."

"I believe," she said.

"And do you feel good?"

Renee smiled, allowing the slow pleasure of it to spread across her face. "Yes, I do."

Mayson nodded with a look Renee could read as easily as her name.

"I know." She leaned into her friend's warmth, touched her lips to the bare shoulder, and inhaled her unmistakable eucalyptus scent.

Mayson kissed her forehead. "As much as I'd love to sit looking at you laze around in bed all day, breakfast is getting cold."

"And the beach is waiting!" Renee bounced up in the bed, suddenly vividly awake. "I'm ready."

They ate breakfast, then set off for Mission Beach with the stereo blasting The Skatalites and Mayson's surfboard sticking up from the backseat of the convertible. At nine o'clock on a Saturday morning, the beach was still half asleep with only a few cars cruising down Mission Boulevard. A man walking his two dogs crossed the street against the light. The dogs, untethered by leashes, danced around the man's intricately tattooed legs, nipping playfully at each other as they ran ahead of their human, then back to him.

"See if you can park by the lifeguard's station," Renee said. "I don't want to get stuck carrying the hamper like last time."

"You can carry my board instead."

"Are you joking? That's heavy too."

"Wuss."

The closer they got to the water, the more sand covered the road, crunching under the tires and floating up around the car in a pale cloud. Mayson parked against the curb between a yellow VW bus and an old blue Volvo station wagon. Out on the ocean, the waves were high, foam-topped, and a sharp blue in the morning sun. A few surfers were already riding high on the water, gliding across the surface like sea-bound birds, their arms outspread.

They unpacked their gear; Renee set herself up on her blanket with sunscreen slathered all over her body and her camera nearby, while Mayson pulled on her wetsuit and plunged into the water with her surfboard.

The water was cold. Renee could tell by the single sinuous shiver that took Mayson's body as she rode into the ocean on her belly, a dark slash against her pale yellow surfboard. A wave rose up and she did too, leaping to her feet on the board and knifing into the thick trough of water, leaping on top of the wave, then inside it. The wave curled around her body, hiding her from Renee's sight, then the wave uncurled, revealing a grinning Mayson trailing her fingers against the water's glassy wall as she rode it down to the beach. Her laughter rippled out on the breeze.

Renee watched her, mesmerized by her grace on the water, the strength in her tall body. Even when Mayson fell, disappearing under thundering water, then reappearing again in her quest to conquer, she was beautiful.

The camera fell into her hands and clicked steadily, capturing images of ocean, woman, and sun. In the zoom lens, May-son's face was a portrait of untamed joy.

A shadow fell across her face, blocking the sun.

"We don't see too many black pearls on this white beach."

Renee looked away from the water, squinting up. The camera dropped into her lap. "I didn't know this was a white beach," she said, keeping her tone deliberately light.

Two guys stood over her, California blond and tan, one with long hair falling into his face, young. The other could have been his twin, only his hair was neatly trimmed—almost military—and his bare chest was half covered by a tattoo. Some kind of large cat. The long stretch of sand around her was empty except for a foursome playing a relaxed game of volleyball a half mile or so down the beach.

"It's not really a white beach," the short-haired one said.

"But, you know...." He gestured to the meager oceanside population—the tanned volleyball players, the dozen or so surfers who were all pale reflections of Mayson.

"Your girl is hot. She's got some totally off-the-wall moves out there."

"Ah...thanks. I'll tell her you said that." Renee pointedly lifted her camera again and turned away from them.

"Come on. At least tell us your name." Long Hair flashed a smile and moved back into her light.

Mayson jogged up on the beach, surfboard under her arm. She was only panting slightly, water dripping from her face, down her slicked-back braid. "What's up, fellas?"

"We were just telling your girlfriend how hot you are." Short Hair snickered, his greedy eyes devouring Mayson's slim form in the wetsuit.

"Thanks, but she already knows that." Mayson propped her board up in the sand and dropped onto the empty blanket next to Renee.

When the surfheads made no move to leave, she arched an eyebrow. "Do you mind? We came here to be alone."

Renee had never seen grown men stumble so much over their tongues, then over their feet as they apologized and hurried away.

"How do you do that?" Renee laughed. "People are never scared of me."

"You look like a kitten in your little striped bikini and sunglasses." She grinned. "Wetsuits are more intimidating."

She stood up and unzipped the suit in question, peeling the slick black rubber off her body until all that was left on her was a bikini not much bigger than Renee's. It was a lot like a striptease.

Renee looked away, rummaging in the duffel bag for a towel. She passed it to Mayson and her friend took it wordlessly, dried off her face, and passed it briskly over her hair and body. "Thanks."

"You didn't have to get out of the water for me, you know."

"Yes, I did. Those assholes were about to start something." She folded the towel and put it under her head. "They need to go smoke some more weed and just sit down somewhere instead of annoying every pretty girl they see." Mayson closed her eyes and wriggled against the blanket. Droplets of water clung to her lashes, glistening against her cheeks. Under the sun, her body steamed.

Renee picked up her camera.

"Let's go in here." Mayson gestured to the shop with the red awning. "They have great bubble gum ice cream." The sun glinted off her smooth hair tumbling around her shoulders, damp and gritty with sand.

Because of the incident with the two surfer boys, Mayson was reluctant to leave Renee alone again. But after they swam together, raced to a far-out buoy, and ate lunch, she sensed Mayson's restlessness. With a laughing promise not to talk to strangers, she sent Mayson back out into the surf while she took her camera and went in search of interesting things. Hours later, it was her friend who hunted her down, insisting it was time for an ice cream break. Renee agreed.

"Bubble gum?" Renee stuck out her tongue, laughing. "Sounds nasty."

But completely like Mayson. Ever since they were kids, she was forever putting strange things in her mouth. She laughed again and squeezed Mayson's waist, feeling the sun-warmed skin against her arms.

They wove through the sun-kissed crowd on the Mission Beach sidewalk toward the ice cream shop, their shoulders and bellies bared in bikini tops, cutoff jeans hanging from their hips.

"Don't judge until you've tried it. It even has pieces of bubble gum in it," Mayson said.

"Definitely nasty. I either want ice cream or chewing gum, not both at the same time."

"Okay, Grandma."

Laughing, Renee followed her into the ice cream shop. The guy behind the counter flashed them a smile of welcome before turning back to his customers, a father with his two kids. The young boy and girl stood on tiptoe to see the flavors in the ice cream case.

Like Renee and Mayson, the kids had their bathing suits on but unlike the adults, they hadn't bothered to put any pants on. And of course, the boy was bare-chested.

At the ice cream counter, Mayson made a show about looking at the other flavors, although it was obvious she had already made up her mind.

"Since bubble gum isn't in your future, what flavor are you thinking about?" Mayson asked.

Renee peered into the case, her eyes drawn to the tamer, pale-colored flavors. She knew if she ended up getting vanilla Mayson would never let her hear the end of it.

"Rum raisin, I think." She chewed on the tip of her finger. "Although I shouldn't get the waffle cone since we're having dinner soon."

"No offense, Renee, but there's no way your parents are going to have dinner ready when we get there. Between all the catching up and talking and usual pressure to play Taboo and the fruity drinks your mom likes to have before dinner, we'll be lucky to eat before nine."

"You're probably right." Renee eyed the case lined with waffle cones of all types and sizes. When the guy asked her what she wanted, she was ready. "Two scoops of rum raisin in a chocolate waffle bowl, please."

Mayson chuckled. "Way to let loose, Renee."

She stuck out her tongue. "Kiss off."

"Here you go, Miss."

Before Mayson could reach for her cash, Renee pulled a ten out of her bikini top and exchanged it for her overflowing chocolate-lined waffle bowl. "Thank you. This is for both of us."

They walked out of the ice cream shop and back into the sunlight.

Renee sighed. "This is so perfect. Cold ice cream. The hot sun."

"Bubble gum." Mayson licked her spoon and grinned. The wind blew hair into her face. She shook it back with a toss of her head.

Renee chuckled and moved closer to Mayson to avoid bumping into an oncoming group of college girls on the sidewalk. A woman in a yellow scarf walked up from behind and between the formation of blond girls, splitting their group.

"Funny running into you here," the woman said.

Mayson came to a dead stop. Then Renee did too, looking from her friend's surprised face to the vaguely familiar woman who'd spoken to them. When Mayson only stared at the woman without saying a word, Renee abruptly remembered where she knew her from.

"You're Kendra, right?" She felt no great joy in recalling the woman.

"Yes, that *is* my name." Kendra stood still on the sidewalk, forcing people to move around her. She turned her back on Renee. "Do you remember it, Mayson?"

"Kendra, I was going to call you up later this weekend."

"When? After your little ice cream date? Or will you wait until after you fuck her under the stars to compare how it was with me?"

At her side, Mayson stiffened.

"Calm down, honey," Renee said to Kendra. "It's not like that. It will never be like that."

"And even if it was," Mayson said, a hard finality in her voice, "it's none of your business. There's no reason for any of this drama."

"Drama? Are you fucking kidding me?" Kendra's eyes became wide in her face, the lashes wet. "I thought we had something special. Why are you trying to blow me off?" Passing eyes flickered to Kendra.

"I'm not trying to blow you off," Mayson said with an impatient lift of her shoulders. "Listen, I'll call you later and we can talk about this. Okay?"

"Whatever. I won't wait for *that* phone call." With one last glance at Mayson, she clamped her purse under her arm, spun, and walked away. The yellow scarf at her throat appeared and disappeared as she slid through the crowd.

"Come on, May. Let's keep walking." Renee looped an arm through Mayson's, propelling her forward. Through their skin-to-skin connection, she felt Mayson's deep, silent sigh. The melting ice cream lost its appeal. She dropped it into the trash, wiped her fingers on a napkin, then stuffed the dirty napkin in her pocket. "That woman is about as handy as a hot rock. You need to drop her," she finally said in the silence.

"I'm starting to think that too." Mayson sighed again.

"I hope the sex was worth it, at least."

When Mayson didn't say anything, Renee stopped and turned to face her. "Kendra wasn't even that good, was she?"

"It was fine." Mayson shoved her hands in the pockets of her cutoff jeans and looked straight ahead, anywhere but at Renee.

Renee burst out laughing. "That's a damn shame."

"Shut up."

"Come on."

She started walking again, pulling Mayson toward the beach. With sunset less than an hour away, the day had cooled down a little. From the water, they would be able to watch the sun fall into the horizon as they floated side by side. Mayson on her board. Renee on her back. The perfect way to end their day in San Diego before heading up to see her parents. Smiling, she grabbed Mayson's hand and moved to the edge of the crosswalk. They waited for the light to change.

A yellow Mustang with a familiar face drove slowly past. Renee stared after it. "Is that Kendra's car?"

Mayson craned her head to look. "Yeah, I think so. Why?"

"That's the car I saw near your place the other night."

"Really? She hasn't spent the night with me in at least two weeks. Maybe three. When did you see the car?"

"When I had my little breakdown and busted in on you in the middle of the night." Renee made a face.

"No. She wasn't with me. At least not really. She came over but I was just too tired to deal with anybody."

"So you sent her away," Renee said.

"I wouldn't put it quite like that."

Renee rolled her eyes. "But she probably saw it that way, especially since she hung around long enough to see me come over later that night."

"Yeah." Mayson nodded. They both watched the road where Kendra had disappeared, each lost in thought.

Chapter 32

She'd taken him in this.

Renee shook out the red skirt and clipped it to a cedar hanger. The straight lines of the silk looked so commonplace in the row of other skirts. But there was nothing common about this skirt. Not in the way it had sat on her bottom as he slid his hands over, then under, cupping her willing flesh, kneading, stroking, before pulling her back into his lap. And though blindfolded, she'd stretched out the moment. She'd held herself above the palpable heat of him, then stroked him with her wetness, back and forth until he trembled.

With her face buried in the silk skirt, she searched for remnants of his scent and hers together, of that night. But the laundry had done its job and all she smelled was fabric softener. With a sound of self-mockery, she hung up the skirt and went back to the laundry basket in the middle of the floor. She began sorting her socks.

There was something that she wanted from him. Just one thing. Would he give it? She folded a pair of white socks and tucked them together. With her murky motives, did she have the right to ask?

Her cell phone chimed Mayson's ring.

"Hey."

"You sound a million miles away," Mayson said.

Renee laughed weakly. "All I said was 'hey.'" She shook her head. "But I was just thinking about a project."

"For the firm or for yourself?"

"Myself. Definitely for myself." Renee sorted her underwear into a silken pile at her side. "So what's up?"

"I'm going to LA early tomorrow morning to hit the waves in Lunada Bay. Just wanted to let you know so you won't send out the guards looking for me."

"You gone the whole weekend?"

"Only if I find something worth staying up there for. Right now the plan is to drive back down Saturday night."

"Okay. Just let me know if you decide to stay up there."

"Why, you planning to host an orgy at my house?"

Renee smiled, hands sifting idly through the smallclothes beside her on the floor. "Well, that's for me to know and for you to maybe find out, isn't it?"

Mayson chortled. "The day you have an orgy—you know what? I won't even say that. My little Renee is growing up a little more every day. Who knows what surprise you'll spring on me next?"

"Whatever it is, I'm sure you can handle it." Renee held a pair of black panties up to the light. Ah, just like she thought. A hole. She balled the underwear up and threw it behind her out of the closet. "But have a great weekend, though, Mayson. Whatever you get into up there, have fun."

"You know I will." Mayson's naughty intentions crackled loud and clear through the phone.

After she hung up, she sat with the phone in her lap, the laundry temporarily forgotten. She turned the phone over in her hands and allowed the earlier idea to resurface. It was the riskiest thing she'd ever asked him to try.

She opened a new e-mail message on her phone. Before she allowed the butterflies fluttering in her stomach to change her mind, Renee typed the message: *Spend the day with me.*

She didn't have to wait long for his response: *When?*

Her heart lurched in her chest. Had it been as simple as asking this whole time?

Saturday? Sunday?

Sunday. Let me plan everything?

Yes.

Good. I'll send the details tomorrow. Sweet dreams.

High on the cliffs of La Jolla, the hotel overlooked the leaping waters of the Pacific and the craggy beach where the sea lions basked in the sun. Sheer curtains fluttered at the windows. Endless sunlight filtered through the filmy white fabric.

After the furtive darkness of their previous encounters, the naked light and soft sounds of normalcy floating up from the street and the beach—laughter, the tinkling of a bicycle bell, friends calling out to each other—felt like the most exotic thing Renee had ever experienced.

The note on the bed, a simple piece of black paper against the pale sheets, had told her to be naked and facedown on the bed when he arrived. She imagined the bed linens pressed against her nakedness, into her face, the flush of heat through her when he walked in.

The room was very Victorian, very feminine, not something she thought he would pick. Not something *she* would pick. Did he think this was the kind of seduction scene she preferred? Renee smiled, rueful. He didn't know her tastes. And that was okay. It was enough that he knew her body.

At the window, she slowly unzipped the dress, easing the zipper down the curved line of her back to the base of her spine where her buttocks began. She slipped the dress off and stepped out of it. Naked, she stood in the room, feeling him everywhere. A comfort. A benediction.

She lay on her belly in the bed, and waited.

Renee wasn't sure what she had been looking for when she thought of spending the day with her stranger. It had simply been an idea and a longing formed even before she'd known him. Her body craved a day with a lover, to be touched and desired. And he would give that to her.

When her lover arrived, it was just like any other time. But it wasn't. The door opened in a quiet rush of sound, a faint squeak. A light breeze from the door's movement brushed over her back. Then the door closed. A breath. Two. The weight of him in the room. Without being able to see him, she knew he stared at her on the bed, laid out for pleasure. The hardwood protested faintly beneath his weight. A whisper of cloth as he approached the bed. Cool fingers brushed her newly bare neck, traced the short hair hugging her head.

"Beautiful." He whispered the word into her neck until it was more sensation of breath than sound.

She felt his eyes on her. Felt him watching her with something different than before. Her heart lurched in her chest. For the first time, she sensed that answering current from him. That he wanted more. That he wanted her to see as much as she was being seen. But what if that changed everything?

In the quiet, his hands firmly grasped her shoulders. His weight, heavy and male, pressed into the bed. He lifted her, trying gently to turn her around without the safety of the blindfold. Renee squeezed her eyes shut. *No!* She stiffened and gripped the sheets.

"Don't end this," she whispered. "Please."

More quiet. His breath, a ripple of air against her lips. Then a backward movement, the weight of the velvet against her eyes. The blindfold.

She slackened in relief (but disappointment too) as he gave

in to her demand. Why couldn't he fight her and become— just once—something she wasn't completely sure that she wanted?

He moved away from the bed, pulling away the unfamiliar tension of their bared emotional desires. And unwrapped their morning.

Her lover didn't talk again. He didn't try to push the sight of him on her again. His mint scent brushed her face as he turned her onto her back, propped her against the pillows. And she trembled, imagining what he saw. The velvet blindfold that covered everything but her mouth. Her brown body against the pale sheets. Her breasts, nipples, woman's heart ready for his mouth. Her skin aching for him.

Renee touched the blindfold. Her security. And lowered her hands.

Something wet brushed her mouth and she parted her lips to receive it. He took it away, teasing, then he brought it close again, trailing the rough-soft thing over her mouth, leaving behind a liquid stain. She licked her lips. Pineapple.

The fruit brushed her mouth again. It touched her tongue. He put it in her mouth, brushed her lips with his fingers, traced the sensitive skin of her inner lips while the pineapple released its juices over her tongue. Before he could draw back, she latched onto his finger and sucked it deep into her mouth. She pressed it and the piece of pineapple between her tongue and palate. Again and again. Press. Suck. Press suck. The itch of arousal trickled between her thighs.

She felt his growl before she heard it. Mission accomplished, she released his finger to chew on the pineapple, smiling. His amusement licked the air. As she swallowed the pineapple, Renee realized that she hadn't eaten breakfast. She'd been so anxious for the morning with him to begin, so excited, that food had been the last thing on her mind.

"More," she murmured.

And he fed her. More pineapple, slices of peaches, avocados, creamy pepper-jack cheese. A tiny croissant he passed to her lips from his lips. She chuckled and slid her arms around his neck, kissing him first lightly then deeply, wrapping her legs around his legs and drawing him down onto the bed on top of her.

Their kisses became touches and moans and slickness and laughter and he lay on his back to pull her over him and there was the sunlight on her skin, his firm body under hers, inside hers, pushing into her in lazy strokes that brought her higher and higher to the easy pleasure of a late-morning orgasm she knew wouldn't be the last.

She must have slept.

They must have slept. Together.

Their bare limbs were tangled. She'd never been able to sleep with Linc touching her. His body had burned too hot or his feet too cold for her to be comfortable. Or simply, his body had smothered when hers had demanded to be free.

As she emerged from the fog of sleep, she felt her lover's absolute stillness under her, his chest moving under her cheek. His body was hard against hers but not uncomfortable, exuding a strength that was as seductive as it was domestic.

She brushed his nipple with her thumb and felt him stir. A low rumble sounded through his chest and vibrated her skin. Under her mouth, the skin of his chest was salty, hard. The nipples like tiny buds under her tongue. He groaned and palmed the back of her neck. His maleness stirred against her thigh, inviting, and she moved toward it, blindly.

They made love again, then ate and slept and loved again in a rhythm that was the most natural in the world. When the sun began to sink beyond the curtains, she felt its loss in the warmth leaking from the room.

Sadness fell like a shroud over her. Although it was irrational, she turned away from him to face the window, rejecting him as if it were his fault the day was ending.

He kissed her shoulder, her neck, touching her lightly. Tears pricked her eyes. Renee pushed against him roughly. He startled and reached, gently, for her again. She slammed her elbow back, connecting with his hard belly. He hissed in pain. With her tears soaking the blindfold, she grabbed his bottom and squeezed. Finally, he seemed to understand what she wanted.

Teeth sank into her shoulder and she gasped. He shoved her thighs open from behind. Despite the role she'd pushed him into, he tested her readiness, two fingers that moved easily into her wetness. He grunted in surprise. But his body was willing enough. He slammed into her so hard she almost toppled off the bed. She squeaked in surprise. His arm latched around her waist, holding her tight, pulling her against him with each grunting, loud contact of their bodies.

She was full and wet and open to him, to his firm grip now lifting her knee toward the ceiling, his body undeniably taking possession of hers as she gasped and moaned with him, shoved back against him. Renee stroked her clit in time to his thrusts, each grunting moment shoving her closer to the fire waiting just on the other side. But the closer it came, the less sure she was that she wanted it.

He took her hard, his gasps and the thud of their bodies exactly what she'd wordlessly demanded of him. Their day together was ending. She didn't want it to. Her fingers moved faster. He moved faster. Soon, he was jerking inside her, spilling into the condom, shouting his completion into her hair.

The fire retreated as he pulled limply out of her.

This is how this should end, she wanted to shout. *Leave me unsatisfied so I won't miss this and beg for another day with you.* She squeezed her eyes shut.

But he was not that kind of lover. He never had been.

He shoved her hands away, turned her. Thick fingers replaced his manhood. His thumb found her clit. He moved effortlessly in her wetness, taking her with intent speed, tonguing her nipples, sucking them, pinching them until her fire came back. Higher. Brighter. And engulfed her.

She wanted to scream his name. But in the end, she just screamed.

Chapter 33

"Let's start over, Mayson."

Kendra stood in the doorway of Mayson's office wearing white. A ruffled blouse, linen slacks, sandals.

Behind her in the hallway, people gave her only a passing glance before continuing on their way. Mayson wanted to keep it that way. "Come in."

With Kendra seated at the chair in front of her desk, Mayson closed the office door. She cautiously approached the other woman, unwilling to sit down just yet. After the unexpected confrontation in Mission Beach, she didn't know what to expect from Kendra. She settled for propping a hip on the corner of her desk and looking down at her visitor.

"Listen," Kendra said, leaning forward with her chin propped up on a closed fist. "I'm sorry about the other afternoon. I wasn't thinking clearly."

Damn right you weren't. Although she'd tried to move past it, Mayson remembered the humiliation of that public encounter, the heavy pulse of anger when Kendra had talked about Renee being just another woman to fuck. She took a steadying breath. "Why are you here, exactly?"

"I told you, I want to start over." The long, thick hair tumbled back over Kendra's shoulders as she tilted her head to look up at Mayson.

"Which means what?"

"I can be what you want. Casual. No strings. Just sex, whenever you want it." Her voice deepened to a purr. "*Wherever* you want it."

Kendra's lashes lowered and Mayson felt the hidden eyes on her, hungry and hopeful.

"No."

Kendra flinched as if Mayson had slapped her. "Why can't this work?" she demanded. "Didn't I do everything you wanted?" She stood up, back straight, her breasts high and firm under the white blouse.

"Yes, you did. But that isn't what this is about," Mayson said. "You know that. I don't deal with drama and you've brought a lot of that." She took a deep, considering breath. "Maybe you've always been like this or maybe I bring out the worst in you." She shrugged. "Whatever the case, this thing between us has no life left."

"Drama?" Kendra spat the word. "That's bullshit. I'm just hotter than your washed-out fuck buddy and all the other dykes you're used to. You don't know how to handle it."

Mayson stiffened. "If it makes you feel better to think that, go ahead."

The chair jerked across the rug from Kendra's sudden movement. "Mayson—!"

Mayson shook her head again, calling herself twenty kinds of idiot for letting things get this far. "It's okay, Kendra. There's nothing else we need to say to each other. Let's write this whole thing off as a mistake and get on with our lives." She moved toward the door.

"Is her pussy that much better than mine? Is it because she has more experience?" She asked the questions with frightening certainty of their answers. "That's old, stale ass, Mayson. You need something new and fresh. I'm right here. All you have to do is reach out." Kendra moved closer, her mouth in a pouting smile.

A wordless noise hissed between Mayson's teeth. "I think

it's time for you to go, Kendra." She yanked open the door. "I hope you'll be able to get past this."

Kendra, with her face set in hard lines and her arms crossed tightly across her chest, looked like she had no intention of leaving.

Mayson set her back teeth. She didn't want any shit to go down here at the studio but if she had to call one of the neighborhood cops...

"Hey, Mayson, I just found this new instructor—" Linette appeared in the doorway. When she saw Kendra, she stopped her progress into the office. The hand holding a sheaf of papers fell to her side. "Oh, I didn't know you had company. Sorry."

"Don't be sorry. Come on in." Mayson forced a smile she knew didn't reach her eyes. "Kendra was just leaving."

The other woman looked at Linette, then at Mayson. Finally she got to her feet and left the office, brushing past Linette without a word.

"That was awkward." Linette wrinkled her nose like she smelled something bad.

"Could have been worse," Mayson said with a dismissive wave. She closed the door and sat heavily behind her desk. "Now what do you have for me?"

Chapter 34

"**I** can't *fucking* believe her!"

Mayson stalked back and forth in her living room like a trapped animal. The energy crackled off her in angry, palpable waves.

"She actually came to the studio to give me another chance to fuck her. And when I didn't take her up on it she insulted you again." Her braid whipped around her shoulders as she turned abruptly to walk the same length of floor. Again.

"Yup. You definitely hit the crazy jackpot with this one." From the couch, Renee sighed. Mayson's pacing was making her thirsty. After a few more minutes of watching Mayson, she got up. In the kitchen, she poured herself a glass of orange juice and some water for her friend. "Where do you find these women, Mayson?"

"Unfortunately, they find me," Mayson muttered. "Or I invite them into my life like a fucking idiot." She accepted the water with a tight smile of thanks and emptied the glass in a few quick gulps.

Renee took the empty glass and slid it onto the coffee table. She sipped her juice. "Honey, it's okay. You already sent her away. Just next time, say no. Coochie isn't worth all this hassle."

Mayson finally stopped walking the floor and sank into

the couch beside Renee. "The advice comes a bit late, darling." She sighed.

"Oh, May..."

They both knew it had been a mistake to get involved with the girl. Mayson felt guilty and angry with herself most of all.

"Come on. Enough of this self-pity crap." Renee smoothed the loose strands of Mayson's hair away from her face. "We should go out. Try to forget about her and your month of thinking with your...privates."

Mayson's head eased back against the couch and she sighed deeply, closing her eyes. The half-moon shadows of her eyelashes fanned across her cheeks. Her chest moved with her deep exhale.

Did these breathing techniques ever work when she was this upset? Renee tugged on the tail of Mayson's braid.

"How about Strokin' Aces? I'm sure we can find something there to distract you."

Mayson laughed weakly. "I'm not going with you to the strip club. Not after last time."

Renee snickered. "Afraid of a little competition?"

Their first and only trip to Strokin' Aces had been for Mayson's birthday a couple of years before. The two of them plus Iyla and another friend from LA. It wasn't Renee's fault that out of all the women at the table, the strippers gravitated toward her, even going so far as giving her free lap dances, buying her drinks, then slipping their phone numbers into her bra. Jealousy didn't suit her friend at all.

"But," Mayson said after a brief silence, "I could do with a drive over to Coronado and maybe some coffee at that place with the triple chocolate cheesecake and sexy waitresses."

"Almost as good as the strip club," Renee said, getting to her feet. It was better than moping around the house all night. "Let's go upstairs and get you in the shower. You stink."

*   *   *

After her shower, Mayson searched listlessly through her closet, dismissing outfit after outfit without pulling them off the hangers. Renee watched her from the bed, tucking the pillow more comfortably under her cheek. If they didn't speed up this process, she was going to fall asleep and send Mayson off to troll for girls on her own. She grinned at the thought.

"You should wear that green shirt I bought you last year. It looks great against your skin, especially with your hair loose."

Mayson obediently began rooting around in the green section of her frighteningly well-organized closet.

"I can't find it," she said after a long search.

"Then never mind. Put on that thin white one. Yes, that one with the black buttons down the front. With black jeans you're all set. The girls won't know what hit them." Renee invited Mayson to share her smile, but her friend was having none of it.

"This better not be a repeat of last time I took you cruising or I'm leaving you to find your own ride home."

"I'm sure none of the girls would mind...giving me a ride." Renee smirked.

She turned in time to see a smile transform her friend's face. A real smile.

Mayson shook her head. "Come on. You promised a good time. You better deliver."

Less than an hour later, they left Mayson's townhouse in the convertible with the top down and Alicia Keys on the iPod. Renee drove. She kept the stereo just above conversation level so Mayson wouldn't feel she had to talk. The mellow voice and piano were the only sounds they needed as they cruised under the moonless sky, the faint stars.

Mayson visibly relaxed, head lolling back against the passenger seat, fingers tapping against her thigh to the music.

She looked moody tonight. Hell, she *was* moody and should have no problem picking up someone to help her forget about Kendra if that was what she wanted. But Renee doubted that was what she wanted.

She turned her gaze back to the road and let her mind float away.

It had been days since she'd seen her lover, and she missed him. As much as she wanted him, she didn't want to want him. It was too much like a relationship. After their last date, he'd sent an e-mail letting her know he would be out of town for the next six days and wouldn't be able to meet her. Renee had tried to see someone else. She was sure that the itch he inspired could just as easily be scratched by another man.

Uninspired but determined, she'd looked through her long-ignored inbox and picked a man she thought would do just as well. But when she walked into the hotel room, shrouded in a darkness that should have been perfect, the wrongness of the man's smell washed over her. She couldn't touch him. She couldn't let him touch her.

Before things could go any further, she made stammering excuses, grabbed her things, and left the room. It had felt too much like cheating. At home, she emptied her inbox of every message, every profile except his. And instead of taking a cold shower like she'd planned, she slid into bed with her favorite vibrator and made herself come again and again thinking about his cool mint scent and the concentrated force of him against her back when he took her from behind. *Next time,* she remembered thinking just before drifting into a dreamless sleep, *I'll have him like that.*

Renee pressed her thighs together and brought herself back to the present with a low sigh.

"Thinking about something good?" Mayson asked.

Renee decided to ignore the meaningful tone in her friend's voice. "I usually am thinking about something good," she replied, slinging an arm outside the car window.

The breeze felt good on her head and the back of her neck, reinforcing the rightness of her decision to get rid of the weave and wear her hair short again.

"I'm sure whoever he is appreciates those good thoughts... and deeds." Mayson chuckled.

Renee smiled back at her despite the sudden heat in her cheeks. A few weeks ago she would have chided Mayson that not everything was about sex. But with the thought of her lover and the deep satisfaction he brought her *every single time,* she realized that sometimes it *was* just about sex. And that was okay.

"You feeling better about things?" she asked Mayson.

"A little. Although I don't know why."

"The healing elixir of my company, of course."

"Of course." Mayson snorted behind her grin.

Renee forced her smile away. "Things will be okay again, May. You didn't do anything wrong. Just remember that. Okay?"

"Okay." Mayson's response was quiet but certain.

On Coronado, they found parking on the street across from the little pastry shop, sliding into a parallel spot right after a black Honda Accord pulled out. Xocolatl was overflowing with women. Through the wide glass windows of the little chocolate shop they could see a line of nearly a dozen customers—mostly women—peering into the case of delicacies as they waited to be served.

"You want to sit inside or out?" Renee asked.

"Outside," Mayson promptly answered, a smile already spreading on her face. On the patio, three of the five tables were already taken by casually dressed women—some with boyfriends—sipping mugs of the café's signature Mayan chocolate blend.

"I'll grab a table while you get our order."

She pulled out her wallet but Renee turned away. No need to fight over who was paying since she was the one who had invited Mayson out.

The smell of chocolate, rich and dark, bathed Renee's face as she opened the café's heavy glass door. This was the real reason Mayson loved this place. Heaven. It put an automatic smile on her face. The woman behind the counter returned her smile with a quick one of her own. Renee took her place at the end of the line.

The glass cases were filled with beautiful concoctions—chocolate cheesecakes, a chocolate-infused strawberry short-cake, fruit tarts with stripes of dark chocolate, tiramisu, platters of fat chocolate-dipped strawberries.

"You have some great little cakes tonight," she greeted the cashier when it was her turn to order.

The woman, pretty in a boatneck blouse showing off her elegant collarbone, grinned back at Renee.

"I know. Some of my favorites are out. The chili chocolate cream is really good." She leaned closer, as if sharing a secret. "There's vanilla cream *inside* the chili pepper."

Renee laughed, surprised into realizing the girl was flirting with her. "In that case, I'll have one of those. Add a chocolate crepe and two cups of house hot chocolate to that too, please."

"Good choice."

The woman—well, she was just a girl, actually, not much past twenty—rang up her order and took her money. The girl let her fingers brush Renee's palm when she passed back the scattering of coins. Inexplicably, Renee blushed, dropped the coins in the tip jar, and added a dollar from her purse.

The girl flashed another smile. "Enjoy."

"I will. Thanks." Renee moved farther down the counter to wait for her order.

Outside the café, Mayson had taken a table with a view of both the street and the entrance to the café. It was a beautiful night. Pedestrians walked down the strip in a constant trickle, enjoying the late spring weather.

A couple walked past, arm in arm, pausing for a moment to peer inside Xocolatl before continuing on. Renee noticed that Mayson watched them go, her friend's admiring glance following the taller of the women, who wore slacks and high heels.

As long as she and Mayson had been friends, Renee could never figure out the type of women her friend liked the most. Over the years she'd guessed but was so wrong that it was ridiculous. It was a good thing she'd never tried to set Mayson up with anybody. Not that she'd ever needed to. Whenever Mayson wanted a woman, there was never a shortage.

Outside the café, her friend continued to watch the lesbian couple walk away, oblivious to a tall flash of legs coming from the other direction. This more obvious femininity was far from Mayson's ideal. The woman with miles of legs bared in a short green dress looked at Mayson, though. Renee did a double take. *Kendra?*

"Here is your order, miss."

Renee absently took the tray loaded down with their dessert and drinks, still staring out the window. It *was* Kendra. And the dress that bared all those legs wasn't a dress at all, it was a shirt, long-sleeved and buttoned down, that she wore with the sleeves rolled to her elbows, one button undone over her considerable cleavage, and a belt strapped tightly to create a high waist just under her breasts.

Mayson still hadn't seen her.

Renee quickly moved toward the door, walking sideways to avoid bumping into the growing crowd of customers and spilling the hot drinks. "Excuse me," she said more than once, clutching the tray to her chest.

A woman opened the door for her as she approached and she smiled her thanks, only vaguely aware of the chivalrous woman checking out her rear end as she walked out.

"Just in time." Mayson pulled out a chair for her, then took the tray from her hands.

"Looks like you found something good in there. Thanks."

Before Renee could say anything, a new clatter of high heels headed toward them. She clenched her teeth, knowing who it would be before she even turned around. So she didn't bother doing it, only gave Mayson a significant look before she sat down.

"Yeah, this place is full of surprises tonight, both good and bad."

Mayson gave her a puzzled look. She still hadn't noticed Kendra's steady approach.

"We should have just gone to Strokin' Aces," Renee muttered.

"I didn't know you were into strippers like *that*, Ren." Mayson chuckled, lifting her mug of chocolate to her lips.

"I'm not, but right now I'd rather be anywhere but here."

"What are you talking about?"

Renee twitched her head in the direction of Kendra's approach. "Trouble."

Mayson turned in time to watch the woman walk the last couple of feet to their table. "This is just perfect," she muttered and put down her hot chocolate.

"For a couple that's not really a couple, you two sure do a lot of intimate things together." Kendra had landed.

Intimate? Having hot chocolate at a café is intimate? Renee stared at Kendra in amazement.

Their uninvited guest sat down on the empty chair, arranging her long legs and cleavage so no one would miss them. To be fair, she did look nice in the dress—ah, shirt. Something that had been squirming for attention at the back of Renee's mind suddenly broke free. Kendra was wearing Mayson's shirt! The same green one they had been searching for in the closet earlier that night. Its black and jade cloisonné buttons were unmistakable against the green cotton.

"We didn't ask you to sit down," Renee wanted to rip the shirt off Kendra's body and beat her with it. This chick wasn't only psycho, she was a thief too.

"Is that jealousy I hear in your voice, honey? You finally owning up to the fact that you're fucking your so-called *best friend?*"

A few startled gazes bounced toward their table, then away.

Under any other circumstances, Renee would have squirmed with embarrassment. But right now she was too pissed off.

"Kendra, this isn't necessary," Mayson said coldly.

"What do you mean this isn't necessary?" Kendra leaned into Mayson's face, hissing. "You dump me for your slut of a best friend and you think I'm just going to slink away like some whipped dog and let you do this to me? Do you know she fucks strange men in hotel rooms all over the city? Do you?" Kendra's voice rose to a near screech. "You deserve better than her and I deserve better than this."

Heat exploded in Renee's face. "Listen to me, you psycho *bitch*. Mayson isn't with you now because she doesn't want you." Kendra gasped but Renee didn't stop. "Accept it. Be a woman, not some pathetic excuse for one." She kicked Kendra's chair hard, jolting the woman. "Now leave before you make me lose my temper."

While she spoke, Renee had kept her voice low but steady so Kendra couldn't mistake her meaning.

Kendra's mouth snapped shut and her eyes narrowed to slits. Her hand flashed out to grab the nearest mug of hot chocolate from the table but Mayson snatched her wrist in the air.

"Don't even think about it," Mayson said.

"You fucking cunt! I should have done more than key your car when I had the chance."

"What?!"

Kendra shook off Mayson's hand and stood up, ignoring Mayson's shocked question. She loomed over them in her high heels before stalking off, her shoes stabbing the side-walk with each vicious step.

"She was the one who keyed your car? Why didn't you tell me?"

"I just found out a second ago like you did. When it happened I thought it was"—Renee shook her head—"the girl. Remember?" *My God, did this just really happen?* She took a shaky breath. "I am officially out of fun." Renee looked around the café, at the people who stared, at the people trying hard not to stare. "Let's call it a night, okay?"

Without waiting for Mayson to respond, she grabbed her purse and jerkily got to her feet. Her hip bumped the table, sloshing lukewarm chocolate over the edges of both mugs.

"Shit!" Mayson jumped away before the leaking chocolate could drip through the scrollwork metal table and stain her pants. "This is so fucked. I'm sorry, Renee. This shouldn't have happened."

"You're right, it shouldn't have but nothing can be done about it now. Let's just go home and try to forget this crappy night." Although it would be hard to forget Kendra's hate-filled face and the frightening way she had claimed Mayson.

They endured a mostly silent ride back to Mayson's town-house, where Renee gave her best friend a fierce hug before getting into her car and driving the short distance home.

"Oh my God." As soon as she stepped into her house, she sagged in the doorway.

Kendra had been awful. Spiteful. Unpleasant. Insane. And the things she said...Renee shuddered with revulsion. It made her sick to realize that this was the woman Mayson had shared herself with, had welcomed into her home and into her bed.

She plucked off her shoes and padded to the kitchen to pour a glass of red wine. Glass in hand, she left the kitchen, turning off the lights as she walked through the condo. With a trembling hand, she massaged the back of her neck, stretched the muscles, trying to get rid of the tension there. It didn't work.

A sense of restlessness kept her moving. She wasn't quite ready for bed yet, but she didn't want to go out either. Aimless footsteps took her into the office. The computer was still on, the screen dark but the power button a sleepy green. She sank into the chair at her desk and flicked the mouse.

*Did you let someone else touch you when I was
gone?*

Renee sat up in the chair, heart thumping in her chest. The words flashed on the instant-message box, heavy and black. The sender was unmistakable. Was he back in town? Was he close?

At the very idea of him, the tension and anger of the past few hours began to drain from her as if they never existed.

The time stamp said the message had been received at 7:46. She had been at Mayson's by then, the two of them batting back and forth the problem of Kendra. Almost three hours ago.

Her fingers hovered over the keyboard, uncertain what to type. Should she tell him that she'd contacted someone else, that she hadn't been able to go through with it?

No one else touched me.

Are you lying?

She blinked in surprise when his reply came almost immediately.

No one can touch me like you can. Guilt at her attempt to replace him scorched at her face.

I know that. You didn't answer my question.

She thought about the various truths she could tell him, then settled on the one that seemed right.

*I arranged to meet someone else, but he wasn't
you and I couldn't go through with it.*

How far did it go before you stopped him?
Did you let him put his fingers inside you?
Did you give him a blowjob to compensate him for his time?
He fucked you, but you couldn't come?
You let him put his dick in your ass, so it doesn't count?
What? Tell me.

The words came at her like bullets, rapid-fire fast. She squirmed at their rawness, blushed at how easily images flashed behind her half-closed eyelids. All of him and her together. Her on her knees, him with his palm against her womanhood, his fingers seeking inside. The darkness pressing them together but nothing hidden between them.

No. Nothing. I couldn't even let him touch me.

A long, wordless pause.

How do I know what you're telling me is true?

But the gentle, almost apologetic way he worded the question told her that he believed her. She could almost see his body relax. The phantom of the other man had already been dismissed from between them.

Do you want to smell me?

Renee shivered as she wrote the words, imagining him sniffing between her legs for evidence of another lover. His nose brushing the soft hairs, his mouth tantalizingly close.

Yes. I want to smell you.

Her fingers were paralyzed by the image abruptly thrust into the center of her brain. His mouth hovering over her aching center, his big hands holding her thighs wide open to his gaze. She was quickly and completely wet. Renee rubbed her thighs together, a hand drifting down to rest on her knee.

And I want to fuck you, he wrote into her silence.

Her hand clenched into her skirt. Her womb clenched, achingly empty, hungry for him to fill her. She couldn't help it. She really couldn't. She slipped her hand between her thighs, under her panties. Sighed.

One-handed, she typed, *Yes.*

Would you let me?

I'd beg you to.

Her words lay on the white screen, naked.

I want to see you, he wrote.

Tomorrow.

Yes. He continued. *Although I'd rather be skin to skin with you right now. You'd feel so good. You ALWAYS feel so good.*

Her fingers moved languorously against her clit, sliding down and inside, imagining they were his fingers. She licked her lips.

He'd never been so talkative before. The flow of words from him was just what she needed. If his body couldn't be there to fill hers, it was only right that his words were there now to overpower her senses, to conjure him there in her office. She could almost feel his breath at the back of her neck. His hands tugging down the straps of her dress to bare her breasts. The cool air teased her nipples to hardness. Like his tongue painting wet circles around them, flicking the hard nubs until she gasped her pleasure.

What are you doing?

Touching myself. There was no need to lie.

A moment of tense silence. *Are you imagining me inside you?*

No, we're not there yet. I'm imagining you playing with my body, the way you like to do. I like how you lick me.

If I was there with you right now, I wouldn't be able to hold off. I'm so—The sentence cut off. *I need you so much. I couldn't wait. I can't wait.* Another pause. *I'd push you on your back over that desk, rip off your panties, and fuck you until you screamed my name.*

The words simultaneously pushed and pulled her into the flames. The scene he sketched was vivid, undeniable. Him moving up behind her to shove her down onto the desk, her back hitting the neat surface, scattering papers, pens, the laptop, all to the floor, her legs lifting to clasp his naked waist, the light illuminating their joined bodies but showing none of his face. His stomach, hard and flexing, muscles rippling as he shoved his hard length into her again and again. Her spine turned to liquid gold.

The pulse beat stronger between her legs. But she was pulled too.

I want to know your name, she wrote.

A pause. *I don't think you do. I've given you chances to know me. Plenty of chances. You didn't take any of them.*

Her hand stilled its movement between her legs. *I was scared.*

Are you scared now?

"Yes." Renee's whisper startled her, as if she weren't the one who had said it. But it was the truth.

She drew a shuddering breath.

If I see your face, everything good between us will end. Our relationship will turn out like all the others I've had.

It will become stale and empty, and then it will disappear.

The silent words echoed in her head. More painful truth. But she couldn't deny her hunger for more of him. She wanted to walk out of the darkness.

"I want to see you," she said to the man beyond the computer screen.

I want to see you, he wrote.

A fine tremor started in her belly, growing until her entire body shook. *When will you be back?* she typed.

I can meet you on Tuesday night.

In three days.

Where?

The first place we met.

She remembered the dark hotel not far from the university. The cool smell of evening on his skin when he'd walked in. His teeth sinking into her palm when she tried to silence him.

Tuesday night at 8 then.

Tuesday night at 8, she echoed, looking at the black words on the white screen, knowing what they meant. On Tuesday she would see him. Really see him. Was she ready?

Chapter 35

Mayson grabbed her bag from the kitchen counter and, glancing quickly at her watch, walked to the front door. She swung it open. And nearly walked into Grant's upraised fist.

"Shit!"

And he *looked* like shit.

"What are you doing here?"

"I didn't know where else to go." He looked behind Mayson into the house. "Have you seen Renee?"

"Not since yesterday. Is everything okay?" A coldness dropped in the pit of her stomach. The duffel bag fell at her feet. "Was there an accident?"

"No, nothing like—" He stopped. "She and I were supposed to get together last night and she never showed."

Mayson frowned. "Did you call her?"

"Yes. No answer."

Before he could even finish talking, she pulled out her cell phone and speed-dialed Renee's number. The feeling of unease deepened when her call went straight to voice mail.

"Ren, it's me. Give me a call when you get this message." She slowly closed the phone and looked at Grant. "Was everything going okay?"

Before he could answer, her cell phone rang. Mayson nearly snapped it in two flipping it open. Grant's eyes fastened on the phone. The phone number on the screen was unfamiliar, but she hoped.

"Renee?"

"No, but she's close."

Mayson turned away from his tense, questioning face. "What? Who is this?"

"You forgot the sound of my voice so soon? I'm crushed. I really didn't mean much to you, huh?"

"Kendra?" Mayson tried to push aside her annoyance. It didn't work. "This is not a good time."

Kendra's abrupt indrawn breath came clearly through the phone. "Well, you better fucking make it a good time or you'll never see your little fuck buddy again."

Mayson froze. "What?"

"Now I have your attention, don't I?" Kendra's laugh sent shocks of fear up Mayson's spine.

"You know where Renee is?"

"Who's that?" Grant demanded, stepping closer. "Do they have Renee?"

"Whoever is there with you is smarter than you look, honey." Kendra chuckled again.

"You have her."

"Of course." Her tone said that was the most logical thing to assume. "Now, all you have to do is find her. And me."

"Why? What the fuck are you doing?" But all she got in response was dead air.

"Oh my God."

Without the distraction of Kendra at her ear, Mayson abruptly realized her knees were shaking. She grabbed at the wall. The phone fell from her numb fingers and crashed against the floor. "Oh my God." The words tumbled in her head, echoed, until she wanted to scream. A roaring noise pressed against her from all sides.

Grant grasped her shoulders. "Who has her?"

When Mayson didn't answer, he shook her roughly, once. "Who has her?" His face was tight with fear.

Helpless fury erupted in Mayson's chest. "Back the fuck off me!" She slammed her palms against his chest, shoving him back. He let her go.

"I'm sorry." He backed off, hands held up in surrender. "But please, tell me who has her."

"Someone I was seeing. Kendra..." She cast around mentally for the woman's last name but couldn't find it. "I think I have her card somewhere in the house."

Her senses abruptly sharpened. *Yes.* Kendra had put a business card in her tux the night they met. The vest pocket. And although Kendra had given her the card under the pretext of Mayson getting the suit dry-cleaned on her dime, Mayson had hung up the suit and forgotten about it.

"I know where the card is." She turned and ran up the stairs to her bedroom.

Mayson pulled open the closet door, stumbling inside. She dragged the hangers along the rack with a long wooden whine, frantically looking for the tux. The card was right where Kendra had left it.

"James." Downstairs, she shoved the card at Grant. "Her last name is James."

He nodded grimly and pulled out his cell phone. "This is Detective Grant Chambers. I need you to check into something and get back to me ASAP." He turned over the card and read off the information to the person on the other end of the line.

When he was through, he turned back to Mayson, his nostrils flared.

"Now tell me everything you know about this crazy bitch who took my woman."

When Kendra called again, they were ready. Grant attached a small device to the cell phone to track the call. They put the phone on speaker.

"Are you coming, Mayson?" Kendra said in a singsong voice. "She doesn't have much time left."

The fear thumped harder in Mayson's chest. "If it's me you want, just tell me where you are. I'll come and you can let Renee go."

Kendra laughed. And the hairs stood up on the back of Mayson's neck. Because she'd heard that laughter more than a dozen times, that sound of teasing amusement that reduced everything to a joke.

"I won't make it *that* easy for you, baby." The laughter eased out of her voice. "Come, find your little girlfriend. Prove that you know *something* about me."

Mayson heard a sound as if Kendra sank into a big, soft chair. Like she had all the time in the world. "Were you even listening when I poured out my life to you, Mayson? Or was it just about the sex?" Kendra paused, giving Mayson the chance to say something.

But she didn't know what to say. Guilt and anger and help-lessness gripped her tongue. Across the room, Grant gave her a frantic sign to keep the conversation going.

"Tell her anything!" he mouthed. The cords stood out in his neck as he hovered over the phone at Mayson's side. His eyes burned in his face.

She cleared her throat.

"I put everything out there for you to take, you know that?" Kendra murmured so quietly that Mayson had to lean closer to the phone to hear.

"That was a mistake I made," Mayson finally said, "not being able to see that. I'll do better next time."

"I was a virgin when we met, you know."

Mayson's teeth snapped shut.

Laughter spilled from the phone. "Okay, that one was a lie, but wouldn't it have been fun for you if I had been." Kendra chuckled. "I wish I could see your face right now." She hung up.

Grant slammed his hands against the counter. "Shit!" He spun toward Mayson. "That wasn't enough time to trace the fucking call. Why didn't you keep her on longer?"

"Do you think I can get that damn woman to do anything she doesn't want to do?" She gritted her teeth, fighting the panic that bubbled up in her throat. Her fingers stiffened at her sides.

"Can you at least *pretend* to be interested in her pathetic little life so we can get Renee back?"

Mayson growled in frustration. "I'm working on it, dammit!"

He wasn't telling her anything that she didn't know. Before Kendra had hung up the phone, Mayson was already flitting through the few intimate conversations they'd had to figure out what the hell Kendra had been talking about. She'd given Mayson everything? They were only fucking, for God's sake!

Mayson turned away from Grant. His intensity was making her nervous. With him battering at her with his frantic worry, his anger, she couldn't think. All she could feel was his passion for Renee and his need to get her back. That was her fault too. But this wasn't the time. The important thing was that they find Renee. And fast.

"You and your cop friends do what you can to find out more about Kendra. I'll go through all the shit she ever gave me—the letters, the cards, everything."

"I'll look with you." He moved to follow her up the stairs.

Mayson stopped. "No. It's okay. I can do it better by myself." When he didn't slow down, she put up her hands. "No. I need to do this alone. If there's anything in those things, I'll show it to you right away. I just need this time alone, okay?"

Grant nodded jerkily and backed away. He raked fingers through his hair. Cursing.

Chapter 36

"**F**uck!"

Mayson slammed her bedroom door. "Fuck!"

This was where she'd brought Kendra. *This* was where she'd pulled that psycho woman into her life and because of her *fucking* bad judgment she could lose Renee. "Goddamn it!"

The anger and fear spilled over her in scalding waves but her cheeks and fingers felt cold. She paced the floor—to the window with its view of the empty driveway, to the wall, then back again. Suddenly she couldn't stand the sight of her room anymore, not the bed, not any of it. Her arm shot out and swept across the bedside table, spilling the phone, her books, her reading glasses onto the floor.

"Stupid fucking fool!"

The anger burned behind her eyes until wetness slid down her face, into her mouth. "I'm so sorry, honey. I'm so sorry." She sank to the floor on her knees. "Please be all right. *Please.* If anything happened to you—" The hardwood bit into her skin but she barely felt it.

A vibration in her pocket shook her out of her trance. She snatched open the phone without looking at the number.

"Yes?"

"Hey, baby. I thought you were coming up to see us this weekend?"

It took her a moment to realize that it was Iyla's voice on the phone and not Kendra's. She sagged with relief. Then instantly tensed again. "Iyla. I—I can't this weekend."

"What's wrong? You sound strange."

Her friend's concern loosened whatever temporary rein Mayson had on her emotions. She bit back a sob. "I fucked up," she muttered into the phone. "I fucked up in a big way."

The entire story spilled out of her. And saying it aloud, telling her friend just how she'd put herself and Renee into this shitty mess, made it even worse.

"Shit..." Iyla's voice trailed off. "I'll do what I can to help," she said without hesitation.

"Thanks. I—I really appreciate that."

"You can thank me after she's safe, Mayson," Iyla said. "Do the cops have any leads?"

"Not yet, but they're looking." Mayson sagged against the wall. "A friend of hers is a cop. He was the one who suspected she was missing. He's doing everything he can to find her."

"But we could always do more. Can you think of anything the woman told you that might give you a clue where she's keeping Renee?"

"Grant asked me the same thing, but I have no *fucking* idea. I just can't remember a goddamn thing that she told me. And I threw away almost everything that she ever gave me." Even the vases that had come with her flowers.

"What about...?" Iyla hesitated. "Does she have a business—or is she in a sorority or something like that?"

A rhythmic thumping made its way through the phone. Mayson imagined Iyla pacing back and forth across the wooden floors of her office, sun streaming through the floor-to-ceiling windows. The image calmed her. Iyla continued without a pause. "Can you think of anywhere she has access to facilities to keep someone locked up without anyone else finding out?"

"Ah—shit, I don't know." She'd never felt so helpless in her life.

"You know something, Mayson. You just don't realize it yet."

"But I don't have the time to fucking meditate on it. God knows what Kendra is doing to Renee while I sit here with my thumbs up my ass." She pushed herself off the wall and paced the room again.

Iyla's voice droned on in her ear. Even from so far away, she was doing something. She was helping as much as she could. And what was *she* doing? Not a damn thing. This was bullshit. She refused to live on her knees while Renee was out there going through something that she had caused.

"Iyla, I have to go."

Before her friend could respond, she hung up the phone and ran downstairs, barely noticing that Grant was already gone. She jumped in her car and sped off toward Lemon Grove.

She'd been to Kendra's house only once, and that was to pick her up before they went off somewhere else. The invitations had just never appealed. She liked the comfort of her own home, the conveniences that it offered—her own bed, her own dildos. But as she got out of the car and approached the stacked hillside apartments, Mayson had to admit that she simply had had no interest in being in Kendra's apartment or in finding out more about the other woman's life.

From the beginning, she'd drawn that boundary between them. Her lesbian life and the straight woman. That was how their relationship started and that was how she planned on ending it after they'd both gotten what they wanted. But Kendra had changed the rules.

She hopped the stairs to unit number 7, partially hidden by a swaying jacaranda tree and, with her hands casually in her pockets, slammed her booted foot into the door just under the lock. Once. Twice. The impact shot up her leg. Mayson grunted. Then with a sound like a muted gunshot, the wood cracked under the third kick, the lock wrenching through the door frame. A shower of splinters fell at Mayson's feet.

She slipped into the apartment and shoved a chair against the door, giving it the illusion of being secure in case someone wandered past. But Kendra had boasted that her top-floor apartment, tucked away in a shaded corner of the small complex, was very private. She'd even invited Mayson at one point to fuck her on the stairs with nothing to shelter them but the purple blossoms of the overhanging tree.

Mayson scanned the spacious apartment. Nothing was out of place. Everything was pinprick neat, bookshelves neatly arranged, even the magazines on the coffee table ordered by size, then color. Her hands shook with the urge to rip it all to pieces.

No. The breath hissed through her clenched teeth.

In the kitchen, she yanked open drawers—knives, dish towels, receipts, and menus—pawing through everything that could mean anything. Kendra apparently liked Asian food. Mayson pulled menu after menu from the drawer, interspersed with receipts from restaurants—Chinese, Japanese, Thai, Vietnamese. She jerked out the receipts and menus, letting them fall on the floor one after the other. Some of these were places that Mayson had been to. Soon the empty bottom of the last drawer stared back up at her.

"Useless." She slammed it shut.

The living room yielded even less. No papers, just books and magazines, old issues of *People* tucked away in the coffee table drawers. On the walls, abstract paintings with reds and golds, splashes of color against the pale walls. All of it pointed to Kendra being a very boring and unimaginative person. Except the part where she was a psycho bitch.

"Useless," she hissed again. And the futility of it struck her like a blow to the chest.

She staggered to the middle of the apartment. For the second time that day, she was on her knees. The apartment smelled like Kendra, sweet and cold. Her hands shook; the breath churned fast in her chest until she was nearly hyperventilating. She jumped to her feet, reason falling away from her like dead weight.

All this is nothing. She ripped a dictionary from the bookcase and flung it hard at the mirror. *Kendra is nothing.* The mirror shattered. She reached for something else, anything else, tearing, breaking, flinging, shattering, screaming like an animal in pain. Renee was everything.

At the end of the storm, she stood in the middle of Kendra's bedroom, gasping. The welts on her hands burned. Drawers lurched drunkenly from the bureau; clothes lay scattered on the floor, spilling off their hangers and out of the closet. Mayson sat down on the bed, her trembling and bleeding hands held palms-up on her thighs.

Her breath gradually slowed.

Her eyes drifted shut.

When she opened them again, the room was gray, painted in soft shades of dawn. Her hands twitched at her sides.

A large shattered frame lay at the foot of the bed. Wrinkled beside it was an antique kimono, its reds and whites muted with age. She barely remembered dragging it from the wall and slamming it into the bedpost until the glass shattered and the heavy black silk, embroidered with red cherry blossoms, tumbled out.

"My stepmother was Japanese." Kendra's voice came to her from a past conversation. She had lifted a hand to Mayson's heavy fall of hair. "You remind me of her." Kendra had pressed Mayson down into the bed with the sticky weight of her body, her breasts on top of Mayson's breasts, their legs tangled together. The fan had whirled lazily overhead. "When I was seventeen, she left my dad for another woman." Kendra's voice had broken.

The old conversation faded away under the steady hum of the air conditioner, the sudden wildness of her heartbeat as she clawed aside the remnants of sleep. She knew where Kendra was keeping Renee.

Chapter 37

"You comfy, Renee?"

Kendra watched her without an ounce of concern in her heavily lashed eyes. She sat with her knees drawn up beside her in the big armchair, a bowl of cherries in her lap. A small knife gleamed in her hand. She used it to split the cherries, separate them from their seeds, before putting the two halves into her mouth. Renee's stomach growled.

It had been two days since she'd eaten. Two days since Kendra had lured her out of her condo and into her car. Her watch had slowly ticked the hours away.

Grunting, Renee twisted her wrists in the handcuffs chaining her to the bed.

Why had she even believed Kendra when she said Mayson was hurt and needed help? From that lie and her mad rush into Kendra's car, Renee only remembered something hard smashing into her face. Then she woke up with her hands cuffed above her head to a massive bed that took up nearly all the space in a small pink-wallpapered room that looked like the set from a porn movie. Another set of cuffs secured her ankles together and to the bed. They rattled when she tried to move.

The room was dimly lit, but glittering gold curtains had been hung over the windows, blocking any natural light, injecting a false note of brightness. A scattering of softly glowing lamps helped to push the darkness to the corners of the room but could not disguise the shabbiness of the furniture, of the armchair where Kendra sat or the end table that held a small, gurgling fountain, a basket of fruit, and a pitcher of what looked like lemonade.

In the two days, Kendra had given her one glass of water and allowed her a single trip to the bathroom, dragging her by the handcuffed wrists down the hall to the tiny room with the mint-green toilet and a bamboo screen on the window.

Somewhere, an old air conditioner creaked but it might as well have been a heater for all the good it did. Sweat slid down Renee's forehead, into her mouth. Her dress was already plastered to the small of her back.

"If I wasn't 'comfy,' " Renee spat the word, "would you do something to fix that?"

"It depends on how good you are."

"Oh, please." Renee sneered.

"Are you only good for Mayson, then?"

From the armchair, Kendra twirled a lock of her hair around a finger and watched Renee. She looked like she was dressed for a party. Or a date. The long hair was gathered at the top of her head with a gold clip, the curls loosened to cascade around her bare shoulders. A peacock-blue dress clung to her body, showing off the reason Mayson had initially lost her head. She slid from the chair and slunk close to Renee on bare feet.

Renee stiffened. It took all she had not to cower against the bed in fear. "Mayson is my *friend*. It's not my fault you're too stupid to realize that." She blinked the sweat from her eyes, dipping her head into her arms to wipe her damp forehead.

But Kendra was unfazed by Renee's anger. She only smiled and circled the bed, the handle of a small knife cradled in her palm. "You talk a lot of shit for someone tied up and at my mercy."

Renee locked her arms and forced herself not to look

away. Kendra looked crazy enough to do anything. That was obvious from the way she stood waving the knife around like an extra from *Crocodile Dundee*.

"Why don't you just let me go and we can deal with this like rational adults?"

"Rational. Are you saying that I'm being irrational?"

Despite the teasing note in Kendra's voice, her question was deadly serious. Her eyes sat hard on Renee's face.

Renee swallowed the sudden surge of fear. "Uh...no. I was just thinking that if the two of you had the chance to sit down and talk, then maybe you'll be able to come to an arrangement. None of this—" She wriggled her chained wrists to encompass the tacky little room, Kendra's knife.

"You *do* think that I'm crazy." Kendra sat at the foot of the bed. The knife, wet with cherry juice, sat beside her on the bed, staining the pale blue sheets. "It's okay." She shrugged. "I know she's not going to want me anyway, not after this." The hair rearranged itself around her face as she shook her head. "This whole thing isn't really about getting Mayson back. It's about getting her to admit that she tricked me into falling for her." Kendra's voice grew soft. "I don't want that selfish bitch back. I want her to see how it feels to love and lose that love."

The breath caught in Renee's throat.

"Ah, now I have your attention." Kendra flashed her sharp white teeth in what could have passed for a smile.

After scaring the crap out of her, Kendra was satisfied with her day's work. She retreated to the armchair. Smiling, she dropped her knife on the table and poured herself some lemonade. She drank deeply from the glass. Renee licked her lips, suddenly aware again of the heat, the uncomfortable weight of the sheets under her already damp thighs. The drip of sweat under her breasts. The dryness of her mouth.

"Feel more comfortable yet?" Kendra asked again, a definite smirk on her red lips. She drank from the lemonade again.

Renee didn't waste her breath on an answer. Kendra chuck-led and opened a book, apparently content to wait. For what, Renee had no idea. It was obvious, though, that *she* did not have that same luxury of time.

She shifted in the handcuffs, wincing when they bit into her skin with each movement. Kendra didn't mean for her to get out of this. The idea frightened her more than she wanted to acknowledge. She raised her chin higher and leaned back against the headboard to take some of the strain off her wrists.

"You're very pretty," Kendra said. Glass clinked against glass. The sound of her pouring more lemonade from the pitcher. "It's no wonder Mayson can't get enough of you." *Like she got enough of me,* was the unspoken rest of that sentence. Renee rolled her eyes, knowing the movement was hidden behind her upraised arms.

"Still, maybe Mayson and I can still work things out." There was a question in Kendra's voice.

"Anything's possible," Renee said finally since the woman seemed to be waiting for some type of reaction from her. Kendra was stupid but she was also completely out of her mind. No need to antagonize her more than she could get away with.

"Yes." Kendra looked at her, unblinking. "Anything *is* possible."

Renee squirmed and finally dropped her gaze. After a long and uncomfortable moment, she still felt Kendra's eyes on her. The longer the woman stared, the more claustrophobic the room seemed. Desperation began to peak in her chest.

She jerked at the cuffs. Her fear-wet palms felt too hot. Her throat was dry and parched.

"You might as well relax, sweetie. You're not going any-where."

"I will not relax as long as you're in this damn room, you psycho bitch." So much for not antagonizing Kendra. "Shit." The word scraped across her vocal cords like sandpaper.

She forced herself to breathe evenly. This was getting her nowhere.

"It's all so hopeless, isn't it?" Kendra tucked her feet under her in the chair. With a coy smile, she flung her hair back off her shoulders. "Just makes you want to cry."

"Not quite," Renee muttered.

"What do you mean, not quite?"

"Does it look like I'm about to lie down and let you do whatever you want to me? I've already had it done and I'm sure he's much better at it than you."

"You mean, she. Mayson."

"What do I have to tell you to make you get it that May and I are just friends? Period."

"Nothing. Because I know better."

"Oh my God, did Mayson's sex really scramble your brains that much?" Renee sighed, suddenly tired. "Mayson's amazing," she said quietly. "Absolutely the best friend that a girl could want. But we've never been lovers. Never."

"Let's say it's all true, this shit you're feeding me. You and Mayson are the absolute best of friends, then what?"

"What do you mean?"

"Where does that leave me?" Kendra crept closer, the knife abandoned on the small table. She perched on the edge of the bed and leaned toward Renee. "Are you saying she just doesn't want me?"

Her voice shrank until it was almost a squeak, mouselike and lost. She held the half-finished glass of lemonade in her hand, her wrist curled in, the glass pressed to her chest like a child watching a disappointing cartoon.

Hell, yes. Who'd want your crazy ass, especially after all this foolishness? "Ah...I don't—" A cough interrupted her already halting flow of words. She cleared her throat. Or at least tried to. Instead another cough doubled her over and she turned her head so she wouldn't cough in Kendra's face.

Kendra held the cup of lemonade up to Renee's mouth and she bent her head to drink, grateful. It tasted only faintly of lemons and was sweeter than she liked but it was wet and eased her dry throat.

"I guess you were thirsty, huh?" she said, holding up the empty glass. "You want some more?"

Renee was about to nod, then thought better of it. She was still thirsty but the thought of another trip to the bathroom with Kendra watching while she squatted over the toilet seat made her head shake in refusal.

"I'm fine. That was perfect, thank you."

"Ah, you're so polite."

Kendra pushed away from the bed anyway to refill the tall glass. She moved back into place beside Renee, curling her legs under her and leaning back against the bedpost like they were best girlfriends. Renee turned her face into her arm to wipe away the sweat.

Kendra watched her.

"This is someplace I never thought I'd be, you know." The woman's words came softly, reluctantly. She rested her head against the bedpost, her eyes turning inward. "When I saw Mayson that evening, I couldn't believe my eyes. She looked just like Toshi. It seemed so strange, yet so perfect. Even though I knew it wasn't really her, I had to talk to her. Then I had to touch her. I couldn't stop myself. It was like I was getting a chance to live all the fantasies I'd had about my stepmother."

Renee squeezed her eyes shut. This was something she did *not* want to hear.

But with her eyes closed, the story still, unfortunately, continued.

"She touched me so perfectly, like she knew me."

At the unexpected silence, she opened her eyes to see Kendra watching her, expecting her to know exactly what she was talking about. "It was like Mayson had read the fantasies in my head," Kendra continued. She looked down into the lemonade glass, blinking into its depths at something only she could see. "After that I couldn't bear to let her go."

Kendra lifted her head. "I told Mayson every important thing about me. I even told her about this house that my stepmother left to me. I told her everything. But I guess she wasn't listening." Tears glistened in the corners of her eyes.

Renee couldn't hide her incredulous stare at Kendra's confession. "Don't you think this is all a little..." She tried to think of a relatively neutral word. "Extreme?"

Kendra's eyes flashed to her. They burned cold, then hot. "But isn't love irrational?"

Kendra was mocking her! Renee drew back. Or at least as much as she could with the handcuffs tying her to the bed.

"I know this is pathetic," Kendra said. "I *know.*" She laughed bitterly. "But there's nothing to be done about it now. It's over."

Cold dropped into the pit of Renee's stomach. "What do you mean it's over?"

Kendra smiled.

"Tell me. What do you mean?" Hysteria climbed into Renee's voice.

But Kendra still didn't answer. Instead she reached into her pocket, taking out a small silver pillbox. The tiny lid popped open revealing a round white tablet.

The headboard started to shake. Then Renee realized she was the one shaking. *This isn't happening. This isn't happening.* Her eyes filled with tears and overflowed. There were so many things she wanted to do. So many... *Mayson!*

"I hope you didn't think this was going to end any other way." Kendra put the pill in her mouth and swallowed it with the last of the lemonade.

"When I first dreamed up this whole stupid thing, I thought she would find us in a couple of hours. But she really doesn't know me and was *never* interested in getting to know me." Kendra put the empty glass on the floor. "But someone will find us, eventually." Her eyes gleamed with sudden malice. "And she'll die inside."

Renee shook her head. "No. Whatever it is you're thinking about, don't."

"It's too late, honey. I think it's been too late for a long time." She swallowed hard and leaned back against the bedpost. A fine mist of sweat broke out on her forehead. For the first time she seemed uncomfortable in the room's heat. Kendra fumbled to undo the first few buttons of her dress and swallowed again.

Renee blinked her tears away in irritation. This would *not* be the end. "Kendra, don't be stupid."

But the other woman was done listening.

"Kendra!"

Renee yanked at her cuffs, pulling against them to get to the other woman, who lay barely two feet away from her but might as well have been a continent away for all the effect that she had.

"Kendra!" she shouted again.

And this time Kendra rolled her head to look at Renee with a faint smile. She grimaced as a shudder shook her wilting frame. Her eyes shot open as if in surprise at what was happening to her body. She jerked against the headboard, shaking with convulsions, arms flailing. Her head thudded against the metal headboard. Foam bubbled up in her mouth and dribbled down her chin.

"Oh my God!" Renee tugged at the cuffs. But they held fast, scraping her skin the more she pulled. Kendra's body tumbled toward her, the wet and foamy mouth falling against her face. Renee screamed. She scrambled to get away but was trapped against the bed, wrists and ankles pulling furiously, uselessly at their manacles. The smell of feces, Kendra's, exploded against her face. "Mayson!" *Oh God.* "Mayson!"

She couldn't stop screaming.

A sound like a gunshot jolted her into silence. Her head whipped up and around. The sound came from the door. It came again just as suddenly and the door buckled. A battering ram.

A gun appeared at the open door. Two men in dark clothes burst in gripping their pistols, moving the weapons from side to side as they advanced inside the room. Renee sat frozen to the bed, Kendra's wet face and cooling body pressed against hers. She shuddered with revulsion.

One of the figures approached the bed while the other—a woman, she realized—looked quickly around the small room. Flashes of gold on their hips said they were police. She sagged in relief. Squeezed her eyes tight. *Now it was over.*

With his finger still on the trigger of the pistol, the officer bent to check Kendra's neck for a pulse.

"Clear!" he called out and Renee looked up in surprise. Grant shoved the gun into its holster and pulled out a small key, quickly unlocking Renee's wrists and ankles. He gingerly leaned Kendra's body away from her and onto the bed.

"Are you hurt?" he asked.

"No," Renee croaked past her dry throat, still looking up at him, unable to believe her eyes.

The thud of footsteps. "Renee!"

At the sight of Mayson's face, her composure disintegrated.

"Mayson!" She gripped her friend tightly, sobbing in her arms, chest heaving, her body wracked with tremors. "God! I thought she was going to kill me."

"I called for an ambulance and the coroner," the other officer said over their heads.

She shuddered at the unnecessary reminder of Kendra's body next to hers. The stink of her loosened bowels, the rictus of surprised fear on her face. Things she would never forget.

"I'm fine, really. Just a little thirsty and hot from being locked up in here." Her voice sounded awful. She coughed.

"I think it's best to check you out anyway. You've been in here for almost two days. Better safe than sorry."

"Okay." She rested her head against Mayson's chest and turned to look at Grant. "How did you find me?"

He opened his mouth but nothing came out. It was his turn to adjust phlegm in his throat.

"He was the one who told me you were missing," Mayson said.

"What?" Renee couldn't get over the way he was looking at her, like he wanted to come closer but was afraid to.

"I'm just glad you're all right," Grant said, his voice low with meaning Renee couldn't even begin to decipher.

Her head felt cottony and thick. It was hard to think. The sweat saturating her clothes made her shiver.

"Come on, let's get you out of here. We can wait for the ambulance outside." Renee couldn't help but notice that Mayson barely glanced at Kendra's body before tucking her under her arm, turning her head away from the sight of the dead woman. It was a brilliant and beautiful day, everything outside her prison golden and bright. Inside, it had seemed like one endless night.

"I'm okay, Mayson." Renee willed her voice to stop shaking. She blinked against the bright sunshine. "I just want to go home in the air conditioning and drink about ten gallons of water." She shivered in Mayson's arms.

"Okay, okay." Mayson turned her head. "Grant, she's really exhausted. I'll just take her back to my place. Come over and get her statement when you're done here. She's not going anywhere."

Grant must have nodded, because they began moving toward Mayson's car. Close by, a siren wailed.

"Thank you," she said softly.

She clung to Mayson, hands fisted in her friend's T-shirt. At the car, she reluctantly released her so that Mayson could get in the driver's seat. Renee huddled against the window as they drove away from Kendra's house and the little residential neighborhood with picture-perfect yards. She smiled gratefully when Mayson eased the top down, inviting the sun over their faces.

Kendra was dead. The girl had meant business. She meant to do them both harm but in the end...In the end, what? She had killed herself just so Mayson could suffer the loss. Even if she had counted on them not being found until Renee starved or died from lack of water. It didn't make sense. Despite the warm sun, Renee's fingers tensed with cold. *I almost died.*

The car door opened, jerking Renee from her spinning thoughts. Mayson reached for her.

"This is your fault." She poured all the ice that had taken over her body into those words.

Mayson flinched. Her hands fell to her sides. "I know. I'm sorry."

"You have no idea what sorry means, Mayson. You weren't in there with her." Renee hugged herself, rubbing her arms trying to find some warmth. "She was trying to hurt you."

"I know that now and I'm sorry. I'm s—"

"Stop saying that. It's useless to be sorry," she snapped. Her teeth chattered. She was so cold.

"If I could have been the one in there, don't you think I'd trade places with you in a heartbeat?" Mayson reached out but stopped before her hand could touch Renee's. "I would."

Anything else Renee would have said died on her lips. She didn't want Mayson to suffer. Kendra might have made it worse for her. Might have even forced Mayson to take the same poison pill that she had. The pulse thudded in her throat.

She reached up to put her arms around Mayson's neck. "Take me inside."

Chapter 38

They'd barely made it inside Mayson's house and closed the door before the doorbell rang.

Mayson looked through the peephole, sighing when she saw Grant's face. She let him in. Without the distraction of having Renee gone, Mayson noticed how exhausted he looked. Had he even slept the past two days?

"Renee." He stumbled past Mayson to get to Renee. "Please consider seeing a doctor. You shouldn't be on your feet."

She looked at him, puzzled, and then pointed to the stairs. "I was just—" Her feet took her toward them but she swayed. Mayson dashed forward to catch her but Grant got to her first. He caught her against his chest, lifted her. And, as naturally as though she'd done it countless times before, Renee slipped a hand behind his neck. She blinked and moved back to look at Grant as if seeing him for the first time.

I made this happen, Mayson thought. *I sent him in my place.* She turned away from them.

"Where do you want to be?" he asked, bending his head to look into Renee's face.

Renee looked stunned.

"The guest room," Mayson answered for her, forcing her footsteps in the opposite direction. "Upstairs to the left. The second door."

While Grant took Renee upstairs, she went to the kitchen

for water and grapes for Renee. Two days was a long time. She had no idea what Kendra had fed Renee during those heart-stopping forty-eight hours. At the kitchen sink, Mayson stopped. She felt the water running cold over the grapes in her hand but her mind suddenly flashed on that last unwelcome image of Kendra. Her eyes wide open and staring at nothing, foam and spit drying at her mouth.

This is your fault. Renee's cold voice echoed back at her. She bit her lip hard. It was the truth. It was ugly and bare and painful beyond any measure of pain she'd ever known. Her hands clenched into fists, squeezing the grapes and seeds through her fingers and into the sink.

Chapter 39

She knew this body.

Despite the remnants of shock and fear and disgust thrumming through her, something in Renee was paying strong attention to the arms holding her, to the heart beating strong and fast under her ear. She knew this body.

Her heart began to beat faster. What was going on? Was this part of the shock from seeing Kendra commit suicide nearly on top of her? Was it her relief at being finally safe? She sagged in Grant's arms. *So tired.*

Grant laid her against the pillows. "Let me look at you." His voice came from a very long way off.

In a fog, she felt his hands on her, clinical yet gentle. On her face, her scalp. When his fingers lifted away the delicate straps of her dress, she thought she ought to protest, but she only sighed under his careful fingers. He turned her over and repeated the procedure. And Renee let him. It was so familiar, so easy.

He eased her dress back up and, after giving her bare feet another glance, disappeared into the bathroom. "Wait," she called out softly to his retreating back. "Tell me why having you here feels like this."

But he didn't stop. He returned a few minutes later with a basin of water just as Mayson's worried face appeared over hers.

"Drink this," Mayson said just as Grant began to wash her feet.

The water—it had to be water—bathed her throat, slipping in a cool stream through her chest, then settled heavily in her belly.

"Should she be this out of it?" she heard Mayson ask.

"It's the shock of this whole fucked-up experience." There was something wrong with Grant's voice. It echoed.

"I think she needs to go to the hospital," Mayson said.

"Renee?" Someone called her name. But she couldn't answer.

Chapter 40

"She's been poisoned."

The doctor's words staggered Mayson on her feet. She swayed but Grant held her up.

"Can you flush it out of her system?" he asked.

He stood firmer than she ever could, though his hands around her shoulders were like ice. His skin had gone a sick shade of gray.

The doctor nodded, her chin-length bob fluttering with the brisk movement. "We're doing that right now. It's not a common poison, so it took us awhile to find it." The name of the poison she rattled off had Mayson and Grant staring at her blankly. "It was designed to work over a period of days, shutting down her systems one after the other." The coolness of her words couldn't disguise that the system shutdown would have been a painful process. "It's a good thing you brought her in when you did, otherwise after another day or two it would have been too late." She sounded calm, efficient. Her tone was factual, not in the business of giving hope, false or otherwise.

"When can we see her?" Grant asked again.

Mayson had called Mr. and Mrs. Matthews, to tell them that Renee was in the hospital. But she didn't have the balls to say that this whole thing was her fault. They were already in their car speeding down the highway to Renee's bedside.

"You can see her right now. She's lucid but a bit weak." The doctor inclined her head down the hallway, an indication, Mayson assumed, that Renee's room lay somewhere in that direction. "Room 517. The third door on the left. If you need anything while you're with her, just press the call button by her bed. Someone will be there immediately."

By unspoken agreement, Grant and Mayson started down the hall together. They hadn't talked about his new relationship with Renee. Mayson doubted that she had the strength for it. In the house, Renee had accepted his presence, although she seemed confused by it too.

"I thought it was all over," Renee greeted them weakly when they came into the room. She lay propped up in the bed, an IV drip in her arm, monitors flashing her vital signs at the head of the bed. Under the harsh fluorescent lights, her lips were dry and peeling, nearly the same gray pallor as her face. Her eyelids drooped.

Oh my God. Mayson dropped to her knees by the bed. Everything inside her broke and fell at Renee's feet. "I should have been the one in that room, not you," she croaked. "Never you."

"It was what it was." Renee's voice was a low whisper that Mayson had to strain closer to hear. "It's okay now." She squeezed Mayson's hand. "Stop beating yourself up over this, please?"

But Renee's faint voice and her wilting body in the hospital bed were like accusations of her crime, impossible to ignore.

Grant sat down in the chair on the other side of the bed. His face was a blank mask. His cop's face. But Mayson noticed the hand resting on the bed near Renee's was tightly clenched.

"The doctors already took care of everything," he said slowly. "They found the antidote to the poison and you'll be fine. Just rest and regain your strength. Before you know it, you'll be back to your normal life like none of this ever happened."

"My normal life," Renee echoed faintly, looking at Grant.

She studied him, her eyes taking in every inch of the man. He sat patiently under her stare, not uncomfortable, simply waiting until she had looked her fill. Then she reached out a hand to him. He clutched at it desperately, like a drowning man at a life raft.

Mayson knew the feeling well. Right now her entire world was a turbulent ocean but she had no rescue in sight. She stood up.

"I'm going to wait for your parents at the nurses' station. I want to explain to them before they see you."

Renee stretched her cracked lips into a faint smile. "Do I look that bad?"

"Yes." Mayson didn't smile back.

Chapter 41

"It's you, isn't it?"

Grant didn't bother to deny her words.

"When you didn't come I got worried," he said. "You never stood me up before."

Her fingers curled around his. "This is strange for me. I hope you know that."

"I know." His voice was rough and low, an echo of one of the rare times he had spoken when they were...together. She shivered.

It seemed suddenly foolish that she hadn't known it was him. That big body. His unfailing tenderness. Even that night she had driven him away. With the hand unhindered by the IV, she reached for his face. He came closer so she wouldn't have to stretch, and she closed her eyes, her hand moving over contours that were abruptly familiar. The stubble was new but the angled planes of his face, the full mouth under her fingers. His hair. She snaked her fingers into the dense, springy curls. Yes, this was her lover.

She opened her eyes to take him in. All of him. In the dark, this had been what was waiting for her.

"Are you all right?" He stood up to lean over her. "Should I call the doctor?"

"Renee!"

They both looked up at the gasping voice in the doorway.

Her parents moved quickly into the hospital room with mingled looks of relief and fear.

She squeezed Grant's hand and he pulled away. "I'm fine," she said softly. "Just a little tired."

"Mama. Daddy." She opened her arms, tears already welling up at the streaks of wetness on her mother's face.

"Renee Michelle." Her father's voice was thick with emotion. He touched her head tentatively, as if she would break.

She opened her arms to receive them both, pushing the tiredness away. With a soft cry, she buried her face in her mother's talc-scented neck and closed her eyes to everything else in the room.

Chapter 42

"Where's Grant?" Mayson sat on the edge of Renee's bed, taking care not to jostle her.

Renee looked better than she had five hours before, but her color was still off, and there were shadows under her eyes.

"I sent him home," she said.

Mayson plucked at the sheet, fighting against an unwanted surge of satisfaction. "He cares about you. He loves you."

Near her hand, Renee's leg twitched. The movement forced Mayson to look up, tracing the body under the white sheet, the slim hand with the IV rig deforming its natural grace. Renee's shadowed eyes watched her steadily. "I know."

The sadness in those words squeezed at Mayson's chest. "I—" But she couldn't go on.

"You sent him to me, didn't you?"

A lie would have been easy. Mayson chose the hard route. "Yes."

Renee's cheeks hollowed. From the look on her face, she had already known the truth but the confirmation of it seemed to shrink her even more in the bed. The stiff sheets crinkled from her clenching hand. "I'm—I'm tired. Can you come back tomorrow?"

The vise around Mayson's chest tightened. She couldn't speak. *I'm sorry.* The heaviness of her regret bowed her head.

I thought that's what you wanted. Her fingers reached for and gripped Renee's leg.

"They're letting me go home in the afternoon. Can you come back then and take me? Mama and Daddy will be here too."

Mayson swallowed hard, fighting for her words. She let go of Renee. "If you want, I can stay away. I understand if you don't want to see me."

"I just need a little time. Until tomorrow. That's all I'm asking."

Mayson's control was slipping. "Are you mad at me?"

"Yes. I think. I—I'm not really sure what I feel. It's this thing with Kendra and now this thing with Grant and there's—there's you." Renee's hands moved restlessly over the sheets. "Everything is so mixed up." She paused, eyes large and confused in her face. "I wish you hadn't brought Grant into this."

Mayson's head jerked up. "But I thought that's what you wanted."

"I didn't *know* what I wanted."

"And now?"

"Tomorrow. Please."

"Okay." Mayson nodded once. "Okay." Her knees shook as she stood up. "I'll—"

The room door opened and Renee's parents walked in. Food overloaded their arms—a basket of fruit and paper bags with what smelled like Chinese.

"Mayson, we're glad you're still here." Mrs. Matthews put the fruit basket on the table. "We brought enough food for all of us to eat."

"I think we brought enough for the whole hospital," Mr. Matthews said, setting the bags down.

Mayson smiled weakly. "Sorry, I can't stay. I have to—" She tried to think of something more important than being at Renee's side but nothing came to her. "I have to go."

"Is everything okay?" Mr. Matthews's eyes latched onto her face.

"Yes. Fine. I just...I—I'll see you later." She knew her stammering excuses didn't make it seem like she *was* okay but she couldn't say or do anything else. With a quick glance at three of the most important people in her life, she quickly left the hospital room and closed the door behind her.

Chapter 43

There was pain. And there was *Pain*. Renee thought she knew what it felt like to hurt but the past month had introduced her to a whole new level of feeling. She'd been released from the hospital and her doctor gave her a clean bill of health. Everything was back to normal. Her *life* should have gone back to normal. But it hadn't.

It had been almost a month since she'd seen Mayson.

The afternoon they released her from the hospital, she and her parents had waited for Mayson to come. Waited and called, then finally left. Her parents took her home and stayed with her, taking care of her completely, feeding her, fluffing her pillows, changing the TV channels. She'd longed for Mayson to be there to complain to, to laugh with. But Mayson hadn't come and all her calls to her cell phone, her house phone, and the yoga studio went unanswered.

After a week when she was well enough to get out of bed and out of the house on her own, she went to find her. But the condo was empty and Mayson had put someone else in charge of the studio.

One month. No word.

Renee's parents couldn't help her.

Their friends had no idea where Mayson had gone.

Grant had tried to reach out but she'd shoved him away. In the dark, he had been a fantasy. A fantasy created for someone who didn't exist anymore. In the light, he wasn't what she wanted.

Renee sat on the wooden steps of Dhyana Yoga, stunned. *Where is she?* In the twenty-four years they'd known each other, this was the longest they'd been apart without at least talking on the phone. She absently shoved up the sleeves of her sweatshirt. Before leaving the house, she'd pulled on thick sweats, anticipating the same brisk temperatures as the day before. But today was an abrupt fast-forward to summer. Scorching hot with only an occasional breeze for relief.

At ten o'clock in the morning, the parking lot of the yoga studio was full. The sun shined brightly over the cars in the paved lot, over the sculpted garden of sand and rocks and the small Japanese maple trees Mayson had planted when the studio opened three years ago. A light wind lifted up to brush against Renee's damp cheeks. *Where is she?*

Renee stood up and wiped her face. There was nowhere for her to go but home.

Walking up from the parking garage, she collected the mail, unlocked the door to her building, and stepped into the air conditioning. The cool air bathed her hot cheeks. It was like Mayson had literally vanished, leaving an immeasurable hole in Renee's life.

At the kitchen table, she listlessly sorted through the mail, putting aside the bills to be paid, throwing the junk mail into the recycle basket. A small envelope slid from the pile in her hands. It had a familiar Los Angeles return address scribbled on the back. When she opened the envelope, a key clattered to the table. *What's this?* She frowned and unfolded the piece of paper.

> *Renee,*
> *She's at my house. Sorry I didn't tell you before when you asked where she was.*
> *She needs you.*
> *—Iyla*

The chair jerked against the tile floor when she stood up. *Thank God. Oh, thank God.* She grabbed her keys and hurried out the door. In the car, she programmed the address into her GPS with nervous fingers and headed north. Past La Jolla, through Oceanside, and into Los Angeles. Her thoughts spun like scattered marbles, slippery and without direction. Why was Mayson in LA? Was there another lover? *Doesn't she love me anymore?*

Halfway into the drive, she shut down her thoughts and cranked up the volume on the '80s station. She sang along to every power ballad, every love song, until the car pulled into Iyla's quiet West Hollywood neighborhood. As she drove past, two men held hands walking their dog down a flower-edged sidewalk. A woman in a white convertible, her black Afro blowing in the breeze, raced ahead of her when the light changed to green. Renee turned in to Iyla's empty driveway and parked in front of the two-car garage.

The key opened the door. There was no alarm.

"Iyla?"

Only silence greeted her. She walked deeper into the house, into the Mexican tiled foyer with its twin ceiling fans, to the living room and the open French doors leading out to the pool. The sound of laughter floated in.

She followed the sound back out into the sun and to the turquoise glitter of the pool. A woman sat on a deck chair, topless, eyes shaded with sunglasses. She laughed again into the cell phone, stretching under the sun. In the pool, another woman swam laps, crawling steadily back and forth in the water. Renee caught her breath.

"Renee." Camille, the woman in the chair, smiled at her in surprise, shoving her shades up into her thick dreadlocks. "I didn't know you were coming up." She moved the phone away from her face.

Renee ignored her. In the pool, Mayson was still swimming toward the deep end, her face moving in and out of the water. Trembling legs took Renee to the water's edge, where she waited until Mayson noticed her. The sleek body spun in the water to do another lap, then, when Mayson noticed her, floundered like a hooked fish. Her head came out of the water and her fingers latched onto the edge of the pool near Renee's sneakered feet.

In the sun, she was as slick as a seal, her hair a black wave over bare shoulders and trailing behind her in the water. Under the shimmering blue, she was naked.

"What are you doing here?" Mayson asked, blinking water from her eyes.

Renee slapped her. She felt the sting in her palm, the shocking vibration of the impact, before she even realized what she'd done. They both gasped.

And then Renee was in the water, sputtering and treading water in her sweats that threatened to drag her down. She splashed against a snap-eyed Mayson.

"Careful. We're not kids anymore." The words came through Mayson's gritted teeth.

"Fuck you!" Renee gasped. She shoved at the slippery shoulders and arms, but Mayson held her firmly. "After you disappear for a month, that's all you have to say?"

"What the hell else should I say to you?"

Renee was vaguely aware of bare feet slapping against the ground near them.

"Is everything all right?" Camille's voice came from above them.

"We're fine," Mayson said without turning. "We just need a minute alone."

The footsteps retreated. Doors clicked closed.

"Is that who you've been doing since you left me?" Renee gestured blindly to the now absent Camille, splashing water into both their faces.

Mayson looked surprised. "I haven't been *doing* anybody."

"Then why are you naked? Why is she?" She struggled in the water, treading against the weight of the sweatpants and shirt on her body.

"Because it's a nice day." Mayson shrugged, looking annoyed. "Because we want to be. Why do you even care? Why are you here?" Her eyes narrowed. "Is Grant with you?"

Renee panted. Her arms and legs moved heavily in the water. "You didn't come back."

Mayson abruptly let her go, splashing backward as if Renee's skin burned. "You didn't want me to come back."

"That's not true." The words burst out of her, breathlessly, vehemently. "I waited for you."

"For what? To tell me how much I fucked everything up?" Mayson flinched, sunlight on the water reflecting off her pain. "I already know that. I think about that every day."

Renee felt like she was cracking at the center. No, she had already cracked at the center and now was falling away from herself. Incomplete.

"Can we—can we just get out of the water, please?"

After a slight pause, Mayson nodded briskly. She disappeared under the water, gliding under the surface to appear a few feet away at the ladder. Water sluiced down her bare body, clinging lovingly to brown flesh, muscled back, tight backside, the long thighs and legs.

"I thought you wanted to get out of the water." She stood, toweling herself dry.

Heat blossomed in Renee's face. She splashed clumsily to the ladder, feeling graceless and awkward in her clothes as she clambered up, grunting. Then gasped when Mayson pulled her up out of the water in a heaving splash. She tumbled against her, undoing all the work the towel had done for Mayson's skin. Her hands clutched at Mayson's arms. Bare breasts against her own, and despite the wet clothes hanging from her, she felt every inch of her skin as if they both stood naked under the sun.

Her hands tightened on Mayson's arms. She felt the quickly drawn breath. Then felt it against her lips. Mayson tasted of chlorine and surprise.

"Renee." Mayson groaned her name and pushed space between them. "What are you doing?"

But before she even finished asking the question, Mayson pulled her close, pressing their mouths together. Gladness tripped through Renee. Yes. *Yes.*

This time they shared the kiss. Renee seeking toward the familiar, the softness she'd always wondered at, testing the texture of that longed-for mouth. Her tongue flicked out and Mayson groaned against her, mouth opening, tasting in return.

Oh God. This is it. This is what I've been searching for. Renee poured her joy into the kiss, her relief that Mayson wasn't pushing her away.

Mayson's body trembled against hers. "We—we have to talk," her best friend said. "And get you out of those wet clothes."

It was Renee's turn to tremble.

Upstairs in the attic room where Mayson had been staying for the past month, she offered Renee some dry clothes, then turned away after an intense look at Renee's body, only vaguely outlined under the sweats. A blush warmed her face again and she wondered, briefly, if she was doing the right thing, if this was what she wanted.

Yes and oh, yes.

In the bathroom, she peeled off the wet clothes and hung them over the shower rod. She hesitated at her bra and panties, but they were wet too. They joined the rest of her clothes on the rod. The oversize shirt Mayson had given her smelled of laundry detergent and not of flesh-warmed eucalyptus mint. Renee sniffed at it in disappointment but drew it over her head anyway, smoothing the hem over her knees. She left the bathroom.

When the door opened, Mayson jumped up from the couch. But once on her feet, she seemed at a loss for what to do.

"Sit, please," she said. Dried at her hair with a white towel. Tossed the towel aside.

Renee looked around the room. It was a suite, really, filled with light from two large windows. A couch sat near the low wall leading to the stairs. Across from it and under the window was a neatly made bed. Renee climbed into the bed and sat with her back against the wall. She pulled her knees up to her chest.

When she sat, Mayson sat, stretching out her long legs on the couch. The T-shirt she wore was painted wet at the shoulders from her hair. Cutoff jeans sagged beguilingly at her hips.

She'd always loved Mayson's body, its strength, its softness, the way it could bend and move so effortlessly. But in the past few years, her appreciation had become more than just aesthetics. She'd wanted to touch. Miraculously, she'd hidden this want from Mayson, who noticed everything.

From the couch, her friend fidgeted, plucking at the frayed ends of her shorts. "I'm sorry about pulling you into the water. You've been sick—"

"I'm okay. There's nothing wrong with me now." Renee smiled in reassurance. "I'm perfectly healed. See?" She spread her arms wide.

She felt more than saw Mayson's quick, hot glance at her body. At her nipples pressed against the shirt. Her bare legs. Renee smiled again.

She bit the inside of her cheek. "When you gave Grant to me, you gave me the wrong person."

This time, Mayson's look held something else. Shock. Fluttering eyelashes. Hands frozen in her lap.

"It wasn't him that I wanted. It wasn't his smell that I was looking for." With a quick breath, she threw her heart into Mayson's hands. "I wish you had come to me instead."

In the dark, all those nights, it had been Mayson she was searching for. Craving the blindfold because she knew once she was able to see her lover, it wouldn't be Mayson. It would be disappointment. And it had taken Kendra's crazy love to finally rip her blinders off and show what she really wanted.

"Say that again." Mayson's voice was low, jagged. She held herself stiff and upright on the couch, a look of disbelief on her face.

"I wish you had come to me instead," Renee repeated. "Will you let me come to you now?"

Without waiting for an answer, she slipped from the bed, padding on bare feet across the cool tile, over the rug, and onto Mayson's lap. Arms wrapped convulsively around her.

"I hate Kendra." She whispered the words roughly into Mayson's throat. "I hate what she did to us. But if she hadn't come along, I don't know if we would have found our way here on our own."

Arms tightened around her. "No!"

She drew back to look into her love's face. "Yes." Her fingers tangled in Mayson's wet hair, pushing back the thick waves. "When she held me in that room, I saw clearly for the first time all the things I hadn't done. All the desires inside me that were ignored or pushed aside or placated with substitutes." Renee shook her head. "I don't want that life anymore."

"Do you realize what we'd be doing?"

The unexpected pain lanced through her chest and she jerked back at the shock of it. "Don't you want this too?"

"God, yes! I do. More than—" Mayson drew in a harsh breath. "I want it so badly that it scares me. But I've loved you all my life. You've been my friend. I don't want to lose that."

"We won't lose *anything*." Renee clenched her hands in Mayson's T-shirt. "You've been telling me for years to stop being afraid and to live my life. Be fearless with me."

Mayson's mouth tilted in a crooked smile. "Is that what I've been telling you to do? Just like this?"

"Yes." Renee grinned. "I've already quit my job and I'm

working on building a Web site for my photography. Now all I need is you."

"Are you joking?" Mayson pulled away to look into her face. "You finally broke the ties with that man?"

"*All* the men. I'm a slow learner, but I do learn."

The hair moved over Mayson's shoulders as she shook her head. Her teeth flashed in laughter. "You know that's not what I meant when I told you that, right?"

"It wasn't?" Renee teased Mayson with a finger against her lips, tracing the full, laughing curve.

Their smiles faded.

They sat, foreheads pressed together, words exhausted. For Renee, love and desire had always been dueling opposites. She'd never been able to feel both for the same person at the same time. But with Mayson's soft breath against her cheek, the beloved shape against hers, desire and love, lust and adoration clicked cleanly together. These elements mingled into a bright flame that illuminated Mayson, her beloved, the woman she wanted to be her lover, for the first time.

She wanted to devour Mayson, to strip off her clothes and look at her, truly, all of her for the first time. The want sparked between their joined hands—up her arms, flooding into all of her. Renee closed her eyes and trembled with it.

"Are you all r—?"

Renee tucked her nose into Mayson's throat, rasping her tongue along the sharp collarbone.

Mayson drew in a sharp breath. Her eyes widened. The flush of darker color under her love's skin drew Renee's eyes. Hungrily, she watched it creep down her throat, below the gaping collar of the oversize shirt.

Renee stood up and swept off her shirt, dropping it on the floor. "I want to see you," she said.

Mayson didn't respond; she only stared. Her fingers fumbled, warm and uncertain, against the back of Renee's knee. "I love you," she said, her voice hoarse.

"I know. Come show me."

She tugged Mayson from the couch to the light-filled bed under the window, under the sun. Mesmerized, Mayson allowed herself to be led.

"Take off your clothes," Renee said. "I want to see everything."

But Mayson didn't move fast enough. Her hands were clumsy at the hem of her shirt as she struggled, trying to watch Renee's every movement and undress at the same time. Renee gently pushed her hands away, lifting the shirt over Mayson's head.

Beautiful.

The buttons on the cutoff shorts easily released their hold on the cloth, separating over the naked sleekness of Mayson's most intimate flesh. Renee's hands trembled. It seemed impossible, deliriously impossible, that this was happening. Against the pale gold bedsheets, her long body was quiescent. Her breasts and belly trembled with each quick breath. Mayson. Cupped in the V of her open shorts, the beguiling flesh.

Renee reached out to touch her, then drew back. She looked at her short fingernails, then at Mayson's seductive receptivity in the sheets.

"One fall, when we were in college, I had an affair," Renee said very carefully. Mayson's body was the most beautiful thing she'd ever seen. Awed, she traced a line between her dark-tipped breasts and down the flexing belly. "She was a chemistry TA."

It had been so obvious then. Why had it taken her ten years to see it?

"When?" Mayson's voice was soft, disbelieving as she lay still slack under her touch.

"Our sophomore year."

She and Mayson had gone to different schools in different

parts of the country. Mayson wasn't there when her hormones took her over, when she started to take chances and
go after what her flesh craved.

"Once, I remember her touching me and she did something—I can't remember what it was now—it reminded me
so much of you that I couldn't see her again."

Mayson lifted her hips to allow her to pull the shorts
down. In the movement, the smell of her eased against
Renee's nose, floating over her taste buds. She swallowed.
Mouth wet. Throat dry.

"I didn't love her," Renee said. "She wasn't you. But I
loved being with her. I loved loving her. It was winter break
when I ended it."

Mayson remembered that winter break. Renee had been
strange, restless. There were entire days during that break
when she avoided Mayson. Other days, she was everywhere,
clinging and quiet. One night, she came into Mayson's room
in her sheep-print pajamas and begged for a story. It was late,
past midnight, and Mayson was tired. But she reached for a
book and settled into the bed next to Renee. In the middle of
reading one of their favorite chapters in *Abeng,* when she
thought her friend had fallen asleep, she looked down only to
see Renee watching her, eyes luminous, an unfamiliar expression on her face.

"Don't stop reading," she'd said that night, her voice a
low hum in the bedroom. "Please, don't stop."

Now Mayson, knowing what had come before those moments on that long-ago night, closed her eyes at the memory
and felt the vibration of its echoes under her skin. There had
been another woman. Another *woman.*

The lover from her past wasn't something she thought
she'd ever share with Mayson, but with the heat of her so
close and this new chapter of their relationship, it seemed important. She wasn't coming to this as an experiment. She'd

already tasted this wine and found it sweet. Now she wanted to drink from it always with Mayson as her loving cup.

She kissed the surprise from Mayson's mouth. She tangled fingers in the thick hair and drew her closer, and closer, feasting. The mouth was plump and wet, like a fig between Renee's teeth, under her tongue. The broad sweep of her cheekbones, the eyes that did not once look away from her. Eyes that remained open during the kissing, during the tasting. The slippery glide of tongues, breaths coming quickly. Renee took it all.

I want to see everything.

Renee didn't ask. She didn't demand. She took. Her hands shaped Mayson's body in wonder. The throat was a hot, long column. Her narrow shoulders. Her breasts. Renee lingered at her breasts. She'd always been envious of their size, then curious, then ravenous to have them under her mouth. She touched them now. She curved her hands around their full weight, teasing the nipples between her fingers. A low moan left Mayson's throat and she arched up, pushing her breasts even more into Renee's hands.

Renee raked her nails over the deep brown nipples that hardened even more. Irresistible. She licked one. Delicious. Sucked the dark berry into her mouth. Mayson's deep rumble under her lips. She drew back to look at Mayson in the light. She couldn't get enough of looking at her. The luscious brown body. The wild growth of hair at the top of her thighs. Nipples wet from her tongue. Mayson's mouth open, eyes closed. Breathless.

Renee leaned over her love, shivering in delight when her nipples grazed Mayson's, their legs slid together. Kissing. She could have been kissing these soft lips *years* ago. She sighed in past regret. Shivered in present pleasure. So perfect together. Why hadn't she seen it before? Mayson's hair clung to her fingers.

The sweetness of her mouth!

She pulled slowly away, nibbling on the full lips, kissing her chin. Mayson's hands gripped her shoulders, but she eased firmly away. There was more she wanted. Much more.

Moving down the long body, Renee touched lightly, confidently, short nails over the responsive skin.

"All this time, you were so soft under your clothes."

Mayson's laugh ended on a gasp when the questing fingers slid between her thighs.

"I dreamed about you like this once."

The fingers teased Mayson's softness. They teased her clit and a quake moved through her that was like plunging into the Pacific on a hot day, her skin eager but unprepared. Mayson flung her head back, gasping, back arched. The gateway to her desire open to Renee. Lust-painted thighs. Hand stretching up, reaching for something, anything to hold on to as the tide heaved up, swept her away.

"Renee!" she gasped, her mind going blank, her body seeking and unmoored. "I don't—"

"Shh..."

With her guidance, Mayson turned over. Light splashed over the warm skin. The muscles in her back bunched and released under Renee's lips, contracted under her teeth. Mayson moaned, grinding her hips into the bed, the muscled ripeness of her bottom clenching as she chased after more sensation. Her thighs were only slightly open but Renee could still see the moisture caught in the wiry hairs, the weeping cup of her sex that she ached to taste.

"On your knees, honey," she whispered, holding her breath as Mayson moved to do as she asked. "I want to see you. Oh!"

Mayson knelt in the bed, crouched low with her arms braced against the window. Light poured over her, showing every beautiful inch of her skin. Renee licked her lips.

Yes.

The smell of chlorine and sunlight lingered on her, in the rough hairs that brushed against Renee's face. She sighed. *Yes.* And felt the soft bottom tremble under her hands. Felt the moan move down Mayson's body into the worshipful place that made Renee part her lips in anticipation.

"I need you," Mayson gasped.

And because she lived to fulfill her woman's every wish, Renee touched her. They moaned together. Deep, body moans. The taste of her—woman, water, desire, love—flooded over Renee's tongue. The shielded intimacy of her sex opened for her, welcomed her with more wetness, the slick lips, salty heat, soft, fleshly desire that fed *her* desire. The more she tasted, diving in for the hard clit and the moans that shook her beloved's body, the hungrier she became. She gorged herself on the delectable flesh.

Mayson gripped the ledge, lips parted, gasping helplessly. Blind to anything outside the window, powerless to the hunger moving through her, making her entire body wet. Sweat, cum, tears, sliding from her. The hot mouth covered her, agile tongue swirling through her folds, diving deep inside her. Searing sensation twisted in her belly. Undone. She was completely undone, like the skin of a mango, slit open, turned inside out, sucked clean.

Guided more by her craving for Mayson than anything Amina had taught her on that ripe and lovely college campus years ago, Renee made purposeful love to her woman with her mouth and with her hands. But it didn't hurt that she knew just how to curl her tongue to reach what she wanted or that she had learned the language of the flesh, of the quivers and quakes that meant "More. Give me more," or the muscle-deep vibrations, constant and powerful, screaming, "That's perfect. Don't stop!"

Mayson's softness trembled against her face, filling her

with scent, the scorching smell of sex, the sound of her wordless cries that increased the slickness between her thighs.

"Oh God!" Mayson stiffened under her, then undulated,
her body a wave of sudden and violent satisfaction. "Renee!"

She panted in the aftermath of her orgasm, arms shaking
from their brace against the window. The glass in front of her
face misted. She pushed her forehead against it, helpless to
the rising and falling inside her body. Renee was still behind
her, loving her. She felt the purposeful pressure of her mouth,
the fingers brushing over her twitching clit, dancing lightly at
her entrance.

"I love that you love my touch."

Breath traveled up her back, Renee's tongue licking her
sweat, soft moans of unsatisfied desire as she kissed her way
up Mayson's shoulder, the back of her neck, pushing the hair
out of her way. Smooth pubes pressed against Mayson's ass.
Hard nipples poked at her back. Her stomach tightened from
the fingers sliding down, diving into the damp hairs of her
pussy.

"I want to feel you, inside," Renee whispered.

And Mayson fell under the tide again.

They knelt upright in the bed together, Mayson's back to
Renee's belly. Flesh to flesh. Mayson was drowning, over-
come by the wetness dripping from her, the sweat coursing
down her body, Renee's fingers on her clit, hips moving
against Mayson's hips.

"Tell me." She spoke the words into Mayson's shoulder,
biting the damp skin. Her finger lashed Mayson's clit in lazy
but insistent circles. "Tell me what you want."

"Fuck me." The words fell from her lips in a low moan.
"Fuck me. Now."

Those were the words Renee had been waiting for.
With Mayson still on her knees, she turned her around,

pushed her back against the wall. Her legs fell open even more, head rolled against the wall. Lips parted, tongue moving over dry lips.

She was hotter than Renee ever dreamed. Hot, wet, and tight around her fingers. Renee bent her head. The rounded breasts, the taste and texture of the hard nipples that kept her from flying apart with rapture at the quickening heat of Mayson's body around her fingers. Her fingers. Mayson's sex. Their moans.

Renee couldn't stay still. She sucked, bit, licked, devoured, fucked. Her arm strained to keep pace with her love's need. But she pushed beyond the discomfort until they panted into each other's mouths. Gasping over the frantic sound of her wet movement inside Mayson, the grunts rising, unfamiliar and primal, from her throat. The wall knocked with the sound of their fucking. Because this was *fucking*. Raw and unequaled.

A wave of perfect heat swept through Renee, rushing up through her fingers, into her breasts, bursting between her legs, exploding in a white-hot blaze. She gasped as tremors took her body.

"Oh, sh—!"

Mayson shouted into her shoulder. Her sex tightening, sucking on Renee's fingers. She sagged against Renee. They fell backward into the bed, rolled apart, pushing sticky flesh away from sticky flesh.

Quick breaths, then slow, the panting downward slope of their desire.

Light from the window swam over them, sending dust motes and the sun's burning heat into the wilting room.

"Did you—"

"Yes." Renee gasped the word in surprise. It was as if she'd never given love before. Her body had found its way to satisfaction, easily, explosively.

The bed shifted as Mayson rolled over and pushed herself up onto her elbows. She licked her lips. "I swear it's not always like that." Her eyes flickered away as a dark flush moved under her damp skin. "Actually, it's never been like that. I'm usually more—"

Renee pressed her fingers against Mayson's mouth. "It was perfect. I wouldn't change a thing about how you showed your love for me."

Mayson flushed again, dipping her head to nuzzle in Renee's neck.

"Are you going to kick me out of bed now that you've gotten what you wanted?" Her eyes emerged from the wet fall of hair.

Renee blinked the sweaty sting from her eyes and dipped her head to look at Mayson. "You," she said, smiling into the light surrounding her lover, her friend, "are not going anywhere."

Chapter 44

It felt awkward to knock on Grant's door with the ring on her finger. She wasn't ashamed but didn't want to rub it in his face either. Mayson knocked anyway. And waited.

Just as she thought about leaving, the door opened. Grant's face looked carved in stone.

She shoved her hands into her pockets. "Can I come in?"

With a single nod, he opened the door wider. But didn't move more than a few feet down the hallway, didn't close the door. Grant leaned back against the wall, mirroring Mayson's hands-in-pocket stance.

"I heard," he said.

"I know." Mayson leaned against the opposite wall, watching the man who stood barely four feet away from her, in pain. She bit her lip. "I'm sorry I brought you into this, I really am."

"Me too," he said softly, meeting her gaze. "But I knew what I was getting into and I knew how she felt about me. She never hid those feelings." His head fell back against the wall with a dull thud. "There were so many ways for it to go wrong but only one way for it to turn out right." He sighed and shrugged despite the pain in his face. "The odds were never in my favor."

When Mayson had called him in the middle of the night

months ago, it was out of desperation. Renee had to be protected. And because Grant had wanted her for so long with nothing to show for it, Mayson knew he would do what she asked: seduce Renee and keep her safe.

"This is yours." He pulled something from his jeans pocket. The velvet blindfold.

For a moment, Mayson stared at it, black against his pale palm, remembering the night she'd given it to him with her hands still smelling of nutmeg. "Don't let her know who you are," she'd told him then.

And maybe she had known what she was doing, offering him the cloth from her bedroom, unable to resist the quick mind's-eye flash of Renee, blindfolded, bent back against the sheets, gasping. Under *her*.

Mayson took the piece of velvet and shoved it into her pocket. "In a million years, I never thought she and I would end up together," she said. "Not like this."

Grant smiled without humor. "You're the only one. Even I—" He shrugged. "Anyway, all that is in the past. You have a future with her now and I don't. It hurts like hell but I'm a big boy."

Mayson nodded. There was nothing else to say. She rubbed her fingers across the velvet in her pocket. A familiar sound lifted her eyes away from Grant. Renee, walking up the steps toward them in high-heeled sandals. Her outfit mirrored Mayson's—T-shirt and jeans belted low at the hips—but she didn't hide her hand in her pocket. The platinum band was blinding against her brown skin. Grant winced.

"It would have been easy to love you, Grant," Renee said when she was close enough to be heard. "But I was already in love with May. I see that now." She stepped into the house, into the hallway, and stood close to Mayson. "I'm not sorry that I love her but I'm sorry that I hurt you."

Briefly, he squeezed his eyes shut. "Yeah." His throat moved as he swallowed.

"We should go." Mayson shoved herself off the wall and met Renee's hand halfway. Their fingers clasped. "Thanks for letting me in, Grant."

"Sure." He looked at Renee, then at Mayson. "Take care of each other." His voice was low but sincere.

And they walked out of his house together, hand in hand, the sunlight falling around their shoulders and on the flower-lined path under their feet.